LOIS CLOAREC HART'S

WALKING THE LABYRINTH

Walking the Labyrinth

ISBN paperback: 978-3-95533-052-1
ISBN mobi: 978-3-95533-049-1
ISBN epub: 978-3-95533-050-7
ISBN pdf: 978-3-95533-051-4

Published by Ylva Publishing, legal entity of Ylva Verlag, e.Kfr.
Ylva Verlag, e.Kfr.
Am Kirschgarten 2
65830 Kriftel
Germany

http://www.ylva-publishing.com

First Edition: June 2013

Credits
Editor: Sandra Gerth
Cover and Formatting: Streetlight Graphics

ACKNOWLEDGMENTS

Thousands of years ago, we told our stories to a few around a cooking fire. Today we tell our stories to millions via social media. The common thread is how we convey so much of ourselves, whether in the form of shared humour, a bit of gossip, or a philosophical observation. This is the human imperative, to leave our mark and to contribute our stories to the cultural tapestry. *Walking the Labyrinth*, within its fictional construct, is my story, more than anything else I've ever written. No story has ever spilled out of me in a torrent the way this one did, but it would not have come fully to life without the help and dedication of some remarkable and talented women.

As every author knows, excellent editing is vital to a polished end product. My wife has edited every word I've written since we first met twelve years ago. Day, words are simply inadequate to tell you how much I appreciate your contributions. When I can make you laugh or cry, when you tell me something lacks the Loie-spark and prompt me to rewrite, and when you signal your approval with a smile and a nod, I know all over again how fortunate I am to have you.

Kathleen GramsGibbs, who has been working with me almost as long as Day, is the best of sounding boards, contributors, and as an added bonus, a dear friend. My deepest thanks, Kathy. I hope to benefit from your insight, vision, and patience for years to come.

For this first book with Ylva, I've had the pleasure and privilege of working with Sandra Gerth, who's done a sterling job of editing. Long before we met, I appreciated her writing ability, having devoured the stories written under her nom de plume, Jae. It was a pleasure to discover that she's equally talented as an editor.

Astrid Ohletz invited me to become a part of Ylva's family at the end of 2012, and I'm so very glad I accepted. From skilled editing to fabulous cover art, producing *Walking the Labyrinth* has been a completely positive experience. Thank you, Astrid. I look forward to a long and fruitful relationship with Ylva.

Day
I love you
That's all
That's everything

CHAPTER 1

LEE LISTLESSLY EYED THE WISP of smoke curling up from the cigarette that dangled between her fingers. The ashtray on her lap had overflowed and left dark streaks on the grimy, white T-shirt hanging on her like a shroud. A silent, flickering television screen was the only illumination in the darkness of the basement den, and nothing diffused the sour air.

Lee reached for the bottle beside her. A wedding ring, too large for her finger, clanked against the glass. It captured her attention, and her hand stilled.

She stared at the ring, remembering the day her late wife had placed it on her finger. It had been a perfect day. Surrounded by friends and family, Lee pledged herself for life to the woman she loved.

"For life...right. Who knew 'life' would turn out to be so little time together, eh, Dana?"

Lee started at the sound of her own voice. It was bleak and raw, and echoed hollowly as if the owner had long ago abandoned using it. She tried to clear her throat, but that only engendered a fit of coughing. In sudden self-disgust, she stubbed out the cigarette and set the laden ashtray aside.

A doorbell sounded upstairs, but Lee ignored it. She knew that her son, Eli, or his girlfriend, Liz, would get it. It wouldn't be anyone to see her. Not after she spent months rebuffing every appeal and invitation her friends had extended until they finally gave up and left her alone in her basement refuge. She didn't blame them.

Lee leaned forward. Her forearms rested on bony knees as she tried to recall when she had last seen any of her friends. Three months ago? Six? She couldn't even remember the last time she'd gone in to work. She shook her head wryly. "Good thing I own half the business or I'd have fired me long ago."

She stared at the faded carpet, now covered with stains and dust bunnies. Dana had been so excited the day they'd found exactly the right colour carpet for the basement of their new home. Lee laughed softly as she remembered how insistent Dana had been on not settling for less than the precise shade of burgundy she had fixed in her mind. It had taken over a year before they stumbled upon a suitable carpet in a country flea market, but once Dana spied it, there was no discouraging her. They had been out for the day on Lee's beloved Suzuki bike and couldn't carry the carpet with them. Dana didn't want to leave it for fear it would be gone by the time they got back, so Lee drove all the way back to the city and returned with a borrowed truck to bring their new-found treasure home.

Lee was ashamed at how dishevelled the carpet was, and she winced as she noticed a cigarette burn by her feet. How had she let Dana's carpet come to this state?

"Maybe I could rent a carpet cleaner." Lee ran a hand roughly through her lank, stringy hair. Several strands snagged, and she recoiled at the pain. She held her hand out and was dismayed by the long, dirty fingernails. She could see the ragged edges where she had broken nails on the weight machine, which had been one of her few solaces the past year.

The door at the top of the stairs creaked and opened.

Lee looked up, half-expecting to see Eli with a plate of food. He or Liz usually came down about this time, even though she rarely ate much of what they offered. To her surprise, however, Lee realized she was hungry. It was an unfamiliar sensation, and she rubbed her concave stomach.

It was Eli, but he wasn't carrying her usual supper plate. He was preceding a small group of people down the stairs.

Lee frowned when she recognized her old friends.

When they reached the bottom of the stairs, Eli flipped on the light.

Lee flinched and covered her eyes with her forearm. "What the hell did you do that for?"

"Because it's time to face the light, Lee. It's time you left this basement and started to live again."

Lee lowered her arm and squinted as the light stabbed at her reddened eyes. She surveyed the small group warily. "Christ, what is this? An intervention?"

Rhiannon stepped forward. "That's exactly what this is. We've given you long enough. We're not going to let you destroy yourself bit by bit any longer."

"Go away."

Rhiannon ignored Lee's half-hearted rejection and knelt next to the chair. "No." She touched Lee's knee, and Lee shrank back. "No, I won't go away, and neither will Marika or Eli or any of us. You never in your life let a friend down, and we're not going to let you down either."

"You're wrong. I let *her* down." The retort was automatic, but Lee realized the emotion behind the words had faded. The guilt that had haunted her day and night for months had subsided. For a split second, Lee didn't know whether to feel culpable or rejoice at its loss.

Marika rested her hands on Rhiannon's shoulders. "That's bullshit, and you know it. Dana fought with everything she had, but there was nothing she, you, or any of her doctors could do to stop the spread of the cancer."

David added, "You didn't let her down then, Lee." When she finally looked up at him, he continued, "But you're letting her down now. In your soul, you know how horrified she'd be to see you like this, isolated, barely existing."

Lee dropped her gaze. She did know. The knowledge had been building within her for weeks, but she'd been unable to summon the energy to break the destructive cycle that trapped her. She had spent so long mired in a morass of despair that she'd forgotten how to live any other way.

Willem stepped forward. "My friend, you dishonour not only Dana, but the life you built. I could count on one hand the number of times you've been in our offices this past year. I'm tired of carrying DeGroot and Glenn Security by myself. I want my partner back."

Shame sliced at Lee, and she dropped her gaze. DeGroot and Glenn had once been her pride and joy, second only to Dana and Eli in its importance in her life. How could she have just abandoned the company they had spent a quarter century building up?

"Liz and I got engaged last weekend."

Her son's blurted words startled Lee. "You did? Why didn't you tell me?"

"Because I didn't think you'd care."

"Not care? Eli, how could you think that?"

Eli dashed tears from his eyes with his shirtsleeve. Lee was sharply reminded of the little boy he'd been when Dana first came into her life with Eli in tow. "Because you haven't cared about one damn thing since the day we buried Mom. More than anything, I want you to be at our wedding this summer, but I don't know if you are even going to be alive tomorrow. Hell, I'm scared to bring the laundry downstairs in case I find your body hanging from a rafter. In the middle of the night, when I'm wakened by the sound of that damned weightlifting machine, I'm actually glad. I'm glad because it's a signal that, for one more night at least, you're still alive."

The shame Lee felt at Willem's words multiplied. "I wouldn't—"

"Yes, you would," Eli said. "Every time you took your bike out this winter, I waited for a call from the police telling me you'd been killed in an accident. There was a time you'd have gone up one side of me and down the other for even riding after the end of October. And there you were, out in every fucking blizzard. You were trying to kill yourself, Lee. Don't tell me you weren't."

Lee stared at him, rocked by her son's insight and her fear that he was right. "I wasn't—I didn't—I just needed to get out. That's all. Sometimes the walls close in on me and I can't take the way I feel for even one moment longer."

Eli shook his head, and David put his arms around him. He regarded Lee compassionately over Eli's shoulder. "Do you remember the day, about a week before Dana died, when she insisted you go home to clean up? It was about the only time you left her that last month."

Lee grunted. "She told me I stunk worse than Eli's hockey locker room." She smiled ruefully, remembering the determined look on Dana's haggard face as she ordered Lee home for a shower and fresh clothes. "She was right."

David hugged Eli, then released him and walked toward Lee. "What you didn't know was that Dana had arranged with Eli to call us to her bedside in the hospice. She wanted to talk to us all without you there."

Rhiannon took Lee's hands. "Dana looked like hell that day. She knew—we all knew—that she had very little time left, and she needed something from us."

Marika regarded Lee sternly. "She had written a letter, and she asked us to make a promise."

"Promise?" Lee looked around, her brow furrowed. "What did you promise?"

David pulled an envelope from the inner pocket of his jacket. "Dana knew you so well. She knew her death would devastate you. She said to give you a year to grieve in your own way, then give you this letter. If you were in a good place, then the letter would be an added comfort for you, but if you weren't handling things well, we were to intervene."

"To say you're not handling things well would be a vast understatement."

Lee flinched at the asperity in Marika's voice.

Rhiannon squeezed Lee's hands. "You're handling things like shit, my friend. That has to end. Dana made us promise not to let you go on this way, and come hell or high water, we're going to keep that promise."

"She told us to give you this." David held out the letter. "We don't know what's in it. It's Dana's final message to you, and it's time you read it."

Lee fumbled as she tried to open the envelope until Rhiannon took it and deftly unsealed the flap.

Marika turned on the table lamp and handed over her own reading glasses.

With trembling hands, Lee extracted the handwritten pages. Her vision swam as she desperately tried to make the words legible.

Marika knelt next to Rhiannon, and both her friends rested comforting hands on Lee's knees. She flashed them a look of gratitude and wiped tears away with shaky fingers. Then, with a deep breath, she focused on the script.

Dana wrote this. These are her last words to me...her last words ever...

Lee tenderly smoothed the pages and began to read.

My darling Lee,

As I write this, I know two things. I know my time on earth grows very short, and I know the pain you're going to have to endure will be almost unbearable. I wish I could spare you what is to come, but I can't. I have to believe that some good will come of it, for when I look at you, the agony in your eyes rends my soul.

You have always been so steadfast, my Lee. Everyone has always relied on you—your grandparents, me, Eli, Willem, Marika, and Rhiannon—I can't think of anyone who has come within your orbit who hasn't been the better for knowing you. I've often thought how ironic it was that you, who had so few biological relatives, created the bonds of family with so many others. But for all your strength, I hear you weeping in the night when you think I'm asleep. Sometimes I reach for you and we cry together. Sometimes I let you have the privacy of your tears. This is unknown territory for me too, my love. Please forgive me if I've sometimes been uncertain about the best choices. Know that each decision I made was with you and Eli foremost in mind.

I believe with all my heart that you have the strength to get through the pain, no matter how lost you're feeling right now. Toward that end, I'm going to enlist our son and our friends to rescue you, if need be, because it is my greatest fear that you will have gone far astray. It is ironic that I have no such fears for Eli. He will grieve for me, and then, with Liz' help, he'll pick up his life again. But you, who are the most valiant soul I have ever known, you are the vulnerable one. Perhaps it is because you love so deeply. It is one of your finest qualities, but it also leaves you so terribly open to heartbreak. I was privileged to be the recipient of your magnificent love. And as I take it with me, Lee, so too do I leave with all the love I feel for you and Eli. It was the only thing the cancer could never touch.

It's time for a little tough love, Lee. If you're reading this, a year has passed since my death. You've either weathered the last twelve months well and are in a healthy, wholesome place, in which case I'm thrilled and delighted for you. Or you abandoned yourself to despair, retreated from life, and pushed away all those who love you and want to help. Truthfully, I suspect the latter will be the case, so as a safeguard I'm going to kick your tail feathers, my dearest one.

Stop it—right now, Lee. I'm not downplaying what you'll have had to endure the last year. I know how horrendous it will be for you, and I'm going to be watching you with the deepest compassion from the other side. But, my love, you cannot exist in a stasis of sorrow. It's past time to pull yourself together and get on with your life. Almost every soul who has ever lived has endured the agony of loss. It is a sad reality of the human experience, and few have the luxury of retreating from that pain, because they have people depending on them to keep on putting one foot ahead of the other, day in and day out.

The thing is, love, though you may have temporarily forgotten, you too have people counting on you. You are our son's only parent now. I need you to be there for Eli. He needs you. He will always need you, even when he is a husband and father himself. And as much as I appreciate Willem's fine stewardship of DeGroot and Glenn, you are the founder, inspiration, and backbone of that company. I know our friends will feel the huge hole you and I left behind, so I'm relying on you to fill in that piece of their lives again. Our goddaughter will be walking and talking by now. You have so much you can teach Marnie, about life, love, and how to throw a curveball. Let that little girl learn about nobility, honour, and loyalty from a woman who lives all these qualities to the utmost.

So, no more excuses, my love. I don't expect you to forget me or even to set aside the grief of losing me. I do expect that even as you remember me, you will resume functioning as the fabulous mother, friend, and business partner you've always been.

Now listen up, Lee, because this is the most valuable admonition I can leave with you. I don't want you to encase our love in amber and set it on a shelf. I don't want you to don a permanent set of widow's weeds. I do want you to open your heart to new possibilities. There is a woman out there waiting for you. She won't take my place. She will have a cherished place of her own, and it's up to you to find her. If I have any say in it, I'll be steering her your way sooner rather than later, because wasting the kind of love you have to give is an offence against creation. So when she crosses your path, don't turn away—turn toward her. And when you do, I'll be dancing with the angels in pure joy.

That's about all I have to say, my love. I confess that I long for an end to this pain. I don't have a certainty of what awaits, but many days I simply crave oblivion if it would end this agony. So when it is my time, understand that I do not have a single regret. I would've loved to grow old with you, but there is nothing else in my life that I would change—nothing. You and Eli are the best parts of me, so I leave you to an uncertain world. It's a pretty messed-up old planet, and it needs you, just as I have needed you all these years.

I promise I'll always be with you and Eli, no matter what. Believe that as you have believed in me...in us.

I love you with everything I am, Lee. And I am so grateful to have been loved by you.

Forever and always yours,

Dana

When Lee finished reading the letter, she stared at the sheets of paper. As much as the contents of the letter, it was seeing the familiar, albeit shaky handwriting that shook her to the core.

Lee felt so many things simultaneously that she didn't know what she was feeling. Grief, gratitude, and shame rose in a tsunami that swept her to the edge of an abyss. One more inch and Lee would plunge so deep she knew she'd never emerge. But she didn't have to take that fall. Dana's words were a lifeline, and Lee hungrily read them again.

Then she looked at the people who surrounded her, offering her unconditional love and support.

Lee slipped the letter back into the envelope and rose to her feet. She met each person's eyes sorrowfully. "I owe every one of you an apology. I never stopped to consider how my behaviour would affect anyone else. I couldn't see beyond my own misery. You're right. You're all right. I've dishonoured Dana's memory. She would be horrified if she could see me."

"There's no 'if' about it," David said softly. "She *can* see you."

Lee tilted her face to the ceiling. "Then I apologize with all my heart, sweetheart. And I promise I'll do better from now on. I swear I'll do better." She lowered her gaze and smiled faintly. "Our family and friends will hold me to that, just like you knew they would."

Lee opened her arms to Eli, and he buried his face against her shoulder. She hugged him and crooned into his hair, remembering anew the boy who had climbed into her lap so many times, waiting for her to read him a story. "I'm so sorry, Eli. I wasn't there for you, and I'll never forgive myself for that. Thank God you had Liz."

"I wasn't alone, but it was tearing me apart that you felt you were."

Rhiannon and Marika embraced the pair, and Marika spoke for all of them. "She was never really alone. I think she finally knows that."

David joined the group hug until the friends started to laugh at the unwieldy arrangement and broke apart.

Lee looked over at Willem, who was surreptitiously dabbing at his eyes with a monogrammed handkerchief. "I'm really sorry for leaving you with the full load for the last year, Wil."

Willem waved a hand dismissively. "We'll simply add this to the many favours you owe me." A relieved smile wrinkled his broad face. "So I will see you soon, yes?"

Lee nodded. "I'll be in first thing in the morning. Well, by ten anyway. I've got to get a haircut first."

"Good. We have a new client scheduled for eleven. We will meet in my office then." Willem extended a hand, and Lee shook it.

"I'll be there. Count on it."

Willem turned and climbed the stairs with surprising speed for one of his girth.

"Rhi, we'd better get going, too. The babysitter said she could only give us an hour tonight." Marika kissed Lee on the cheek and wrinkled her nose.

Lee grinned wryly. "Yes, I know. Hit the shower and put on some clean clothes. Job one."

Rhiannon leaned in for another hug. "Marika's right, we've really got to get going, but damn, it's good to see you smile. We'll catch up soon, though, okay? It's just that at the moment your goddaughter is a holy terror. The Terrible Twos is not an old wives' tale, believe me, and I don't want to have to find yet another new babysitter."

Lee felt a surge of regret. "I've been a lousy godmother, haven't I?"

Rhiannon shrugged. "So you'll make up for it. Marnie's two. It's not like she's going to hold it against you because you missed her birthday."

"And Christmas and who knows what else. I've missed time with her, with all of you, and that can't be replaced."

David laid a gentle hand on Lee's shoulder. "Don't focus on time lost, focus on how best to use the time ahead."

Lee took his hand and squeezed it. "That sounds about what I would expect from an ex-priest, but I take your point. And David, I don't know if I ever thanked you for the beautiful sermon you gave at Dana's funeral. I appreciate it more than I can ever tell you. I should've said something long before now."

David hugged Lee and started up the stairs with Rhiannon and Marika. Their voices faded away as they closed the basement door behind them.

Eli regarded Lee warily. "Is it really okay? Are you truly going to be all right now?"

"I can never apologize enough for what I put you through this year, but I swear, it ends tonight." Lee extended her hands, and Eli took them. "I can't promise you I'll never have a bad moment, or that I'll ever stop missing your mom, but I can promise you I'll try to live in a way that will make you proud of me."

"I never stopped being proud of you." Eli's eyes welled up again. "I just felt like I lost both my moms."

Lee pulled him into her arms, revelling in the feel of her son's embrace. "Temporarily misplaced, but not lost, I swear. I'm going to dance at your wedding, and I'm going to be an insufferably indulgent grandmother to all your kids."

"Kids? Liz and I are way too young to have kids."

"Then I'll wait a few years. I can be patient."

Eli chuckled, and Lee pulled back. "So..."

"So...do you want your old bedroom back, Lee? Liz had to work late tonight, but she should be home soon. We can move our stuff into my old room."

"Thanks, but it's not necessary. I'm fine in the basement guest room, though I should put on a clean set of sheets."

"I'll run up and get them. Hey, would you like some supper too? There's leftover meatloaf in the fridge. I could make you up a plate."

"You know what? I'm tired of eating down here. How about I meet you in the kitchen after I have a shower? Make a pot of coffee, and we'll sit down and talk. I'd like to hear all about how you popped the question and what plans you kids have for the wedding."

Lee hadn't seen Eli grin so widely since the day she and Dana had surprised him with a used car on his seventeenth birthday.

"Excellent! I'll go put the coffee on. I think Liz may even have some homemade cookies stashed in the cupboard. C'mon up when you're ready."

Lee watched Eli run up the stairs. She smiled affectionately as she reflected on the dramatic intervention her loved ones had staged. "It's not everyone who'd have had the courage to brave a deranged widow in her lair. I'm a very fortunate woman." Then she laughed outright at the thought of calling herself fortunate. "Half an hour ago I'd have thought that impossible. Just goes to show, I guess. Miracles can happen. They always could around Dana."

The earlier stirrings of hunger had become a full-blown onslaught, so Lee left the den and crossed the basement to the former guest bedroom. Since the day Dana went into hospice care, Lee had been unable to enter the room that had been theirs. This spare room was nothing more than a place to catch a few hours of sleep at night, but at least its walls didn't echo with memories of all the love she and Dana had shared in the decades they'd owned their home.

Lee sat on the edge of the bed and pulled Dana's letter out of the envelope. As she re-read it, she traced the familiar handwriting with her finger and heard her wife's voice in every loving, encouraging word.

One letter, even one as poignant as this, would not single-handedly heal the hollow wound in her heart. It would not fill Lee's barren arms or take the place of the laughing, giving woman who had once slept beside her.

But it was a start. And it was a gift.

CHAPTER 2

LEE STUDIED HER REFLECTION AS the stylist put the final touches on the long-overdue haircut. The sallow, drawn woman looking back at her in the mirror was oddly unfamiliar. Lee's once dark hair, considerably shorter as Angie finished the cut, was almost completely white. Shadows deepened her hazel eyes despite ten hours of sleep.

Angie met Lee's eyes in the mirror. She opened her mouth to say something, but with a small shake of her head, apparently thought better of it.

"It's okay, Ang. I look like hell; I know it."

"You look like someone who's been *through* hell," Angie said gently. She picked up the blow dryer, and for a few moments the whir of the small appliance didn't allow for further conversation. "There, much better."

Angie whipped the cape away, and Lee stood, brushing stray hairs from her suit. Angie frowned and plucked at Lee's sleeve. "You could put two of you in that suit. I think you need to do some shopping."

Lee nodded ruefully. She hadn't donned any of her business suits for so long that she was shocked when she'd had to borrow one of Liz's belts to keep her pants up. “I will, but I’ve got a meeting this morning.” She followed Angie to the front of the shop, where she took out her wallet.

“This one is on me. I’m just glad to see you in here again.”

“That’s awfully sweet, Ang, but I can’t let you do that. This is your livelihood.” Lee held out her credit card, only to have it pushed firmly back at her.

“You and—You’ve been coming here for over twenty years. I think I can spring for one haircut. Call it a loyal customer bonus. After all, it’s my name on the door.” Angie leaned forward with a little smile. “Just don’t let word get around.”

Lee shook her head in amusement. “Am I at least allowed to tip?”

“Not today.” Angie gave Lee a quick hug, handed over her coat, and then turned to open the door. “Now shoo, I’ve got clients waiting, and so do you. I’ll see you next month. Call me for an appointment.”

“Definitely.” As Lee exited the shop, she made a mental note to double her usual tip at the next appointment. A sharp wind hit her face, and Lee flipped her collar up. It was too early in the spring for the morning sun to provide much warmth. She shivered as she strode along the downtown street toward the offices of DeGroot and Glenn Security.

Lee checked her coat pocket for her cigarettes and only then remembered she had smoked her last after breakfast. “Shit.” Her first inclination was to duck into the nearest convenience store, but then she stopped short, recalling the previous night’s promise to her son.

Finally, Lee shook her head and shot an apologetic look skyward. "Sorry, sweetheart; I meant what I said to Eli. I am going to do better, I swear. It's just too hard to give up all my vices at once."

She walked into the convenience store and bought a pack of cigarettes. As soon as she exited the shop, she lit up and drew in a deep lungful of smoke. When she reached the high-rise that housed DeGroot and Glenn, Lee put the cigarette out, exchanging knowing nods with two others who had fled the building's "no smoking" policy.

Lee glanced at her watch as she rode the elevator to the nineteenth floor. She had an hour before their eleven o'clock appointment. It would give her time to get up to speed on their new client. *Knowing Ann, she'll have the file ready and waiting.*

The thought of her long-time assistant brought a smile and then a guilty frown. She hadn't asked Willem if Ann was still in their employ. Perhaps the woman had given up on her long-absent boss and left for more interesting fields. Lee held her breath until she rounded the corner to her office and saw Ann working at her usual desk.

Ann looked up and instantly burst into tears.

Lee stopped short. In twenty-five years, she had never seen her ultra-competent assistant get emotional about anything. "Aw, damn, do I look that bad? I swear I'll go find a tailor today."

Lee's lame jest was ignored as Ann flew around the desk and wrapped her in a bear hug. "You look wonderful. And I could just...just..."

"Squeeze me to death?"

Ann drew away and smacked Lee's arm with a stinging slap. "How could you give up like that? On yourself, on all of us? Dana would've kicked your ass—"

"From here to Vancouver and back. I know, Ann. I'm so sorry." Lee shook her head contritely. She had the feeling that she was going to be making a lot of apologies over the next few days.

"Lee? Is that you?"

Lee and Ann turned at the sound of a familiar voice.

"Damn! As soon as I heard the news, I had to come see for myself. Sonofabitch. I'm so glad to have you back. And about friggin' time, too."

Lee laughed and extended her hand to the head of their technical department. "Happy to see you too, Barb."

Barb shook Lee's hand enthusiastically. "You back for good? You're not just showing your colours, then disappearing again for six months?"

"She's back for good. Aren't you?"

Lee chuckled at Ann's firm statement. "You heard what the lady said. Ann's going to keep me chained to my desk from now on."

"Excellent. Hey, you wanna go for lunch today? The Tudor Rose almost went under this past year without your patronage."

"I'd love to, but Willem and I are meeting with a new client at eleven. I'm not sure how long that will take, but afterwards, I'm going to need to buy some new clothes. How about a rain check?"

"Sure. No problem. You know where you can find me." Barb ambled out of the office and disappeared around the corner.

Ann plucked at Lee's suit jacket. "I'm relieved to hear that you're going to do some shopping. You look like a refugee from a hobo's yard sale."

Lee smiled at Ann affectionately. "I missed you too."

Ann gave a tart sniff and turned away. But by the time Lee entered her office and hung up her jacket, Ann had returned with a cup of coffee. "You'll find the information you need for the meeting filed under 'Britten'."

"Thanks. And Ann, thank you for...for holding down the fort. For not abandoning ship. A lot of people would have."

Ann's face softened, and her eyes glistened with tears again. "None of us gave up on you; none of us ever would. I hope you know that."

"I do now. I just forgot for a little while."

"Perfectly understandable. Now, do you want some time with Willem before eleven?"

"Yes. Ten minutes or so should be good. Thanks."

Ann left the office and closed the door behind her.

Lee leaned back in the leather chair and slowly spun around, admiring the western view of the mountains through floor-to-ceiling windows. Her chest tightened as she remembered the first day she so proudly brought Dana to see her new corner office. For a long moment, Lee indulged the too familiar despair. *No. Not now. I can't do this now. I won't do this now.*

She turned back to her desk and, with a deep breath, switched on her computer.

Lee entered Willem's outer office, the twin of her own, at the opposite end of the long hallway. A new face sat behind the desk. Lee grinned inwardly as she wondered if Willem's wife had laid down the law yet again. Willem had a weakness for lithe, blonde assistants, but the stout, middle-aged woman currently occupying the desk looked as if she had been handpicked by the formidable Mrs. Meena DeGroot.

"May I help you?"

"Yes. Would you please tell Willem that Lee Glenn is here to see him?"

"Oh, Ms. Glenn. I do apologize for not recognizing you." The assistant's gaze flashed to the picture on the wall. She stood and held out her hand, which Lee shook. "I'm Sophie Winston. I started with Mr. DeGroot four months ago. I'll let him know you're here."

Lee nodded. She didn't blame the new assistant. These days she didn't look much like the picture taken when she and Willem had opened their security company twenty-five years earlier.

The inner office door burst open, and Willem hustled out. "Lee. I'm delighted to see you." He shook her hand vigorously and regarded his partner with approval. "Why, you look a hundred times better already. Come. Come." As Willem led Lee into his office, he called back over his shoulder, "Sophie, when Miss Britten arrives, show her right in."

"Yes, sir."

Willem closed the door and motioned Lee to the couch on the side of his office. "Sit. Can I have Sophie bring you a coffee?"

Lee took a seat and sank back in the soft leather. "No, thanks. I've been drinking Ann's brew for the last hour, and you know how potent that stuff is."

Willem laughed as he lowered his ponderous bulk to the couch. "I do indeed. She should market it as a guaranteed cure for fatigue. Remember how we used to rely on her coffee after we'd been out all night working?"

Lee laughed wryly. "Back when it was just you, me, and Ann, all crowded into one tiny basement office."

"DeGroot and Glenn. We've certainly grown since then, haven't we?"

"Yup. Which reminds me, we should probably update our corporate portrait. Neither of us looks much like that now."

Willem patted his generous girth. "True. I think I put on ten pounds for every one that you've lost since then. But let's keep the photo so I can remember the days when I could still outrun you."

"Me and just about anyone else."

"Now I can barely keep up with my grandsons. But it's not so bad, eh? All those twenty-hour days and seven-day weeks? We've done all right for ourselves, yes?"

"I wish... No, you're right. We've done just fine."

Willem regarded Lee keenly. "You wish maybe we'd worked fewer of those long hours so you could've spent them with Dana."

"I never knew the hours would run out, Wil. I thought we had all the time in the world. I figured it would all pay off because we'd have the means to retire early and sail around the world if we wanted to."

Willem was quiet for several long moments, and then he laid a hand on Lee's arm. "My friend, if you want to retire, you have the means to do so. Our hard work has paid off, and very handsomely, I might add. I want you back in the world of the living, but it doesn't necessarily have to be back in these offices. If there's something else you want to do, somewhere else you want to make a fresh start...well, I'd understand and support you one hundred per cent."

"I realize that, but honestly, I've lived and breathed our company so long, I don't know what else I'd do with myself. Retirement without Dana wouldn't mean a damned thing." Lee shot Willem a weak smile. "You'll probably find me expired at my desk some day. When you do, just send for a mortician."

"Or put a cup of Ann's coffee in your hand. If that doesn't revive you—"

"Nothing will. Okay, enough kibitzing. Tell me more about our new client. I read the file, but I can hardly believe it."

"Neither could I, but Stu swears up and down that's how it happened."

"Our Stu? Suspenders, bow tie, and horned rim glasses? *That* Stu rescued a damsel in distress?"

"So he claims, and I have no reason to doubt him. I sent him to London last week on business, and four days later I received a priority call about this woman."

"This Britten. And is that supposed to be her first name or last?"

"Her only. Apparently she wishes to be known

only by one name, like that Madonna woman."

Lee chuckled at Willem's faintly disapproving air. "So, according to the report I read, Stu was at his hotel and he heard a fight in the next room. Somehow I can't imagine him riding to the rescue and engaging in fisticuffs with some miscreant."

"He didn't. He called hotel security. That would've been the extent of his involvement, but before security could arrive, there was a frantic knocking on his door."

"I can just picture Stuey peering out to see who it was."

"According to Stu, he did take the precaution of leaving the door chained. When he opened it, he found a beautiful woman standing there with blood on her face."

"Huh. So he let her in? Doesn't sound like our Stu. She must've been a real knockout, or a real mess, to overcome his caution. The man won't even order lunch until he analyzes all the possibilities."

"Apparently she is, or was at some point, a model. Stu tried to tell Miss Britten that he had summoned security, but the woman begged hysterically so Stu felt compelled to give her sanctuary. He assumed it would be temporary, but when she found out he is Canadian and that he represented an internationally known security company, she prevailed upon him to hear her story."

"And that's when he called you?"

"He did. I'd normally have referred him to Louise, Khabir, or Rick, but Stu believed that Miss Britten's crisis was serious enough to warrant my help directly. He was afraid that he'd lost control of the situation, particularly as Miss Britten had convinced him, quite against his better judgment, to return to her room and collect her luggage once hotel security had removed her assailant. Stu felt that the entire incident was outside his purview."

"Finding a lost dog in a park is outside his purview. Jesus, Wil, he's a numbers cruncher; no wonder he didn't know what to do with a victim of violence. So, who was it—her husband or boyfriend or some unidentified low-life?"

"I'm afraid I'm not clear on that. Stu apparently had reached his explanatory limits. Since Miss Britten possesses a Canadian passport, I told him to escort her here, if she wished, and I would hear her out. They arrived last evening. I picked them up at the airport and deposited them at our safe house."

"*Them*? Stu stayed with her?"

"She appears to have become somewhat dependent on him, and I felt it better to allow them to remain together until this morning's interview."

"What did Stu's wife think about that?"

"I didn't feel the need to ask. Our employees' domestic affairs are their own concern."

Lee grinned as she tried to imagine mousy little Stu involved in a torrid affair with an international model.

A deep, rumbling chuckle from beside her indicated Willem was trying to picture the same thing. Within seconds they were laughing together, and only a sharp rap on the door put a damper on their hilarity.

The door swung open, and Sophie entered. "Miss

Britten and Mr. Lambert are here to see you, sir."

Still chuckling, Willem stood. "Show them in, Sophie." He turned to Lee. "Do you want to take the lead?"

Lee shook her head as she also stood. "No, I'm a little rusty. You go ahead; I'll listen."

Stu Lambert entered the office with a slender, dark, exotic beauty clinging to his arm. Lee casually passed a hand over her mouth to hide a smile. Miss Britten towered over Stu by a good ten inches, but he strutted like a royal guard escorting a queen. He officiously saw her to a chair and assumed a rigid posture behind Miss Britten, resting one hand on her shoulder.

"Thank you, Stu. I'm sure Miss Britten deeply appreciates your kindness, but I'll need your report and numbers from the London office as soon as possible."

Stu bristled at Willem's order, and Lee could tell he was about to protest—unprecedented behaviour on his part—but Miss Britten patted his hand. "It's okay, Stuey. I know you have to get back to work. I'll see you later, okay?"

Stu nodded stiffly, straightened his bow tie, and marched out of the office.

Willem extended a hand to their guest. "Miss Britten, I'm Willem DeGroot, and this is my partner, Lee Glenn."

Miss Britten gave Lee an absent nod as she shook Willem's hand.

Lee could tell she'd been instantly assessed and dismissed. *Huh. Must be the suit.*

Willem continued, "Mr. Lambert told me

something of your situation, but if you wouldn't mind going over the details for us, I would greatly appreciate it. As I understand it, you're looking for protection from...whom?"

"My husband. Willem...may I call you Willem? My husband is a cruel, violent man. He believes our marriage gave him the right to dictate my every move." Britten dabbed at her eyes with a tissue. "He forced me to leave my career in fashion, and my life has been hell ever since."

Willem had resumed his seat behind his desk and was taking notes while Lee watched and listened to their potential client. *Interesting accent, Miss Britten. Somewhere between England and North America, but not grounded in either.*

"What is your husband's name, Miss Britten?"

The former model flashed a smile at Willem. "Just Britten, please, Willem. His name is Michael Saberi." When Willem didn't react, she added, "From the Dubai oil family?"

"I'm not familiar with them, but please do go on."

Britten frowned momentarily. "Well, he's not really involved in the family business anyway. Michael is much more interested in the arts. That's how we met—at an event to raise funding for a new gallery he decided to invest in."

Lee suppressed her instinctive eye roll. *Translation: he's never had to work a day in his life, and he never will. So he fills his time with pretty baubles and pretty women.* Lee knew she was being overly cynical, but she had swiftly sized Britten up and wasn't impressed by their new client. She would compare notes with Willem after Britten left, but she had already lost interest. Unless she missed her guess, this would be a standard personal protection detail, right up Rick's alley. Miss Britten would engage their services until she got bored being away from the high life and returned to her husband or until she found a lawyer good enough to break the pre-nup that Saberi's family had no doubt insisted on. In either event, the case didn't appeal to her.

"How long have you been married, Britten?"

"Almost a year." Britten dabbed at her eyes again, though Lee was willing to bet the tissue came away dry. "And it's gotten so much worse lately. He's suffocating me to the point where I've seriously considered suicide."

Willem shot Lee a glance.

She subtly shook her head in response to his unspoken query. *She might fake a try, but only if it got her the attention she craves. No need to worry about that, my friend.*

"What would you like us to do? How can we help?"

Britten lowered her gaze and wrung her hands. "Protect me. Stop him from killing me!"

"Do you genuinely feel this is a possibility? That your husband would actually seek you out and murder you?"

Lee noted the split second hesitation before Britten began to sob.

"He wouldn't do it himself. He'd never get his hands dirty that way. He'd send his men after me. Oh God, I'm so scared. You must help me!"

Lee openly rolled her eyes as Britten buried her

face in her hands and wailed histrionically.

Willem came around the desk and patted Britten's shoulder comfortingly. He shot Lee a disapproving glance.

She sighed and went to the small fridge. She extracted a bottle of water, twisted off the cap, and handed it to Willem.

"Britten. Miss Britten. Please try to get hold of yourself. You may rest assured that we will not allow any harm to come to you." Willem offered the bottle, and Britten wrapped her hands around his as she focused a teary, pleading gaze on him. "There, there. Everything is going to be all right. We'll work out the details. For now you'll be perfectly safe where you stayed last night."

"No, I won't. You don't understand. I've tried to leave Michael before, and he always tracks me down. He keeps an investigator on retainer, and the man is very good at what he does. Michael will find me within the week. I can't even access my accounts, and I've got less than seven thousand Euros with me."

Lee cocked her head. For the first time Britten sounded genuinely distressed. "Did I understand Stu correctly that you are originally from Canada?"

Britten turned toward Lee, her expression faintly startled, as if she'd forgotten Lee's presence. "I am, yes."

"Has your husband met your family? Would he be able to track you through them?"

Lee was taken aback at the momentary look of embarrassment that flashed across Britten's face.

"No. I, um, didn't exactly tell Michael the truth

about my background. He doesn't even know my birth name."

"Does anyone in your circle have that information? Anyone who might relay it to your husband?"

Britten shook her head. "No. I thought it best to reinvent myself completely when I went to Europe. I even legally changed my name."

"Your passport. In what name was it issued?"

"Britten Saberi. I took Michael's surname when I got married last year."

"That's unfortunate. It would've slowed his investigator down if you'd flown here under your original name. However, it's not the end of the world. Since his search will begin where your flight ended, we'll simply have to get you out of Calgary by car."

Britten turned back to Willem. "I suppose I could seek refuge with my family for a short while." She scowled and flicked a dismissive hand. "Donegal, Saskatchewan is so far off the beaten path that even Michael's bloodhounds wouldn't find me there. God! I don't know if I can stand going back. There's nothing there but gophers, grasshoppers, and grain elevators. I left to save my sanity, and I doubt much has changed."

Willem reached inside his jacket and withdrew his cell phone. "Rick? Could you come to my office for a moment, please? I have a new assignment for you." He ended the call and gave Britten a reassuring smile. "Rick will take you back to the safe house and stay with you until we've made arrangements to convey you to your family's home. Sophie has a copy of our standard contract. You may take it with you and peruse it at your leisure, but I will need it signed and returned with a deposit before you leave Calgary."

"Fine. Will Rick stay with me in Donegal? If Michael's man is able to track me, I'm terrified about what could happen to me—and to my family, of course."

"We've never lost anyone under our protection. You'll have a bodyguard for the duration, I assure you."

A light knock sounded on the door, and Sophie poked her head in. "Rick is here, Mr. DeGroot. Should I show him in?"

"No. We'll come out there." Willem offered an arm to Britten. She took it and the two of them followed Sophie into the outer office.

Willem returned a few minutes later. "Well?"

Lee shrugged. "Well, what?"

"Your instincts have always been dead on. I want your assessment."

"My assessment? Britten has coasted through life on her looks, getting what she wanted, when she wanted it. She's used to wrapping men around her little finger and dismissing women as irrelevant."

"You saw that?"

"Of course. I'm rusty, not blind. I don't have enough background information to evaluate her claim about her husband, but I plan to remedy that this afternoon. Before Rick drives her to her family's place, we should know whether Michael Saberi poses a legitimate threat. We can work from there. I doubt it'll be more than a routine personal protection detail, and Rick's certainly had plenty of experience with those."

Willem resumed his seat on the couch. "What if we didn't assign Rick?"

"You can't assign Khabir. If her husband is of Middle Eastern extraction, Britten is unlikely to accept Khabir as a bodyguard. And you can't send Louise, either. Britten wouldn't think she was getting her money's worth from a female bodyguard, even though Louise is more dangerous than Rick and Khabir put together."

"Actually I had someone else in mind."

"We've got someone new on staff?" Lee tried to smile, but the reminder that the world hadn't stopped when she withdrew from it stung.

"Several, actually, but I was thinking about a veteran. Someone who knows the business inside and out, has ample experience, and the skill to assess the situation immediately."

"Who...? Oh no, Wil. You don't mean me?"

"I do." When Lee began to object, Willem held up his hand. "Hear me out. You and I founded this company on nothing, and we both worked every angle of the business while building it into the entity it is today. You are a director, not a field officer. You've earned that big corner office, and you have the right to never leave your desk again, if that's what you want. But even before Dana... even before Dana got sick, you were getting bored. Handling contracts, schmoozing with potential clients, setting up branch offices, overseeing employees, and balancing budgets...that end of our business is not your passion."

"No, the admin side has always been your bailiwick. I know that, but I hope you feel I've contributed equally, except of course since Dana..."

"God, yes! We wouldn't have lasted past the first year without your knowledge and experience. Our diverse strengths have made us an excellent team over the last two and a half decades."

"They have." Lee sighed and took a seat opposite Willem. "Are you telling me you think that's in the past? That I can't come back and be a productive partner."

"Phfftt. I'm not saying that in the least, and shame on you for thinking it. If you truly want to return heart and soul to our company, then DeGroot and Glenn would only be the stronger for it. But I'm worried about you. I'm well aware of how losing Dana affected you, and I would never begrudge you the time to grieve and heal. But are you healed, my old friend? Do you genuinely want to return to the corporate grind for the rest of your life? Or is there perhaps something else that would restore the joy that is now missing in you?"

Willem was silent as Lee contemplated his words. Finally, she shrugged and shook her head. "I don't know, Wil. I really don't. Two days ago, if I thought about it at all, I didn't picture being back here. But last night you said you wanted your partner back. You said you were tired of carrying the business by yourself. I want to take back my share of the burden."

"I said that because we were all trying desperately to reach you. But we pay very good people to carry most of the burden, including my son and sons-in-law. What's left is what I enjoy doing. I'll never retire, you know that."

"Meena might have something to say about that."

"Ah, my wife is happy as long as there are grandchildren about. Lee, I'm serious. I learned two things in your absence. One is that none of us are irreplaceable. We may have stumbled initially, but the business is running like a well-oiled machine now. Two, I cherish you too much to see you unhappy in our partnership. Which is why I think you should take this detail with Miss Britten."

"I don't get the connection."

"You could do this sort of thing with your eyes shut. Whether Miss Britten is genuinely in danger or merely a hysterical flake, you'll keep her safe until her lust for the bright lights overcomes her good sense."

"You think she actually *has* any good sense?"

Willem chuckled. "I think every human being, even those lacking in common sense, harbours a strong survival instinct. If she truly feels herself in danger, she won't cause you any problems, and if she doesn't, it will be a short hiatus. It's a win-win situation. You fulfill an easy contract and get away to where it is easier to think. My only concern is if you're physically up to a personal protection detail." He gave an apologetic shrug. "A year ago this would not have been an issue, but—"

"It's okay, Wil. I get it." Lee ruefully clutched the copious loose material of her jacket. "I'm not exactly the woman I once was, but if it makes you feel any better, I spent more hours than I could count exercising this last year. I'm sure I drove Eli and Liz crazy using the basement gym at all hours. And I'd slip out of the house when they were asleep and just walk for hours until I was tired enough to go back to bed for a few hours. I doubt I could run a marathon tomorrow, but I'm still up to fighting off a baddie or two."

"If you quit smoking, I'm quite sure you could run a marathon."

"I know, and I'll get around to it. Just not today, okay?"

Willem nodded. "If this Donegal is as remote as Miss Britten indicates, then I suspect you'll have much time on your hands. Use the opportunity to contemplate what you genuinely want from life. When you return, we will talk again, yes?"

"Let me think about it. I'll get back to you before the end of the day, okay?"

Willem heaved himself to his feet and held out his hand.

Lee rose and took it. They shook firmly, and then, to Lee's surprise, Willem pulled her in for a hug.

"Do what's best for you, Lee. Base your decision only on that, because that is all your friends and family will ask of you. Yes?"

Lee gently pulled away. "Yes. And thank you. As always, I owe you."

Instead of dismissing her remark with his customary jest, Willem shook his head. "Any debt you ever owed me you've paid in full. This time, you owe only yourself."

CHAPTER 3

Lee pulled to the curb and turned off the engine. She eyed the bungalow. There was nothing remarkable about the exterior of the house, but having once been a frequent visitor, she knew it was a welcoming place, filled with warmth and love. For a moment, the longing for the home life she had shared with Dana almost overwhelmed her. But as she had done repeatedly that day, Lee firmly pushed the sorrow aside.

Marnie appeared in the front picture window. Lee grinned as the child started to hammer her tiny fists against the glass. When a familiar form arrived to scoop her squirming daughter away, Lee laughed aloud. Rhiannon beckoned to her, and with a lighter heart, Lee exited her vehicle and walked to the front door.

The door swung wide, and Rhiannon stood with Marnie in her arms. "You're just in time. Marika texted that she's on her way home. Supper will be on the table in about twenty minutes."

Lee stopped abruptly. "Damn, I should've called. I thought you guys would be done with supper by now."

Rhiannon grabbed Lee's arm and tugged her

into the foyer. "Nonsense. You know you're always welcome. Marika had to work tonight, so we're eating late. Actually, this works out perfectly. The tiny terror has been fed. I was about to bathe her and put her to bed, so we'll have lots of time to talk." Without waiting for Lee's agreement, Rhiannon walked down the hall toward the bathroom.

Unsure if she should follow, Lee hung her coat in the closet.

"Grab an umbrella and c'mon in, Lee."

Amused, Lee followed the sound of running water and Marnie's high-pitched squeals of delight. After rounding the corner, she saw Rhiannon wrestling her daughter's clothes off while Marnie tried to climb into the tub.

"Umbrella?"

"Yup. Marnie is a splasher. She likes everyone to share her love of water." Rhiannon lifted the toddler into the tub and ducked when Marnie slammed her hands down.

Lee retreated to the doorway and smiled while she watched her old friend deftly shampoo golden curls. Rhiannon had changed so much from the scrawny, reclusive young woman Lee had first met more than a dozen years before. She still had some of the weight put on during her pregnancy, but it suited her. Lee couldn't tell who enjoyed the bath ritual more as mother and child exuberantly splashed, rinsed, and laughed in equal measure.

When Marnie was clean, Rhiannon tossed some bath toys into the tub and leaned back.

Lee handed her a towel and got a grateful look.

Rhiannon dried her face. "Thanks. Usually we

just get in the tub with her. It saves me doing laundry five times a day." She leaned forward and tickled Marnie's belly. "But Mama was late this time, wasn't she, sweetie? So, no bath for us tonight." Rhiannon winked up at Lee. "At least not until after one little girl is long asleep."

Lee chuckled, then swiftly reached out her hand and snagged a well-chewed rubber duck that was launched her way from the tub. "Wow, that's quite the arm she has."

"Uh-huh. Terry's already taught Marnie how to catch. We figure she's going to have an arm like Dana's in a few years." Rhiannon's face fell, and she glanced at Lee apologetically.

Lee forestalled her with a smile. "No, it's okay, Rhi. I think it's wonderful that Dana is remembered. She'd be thrilled to know our goddaughter is going to follow in her footsteps. Heck, if she were here, she'd have Marnie running bases already."

Rhiannon leaned back against the side of the tub. She absently pushed toys toward Marnie and regarded Lee. "How are you doing? Did it go all right today? Being back at work, I mean."

"Pretty well. Actually, I wanted to get your advice—yours and Marika's."

"About something work-related?"

"Sort of."

Their conversation was interrupted by the sound of the garage door opening, and Marnie instantly tried to stand up.

"Uh-uh, sweetie," Rhiannon said while she wrapped the towel around the excited toddler and lifted her out of the tub. "I know you want to see

Mama, but she's not going to be happy if you have a big owie on your head."

Marnie babbled and rocked in Rhiannon's arms as footsteps sounded in the hall.

Lee stepped out of the way when Marika rounded the corner and stopped short.

"Lee! How wonderful to see you!"

Marnie lunged for Marika, who caught her and spun her around. "Who's Mama's big girl?" She leaned forward and kissed Rhiannon before returning her attention to Lee. "I hope you're staying for supper."

Rhiannon answered, "I already asked her, love."

"And did she say yes?"

Both Marika and Rhiannon looked at Lee, who laughingly held up her hands in surrender. "I know when I'm out manoeuvred. I'd be glad to stay for dinner. I just wish I'd brought something."

Marika hugged Lee with her free arm. "Having you here again is the best gift we could ask for."

Rhiannon nodded emphatically. "Besides, you can help me finish getting dinner ready while Marika changes and gets Marnie into her jammies."

Lee followed Rhiannon to the kitchen and was put to work setting the table for three. When Lee was finished, she sat down and watched as Rhiannon assembled a salad. "You're happy, aren't you?"

Rhiannon glanced up at the quiet words. "I am. How could I not be?"

"You don't miss work at all?"

"Sometimes. But I'll go back once Marnie is in school. For now we just really want to give her the love and security neither of us had."

That didn't surprise Lee. She was aware of the chaotic and broken youths both women had endured. She found the determination in Rhiannon's voice reassuring. Her goddaughter would be raised with love and devotion. "Can't ask for more than that."

"Pardon?"

"Oh, nothing. Mind you don't slice your fingers along with that tomato."

Marika entered the kitchen with Marnie snuggled against her shoulder in bright yellow, footed pyjamas. "I most heartily concur. I'd prefer you keep all your digits intact."

Rhiannon and Marika exchanged looks of knowing intimacy, leaving Lee feeling like an intruder.

"Um, maybe I should just go. I shouldn't have come without calling first. We can talk later."

"No," Rhiannon and Marika answered at the same time. Rhiannon hastily dried her hands and reached for Marnie. "Just give us a few minutes to settle Her Highness, and we'll be right back."

Lee watched the family leave the room, then looked around the large kitchen. She and Dana had helped paint every room in the house when Marika and Rhiannon bought it five years ago. She allowed herself to get lost in the memory of the laughter and the mess as the four worked in concert. A wistful smile curled Lee's lips when she recalled worrying about Dana standing on a wobbly stepladder to reach above cupboards.

I was afraid you'd sprain your ankle if you fell. Little did I know that should've been the least of my concerns, eh, sweetheart?

Instead of pushing the sorrow away, this time Lee allowed herself to feel it, to grieve for the carefree innocence of those ten years between Dana's first victory over cancer and the beginning of her final fight.

When a gentle hand touched her cheek, Lee became aware of the tears rolling down her face. She blinked and looked up to find Marika watching her with glistening eyes. "Oh, I'm sorry. I just—"

Marika wrapped Lee in a fierce hug. "Don't you dare apologize, Lee Glenn. This is what you should've been doing all along—letting us in, not shutting us out. Don't think for one moment that we haven't cried buckets for her—and for you, too."

Lee let Marika's embrace comfort her, slowly realizing this was the first time she'd allowed anyone to do that for her. When Rhiannon returned and immediately joined the group hug, Lee felt the first stirring of long-forgotten serenity.

"So, do you think this Britten woman is actually in danger from her husband?"

Lee shook her head at Marika's question. "None of the research I did this afternoon turned up any evidence that Saberi has a violent background."

"But didn't you say she had blood on her face when Stu answered the door?"

"So Stu said, Rhi, but all she needed was a Band-Aid, so it was pretty minor."

"I dunno," Rhiannon said. "Remember my encounter years ago with that crazy Jordanian who was looking for his sister at Marika's office?

Middle Eastern men can be pretty controlling with the women in their family."

"As I recall, that encounter jump-started the relationship between you two, so in a way, you owe that psycho."

"You have a point, though we really owe *you* more than anyone else. If you and Dana hadn't facilitated breaking the ice between us, who knows if we'd ever have gotten together."

Lee shook her head. "No way, Marika. You two were meant for each other. One way or another, you'd have figured that out. But back to Saberi. I grant that given his origins, he's probably not all that evolved about women's issues. But he seems to be exactly what his bio says: the fifth son of a Middle Eastern oil billionaire, who was sent to all the best schools in Europe and who has spent his adult life dabbling in the arts and buying pretty things."

"Including his wife."

"Rhi, that's not very nice."

Rhiannon shot Marika an unrepentant look. "Maybe not, but I'll bet it's true."

"It could be. I also researched Britten's background this afternoon. From what I could tell, she was on the dwindling end of a very minor modelling career by the time she met Saberi. They dated for four years before getting married. She may have viewed him as a meal ticket and a way to stay connected, and he may have viewed her as a trophy wife. Who knows? I suspect Britten will rapidly tire of northern Saskatchewan and return to the gilded fold sooner rather than later, even if

Saberi isn't a perfect husband. Nonetheless, given Saberi's resources, he could make things difficult for Britten if he chooses. So if I do accept this assignment, I won't take it lightly."

"And that's it in a nutshell, isn't it?" Marika said. "You know you could practically handle this assignment with your eyes closed; you're just not sure if you want to."

"That's it exactly. It's way below my pay grade, but Willem obviously thinks I should take it. I owe him big time for carrying the load this past year, and I'm inclined to take it for that reason, if no other."

"It's so good to see you animated about something again." Rhiannon's eyes sparkled with enthusiasm. "I think you should go. Shake off the rust, clear your head, and see some new horizons."

"I don't think there's much in Donegal *but* horizons, so you're right that it would give me an opportunity to clear my head." Lee shot her friends an apologetic look. "God knows I need to clear my head after this past year. I'm so sorry for what I put you all through. I know how hard you tried to be there for me, and I just kept pushing everyone away. I don't know how I can ever make it up to you."

Rhiannon and Marika reached for Lee's hands. "You don't owe us a thing." Marika spoke for them both, her voice choked with tears. "No, strike that. You do owe us something, but you mostly owe it to yourself and to Dana's memory. You owe those who love you the joy of seeing you come back to life. And if that means exiling yourself to the boonies for a while, that's what you should do. Go breathe some fresh air and walk under the prairie skies. It'll be a vast improvement over your self-imposed exile this past year."

"So you both think I should take it?"

"I think so. Marika?" Marika nodded her agreement, and Rhi continued. "Eli and Liz's wedding is in July, right? That gives you three months to wrap up this assignment and come home a new woman."

"Babysitting a spoiled ex-model is not my idea of a choice assignment, but I admit my gut instinct is to do this."

"Then trust your instinct. We do."

"You know what? You're right." Lee pushed back from the table. "Will you excuse me for a moment? I'm going to call Willem and tell him."

Rhiannon clapped her hands and whooped.

Marika said, "Excellent. And hurry back, because I do believe my wife has your favourite ice cream in the freezer—that is, if she and Marnie didn't finish it while I was at work."

Lee left the room, grinning at the mock squabble echoing behind her. As she pulled out her phone and placed the call to her partner, she savoured the satisfaction of making her decision. It was her first resolution since Dana's funeral, and she sensed that it was the right one.

Britten stared at Willem in dismay. "Are you kidding me?"

Lee watched the proceedings with a concealed

smile as Willem projected his most soothing manner to their perturbed client. It was no skin off her nose if Miss Britten refused to accept her services. It wasn't as if Lee was looking forward to a long drive in the company of the dismissive woman.

"You told me that Rick would be my bodyguard, Willem."

"Actually, I didn't. If you recall, I simply assured you that you would have a bodyguard for the duration of your stay in Donegal. Lee is not only a founding partner of the firm, but the best we have. She rarely takes such low-level assignments, but we feel your situation warrants it."

Lee was amused equally by Willem's diplomacy and the disdainful look Britten shot her way. *Huh, guess she's not impressed with my new suit.*

"I assure you, if your husband's people pursue you, Lee is the one you want by your side. If you wish to review some of her previous casework, you're more than welcome to do so."

"I don't want to read a bunch of files; I want what you promised me. I want Rick."

Willem adjusted and readjusted his tie, a clear indication that he had reached the end of his prodigious patience after calming and coaxing their client for fifteen minutes. "I'm afraid Rick is on another assignment, Miss Britten. If you feel that our agency is not able to meet your needs, I would be happy to make a recommendation for one better suited."

"No, it's too much bother." Britten heaved a heavy sigh. "Fine. We'll do it your way. I'll accept... um..."

Lee stepped forward and extended her hand. "Lee Glenn, at your service. Now that that's settled, can you be ready to go in an hour?"

Ignoring Lee's hand, Britten shook her head indignantly. "An hour? It'll take me at least that long just to pack up my makeup."

"Then shall we say noon? I'll see you back here at twelve."

Britten nodded sullenly and flounced out of the room.

Willem hit his intercom. "Sophie, would you see Miss Britten back to the safe house and ensure she returns with all her belongings by noon?"

"Yes, Mr. DeGroot."

Willem turned to Lee with a sigh. "I'm so sorry, old friend. Perhaps I've done you no favour in urging you to accompany this...troublesome client."

Lee chuckled and patted Willem's shoulder. "No worries. I wasn't under any illusions."

"But what a way to get your toes wet again."

"I've always found it's best to jump into the deep end of the pool. I do have a couple of thoughts I want to run by you, though."

"Of course, but you're the field expert."

"A *rusty* field expert after this past year."

"Rust or no, you're still the best, and that woman is lucky to have you."

"You'd better be careful, or you're going to ruin your carefully cultivated image. Who, besides Meena, knows what a softie you are underneath all that stoicism?"

Willem stiffened at Lee's teasing, but she didn't miss the amusement in his eyes. "Softie? I'll have you know I was prepared to toss that irritating woman out on her ear."

"I know, but I'm glad you didn't. Now, about those thoughts. From what I found in my research, Britten was never more than a small fish, even at the height of her modelling career, which was about ten years ago. I don't think there's any danger of her being 'celeb-spotted' on our journey north, but I thought I'd stick to secondary roads anyway, just in case."

"Excellent."

"Also, I called Rick last night to confirm that he'd warned our client away from all social media. The last thing we need is for her to tweet her disgust with her new situation or post photos of gophers, grasshoppers, and grain elevators on Facebook."

"Do you think she would be so foolish?"

"I do. She apparently gave Rick a hard time when he looked into which sites she'd been logging on to since she arrived. She'd already left bread crumbs online but fortunately hadn't mentioned her ultimate destination, so I think we're okay for now."

"Social media. What a scourge."

"C'mon, Wil, you know it's made our jobs a lot easier in many ways."

"But not in this case."

"No, probably not, but I'll keep reminding the client to be careful."

"Good luck with that. Good luck with everything. Keep me advised, all right?"

Lee winked before she turned to leave. "I'll text you."

Lee glanced over at her brooding passenger, who was plugged in and tuned out. Since they'd left Calgary hours earlier, Britten had barely uttered ten words beyond complaining about her smart-phone connectivity. She'd spent the last couple of hours listening to music turned up so high that Lee could hear it leaking around her passenger's earbuds.

With a small shrug, Lee returned her attention to the road. It wasn't her problem if Britten needed hearing aids before she was forty.

An hour later, Lee felt the still unfamiliar stirrings of hunger. Over the past year of ignoring her body's basic needs, she'd almost forgotten what it was like to look forward to her next meal. It was a welcome reminder that she had officially rejoined the human race.

"Hey, Britten."

Britten ignored Lee, gazing out the side window and beating out the rhythm of the music on her thigh.

"Yo, Britten."

When her passenger still ignored her, Lee reached over and tugged an earbud out.

"Hey!"

Lee ignored the indignation. "I need some guidance here. We're just about to your old stomping grounds. Where's a good place to stop for a bite to eat?"

"I haven't been here in almost fifteen years. It's probably completely changed."

"You're the one who said things never change around here. Gophers, grasshoppers, and grain elevators, remember?"

Britten huffed but appeared to give it some thought. "Well, there used to be a café just west of Donegal, the Four Corners Café. We're about forty minutes from it."

"Good enough. We'll stop there."

Britten popped her earbud back in, and Lee resumed perusing the landscape. It was clearly farming and ranching territory, though too early in the year for crops to be growing. They had passed a lot of cattle, with an abundance of calves in the herds. Lee wondered if Britten's family was involved in growing wheat or raising cattle, but she didn't feel like trying to start a conversation.

Half an hour later, Britten's voice jolted Lee from her reverie.

"There, ahead on the left. See it?"

A cluster of pickups was parked next to an old but neatly kept restaurant. A sign advertised the Four Corners Café, and Lee slowed to make her turn.

"Watch out. This is Dysfunction Junction. I can't begin to tell you how many accidents have happened at these crossroads over the years."

Lee was surprised at the almost friendly tone in Britten's voice and glanced over at her passenger. Britten had a look of suppressed anticipation, and Lee wondered if she was genuinely excited about returning home after all the years away. Certainly nothing in her previous manner had suggested the possibility, but Lee remembered how it had always felt returning to her grandparents' home after long absences. Possibly her client wasn't immune after all.

Lee pulled into the parking lot and took a spot between a blue F-150 and another pickup that was too covered with mud to detect a colour.

Britten was out of the SUV almost as soon as it stopped. Lee followed at a slower pace, her body feeling the ache of long hours on the road.

They seated themselves, and before they'd even had time to open the menus on the table, a heavy-set, middle-aged waitress was at their side with a pot of coffee. Looking at Lee, she said, "You look like you could use a cup, hon."

Lee nodded gratefully as her cup was filled before the waitress turned to Britten. "What about you, hon?" Then the waitress did such a classic double-take that Lee almost laughed aloud. "Well, turn me over like a turtle! Heather Ann, is that you?"

"It's Britten, Aunt Eileen. Heather Ann left here long ago."

"Huh. Well, I changed more of Heather Ann's diapers than I could ever count, and I've never met this Britten you speak of."

Lee watched the two glare at each other, then the waitress broke the stalemate. "It's real good to see you again, hon, by whatever name you want to use. I'm surprised, though. We had a family get-together last weekend, and Gaëlle never said one word about you coming home. Of course, your mother can be more close-mouthed than a priest when she wants to be."

"Mom doesn't know."

That got Lee's attention. When they'd finalized their plans, Britten said she'd called her mother and everything was in order for their arrival. Obviously, that had been a lie, so Lee began making back-up plans in the event Britten's mother refused to welcome her prodigal daughter home.

"Well, that won't matter. Gaëlle never turned a soul from her door in her life, and she's certainly not going to start with her baby."

Lee relaxed a little on hearing Eileen's assessment but still calculated where they might find a night's lodging, just in case.

"So, what'll you two have?"

They placed their orders, and Eileen left.

Britten fidgeted, but Lee ignored her. She wasn't about to give her client absolution for the blatant lie, so she gazed out the window instead.

Suddenly, Lee blinked and stared. The strangest creature was riding by on a bicycle pulling a homemade cart, loaded to unbelievable heights with bags, boxes, wheels, pieces of wood, metal, and glass, and clothes stuffed into every crevice. Abruptly, the man stopped and looked through the café window at Lee.

"Oh, for God's sake. Is that loon still around?"

Lee ignored Britten's disparaging comment and examined the apparition. It was impossible to determine his age. A floppy, weather-beaten hat shadowed his deeply lined face. An unkempt grey beard hung to his chest, and his thin frame was dwarfed by an oversized, tattered greatcoat. Most startlingly, ribbons of every colour were pinned all over the coat. The steady prairie breezes caught the ribbons and lifted them in an illusion of multi-coloured feathers. Lee half expected the man to take flight, but he only stared at her with intense, light-coloured eyes. Finally, he nodded at her, pushed his bike into motion, and pedalled away as his treasures clanged and swayed dangerously on the cart.

"How the hell does that not knock him right over?"

Eileen had returned and chuckled as she slid their plates in front of them. "Oh, don't you worry about Wrong-Way. He's been riding that thing for over forty years, and he hasn't fallen yet."

When the waitress left, Lee eyed Britten over her hamburger. "Wrong-Way? There has to be a story there."

Britten pushed disdainfully at her salad. "They still don't know anything but iceberg lettuce here." She set down her fork and picked up her coffee cup. "Wrong-Way Wally Woodson is the town eccentric, to put it mildly. He got the name when he was a boy, because he'd ride that stupid bike through town with no regard for direction signs. One time he even made it as far as the highway and got on that going in the wrong direction, so the name just stuck. He's a complete idiot, and no one ever listens to what he says, even though some people—some really ignorant people—think he's got the gift of second sight."

"You don't sound too enthralled with him. What did he ever do to you?"

"Nothing!" After a brief, uncomfortable silence, Britten continued, "It's just so damned embarrassing. Wrong-Way and my mom have been best friends since they were born on the same day in the same hospital. Do you know what it's like to have your friends make fun of you because your mother insists on treating a freak like he's normal? Everyone in town knows he's demented, except my mother. Hell, he's one of the reasons I left here. I couldn't stand the humiliation one day longer."

Lee's estimation of Britten's mother instantly shot up. "Are they...involved?"

"God, no!" Britten glared at Lee as if she'd just suggested that her mother dated goats. "As far as I know, my mom hasn't been involved with anyone since my dad died, and even she wouldn't take up with Wrong-Way. Jesus, how can you even think that?"

"I didn't. I was just extrapolating from your words. You haven't really told me anything about your family, so I was curious."

"Well, we're not freaks, if that's what you mean. Even Mom is just...unusual, but she's not nearly as weird as he is."

"Tell me about her. Tell me about your family."

"Why?"

"Since you didn't want to alarm your mother, I'm supposed to be posing as a friend of yours. It stands to reason that you'd have talked to me about your family at some point."

"Not really. I don't think I've talked about my family since I left here."

"Not even to your husband?"

"No. I sort of...made up my background. I told him I'd been abandoned in a Russian orphanage and adopted by American parents who died a long time ago."

"Okay, but if we're good enough friends that you're taking me along for a long-overdue visit, then it would be good to brief me on what to expect."

"All right, but my information may be a little dated. We exchange Christmas and birthday cards, and Mom writes at least once a month, but we're not best friends by any means."

"Start with your dad. You said he passed away? How long ago was that?"

"I was a baby; I don't even remember him. He was driving my older brothers to a hockey tournament when he lost control of the car on icy roads. They were hit by an oncoming truck, and my dad and brother Owen were killed. My brother Dale was in the back seat. He survived, though he had some broken bones."

"So you grew up with your mom and brother?"

"And my older sister, Jill. Not to mention my grandmother, uncles, aunts, and a bushel of cousins."

"You were lucky to have a big family."

"Hah! That's what you think. Everyone knowing your business; everyone butting in with an opinion. It drove me crazy."

Lee flashed back on her solitary childhood. She adored the grandparents who'd loved and raised her, but she'd often longed for siblings. "My parents were killed in a car crash, too. I was only three when it happened."

"Oh. Sorry."

Lee waved a dismissive hand. "Long time ago. So, what did your mom do while you were growing up?"

"Do?"

"Yeah, with your dad gone, did she have to work outside the home to support you?"

"I don't think so. My dad was partners in a family ranch with his four brothers. I think my uncles just kept paying Mom his share so that she had enough to raise us. I never really thought about it much."

Lee suspected Britten had rarely thought about much beyond her own concerns. Conversation lapsed, and Lee finished her burger. Finally, she pointed at the salad Britten had ignored. "Are you going to eat that?"

"No."

"Do you want something else instead?"

"No."

"Then let's pay the bill and get going. If we're going to surprise your mother, I'd rather do it while there's still some light."

CHAPTER 4

TEN MINUTES AFTER LEE AND Britten left the Four Corners Café, they reached the outskirts of Donegal, population 3,214. Five minutes later, they were through Donegal and on the road out of town.

Britten pointed ahead. "Take the next left. Mom's place is about fifteen minutes north of here."

Lee turned the SUV off the paved thoroughfare and onto a gravel road. They were rapidly losing daylight now, so she slowed and peered into the dusk. Two deer were feeding next to the road. They threw up their heads as the vehicle approached, then wheeled and darted away.

"You weren't kidding about your family's place being out in the country."

Britten snorted. "When I was a teenager, I hated being isolated in the sticks during summer vacation. I couldn't wait until the school bus started coming again in September."

"Did you go to school in Donegal?"

"Yes. I had to join the basketball team just so I could travel to some decent-sized shopping centres when the team played away games. I sucked, by the way. I had the height; that's about all I had going for me. I remember once when I missed a big game during a weekend tournament in Moose Jaw. My coach was mad, but Mom was madder. She had to drive down and pick me up after I was booted from the team."

"Was it worth it? Making everyone angry?"

"I guess. I went home with some awesome swag. Or so I figured at the time. God, I can't believe I once thought a Moose Jaw mall was the height of fine fashion. My standards were so low then."

"And now?"

"And now… I don't know. I don't know what to do, what to plan. I certainly don't want to spend the rest of my life back here. I fought too hard to escape."

Lee thought that was the most honest thing Britten had said since they'd met. It also solidified her belief that this assignment would not last long before her rootless client fled back to brighter lights.

They drove in silence for another ten minutes before Britten directed Lee onto an even narrower gravel road. "There. Up ahead on the left. Can you see the light down that long driveway?"

"Yes."

It was almost dark, but a soft, yellow light mounted high on a pole near the garage illuminated the farmhouse. Lee eyed it curiously as they approached. It was an old, three-story farmhouse with grey siding, white trim, and a large porch that fronted the house. Someone rose from a corner chair as if they'd been awaiting the unexpected guests.

While Lee guessed the home's age at around a hundred years, modern touches abounded.

The skylights on the roof, the decorative front door, large, late-model windows, and a three-car detached garage were clearly more recent additions. Traditional lines of caragana, poplar, and Manitoba maple trees lined the driveway and formed a shelterbelt around three sides of the farmhouse. A seasonally barren garden lay to the leeward side of the house.

Lee stopped where directed and followed Britten up the walkway where a woman stood to greet them.

"Mom."

"Britten. It's good to see you. Welcome home."

"Thanks. Um, sorry I didn't call first."

"This is your home. You never need to call first." She looked at Lee with a smile. "And you brought a guest."

Lee noted that the woman didn't seem in the least bit surprised at their arrival. She wondered if Eileen had called ahead to alert Britten's mother.

"Uh, yeah. Mom, this is a...a friend of mine. Her name's Lee."

Lee stepped forward and offered her hand. "Lee Glenn. I hope it's not too much of an imposition, ma'am."

"Gaëlle Germaine. And it's no imposition. My children's friends are always welcome in our home."

Gaëlle was thin and almost as tall as her daughter. Long, silver hair fell over one shoulder in a single braid. Dark eyebrows shadowed equally dark eyes that regarded Lee calmly. Though she had welcomed them with warmth, there was reserve in the way she turned to Britten and offered a hug.

Lee thought Britten might refuse her mother's

embrace, but after a momentary hesitation, Britten stepped forward into Gaëlle's arms and offered her own double air kiss.

"Your room is made up, Britten, and we'll put Lee in Dale's room. He won't be home for another ten days."

As Lee returned to the SUV for her client's luggage, she marvelled that Gaëlle hadn't asked anything about why they were there or how long they planned to stay. *Maybe she plans to grill her daughter privately.*

When Lee returned to the porch with several suitcases, Britten had gone inside.

Gaëlle reached out and took a large bag from Lee's hands. "I suspect these are all for my daughter. You don't really seem like the lilac and green floral print sort. Why don't you leave them here, and I'll take them upstairs. I'm sure you want to get your own things from the car."

"I just have one bag, ma'am. I'll get these up to Britten and return for the rest."

"It's Gaëlle, please. And since my daughter abandoned you, the least I can do is lend a hand."

Gaëlle took another small bag from Lee and led the way inside. A staircase was to the right of the entrance, and Lee followed her hostess up to the second floor. When they reached the landing, Lee heard Britten moving around inside the first room on the right. They set the suitcases down by the door, and Gaëlle directed Lee farther down the hallway to a room on the opposite side.

"When the kids were little, this floor had three bedrooms—one for the boys, one for the girls, and the master bedroom. I moved up to the attic ten years ago and converted two of the bedrooms into a suite for my son. That's where I'm putting you. I hope you'll be comfortable."

Lee poked her head into the expansive bedroom/sitting room and had to restrain herself from whistling. Whatever the original set-up had been, the suite was now the equal of any five-star hotel. "Are you sure you don't want to put your daughter in here?"

Gaëlle chuckled and shook her head. "Unless things have changed a lot over the years, Heather...I mean, Britten, will want to spread her things all over the bathroom. Dale's bathroom is too compact for his sister's needs, so she's better off in her old room with access to the original bathroom."

"Good point. And you're sure Dale won't mind?"

"I'm sure. Please make yourself at home." Gaëlle turned away, then stopped. "Have you had any supper? I can easily fix something."

"No, thank you. We stopped at the Four Corners Café for a bite."

"Good. My sister-in-law Eileen works there; I often drop in for supper. I don't think she's working tonight, though."

There goes that theory. I guess Eileen didn't call with a heads-up. "Actually, she was our waitress. She and Britten had a little disagreement about your daughter's name."

"That's Eileen, all right. She's a kind, generous, giving woman, but she's set in her ways and has no use for airs. Britten will always be Heather Ann to her aunt."

"But not to you?"

"My daughter has the right to be called by whatever name she chooses. I rather hope she doesn't adopt Persephone or Gertrude, however."

With a chuckle, Gaëlle went to her daughter's room, and Lee went downstairs to retrieve the rest of the luggage. On her return, she mounted the last stairs, only to encounter Gaëlle, who turned to let her by.

"Please don't feel you have to stay up and keep us company, Lee. Britten and I have lots to catch up on."

"Would you mind if I just stretch my legs a little before I retire?"

"Not at all, but do be careful if you go into the fields north of the house. A winter storm this year took down the old fieldstone barn, and the debris is all over back there."

"Geez, I'm sorry. I hope no one was hurt in the collapse."

"No, we hadn't used that barn in probably thirty years. Other than a lot of startled field mice, it was really a non-event. Though I do have to get around to cleaning it up now that the snow is gone."

Lee dropped off the rest of Britten's suitcases and tossed her own bag into the suite. As much as she'd have loved to crawl into bed, she wanted to do a perimeter sweep and assessment before retiring. She also needed to text Willem. So Lee headed back outside into the cold night air and began a slow amble around the house, her keen eyes raking over what she could see of the landscape. Other than the shelterbelt providing potential cover for interlopers, the house's isolation provided decent sanctuary, though she intended to do a more careful assessment in the daylight.

Lee stopped under the exterior light. Checking her phone, she was relieved to see she had access, and she quickly sent Willem a text. With that task done, Lee put her phone away and tilted her head back. The vast panoply of the clear prairie sky took her breath away.

Lee had no idea how long she stood watching the stars. It was only the cold piercing her jacket that finally forced her to return to the house. As Lee approached the porch stairs, a curtain moved in the front window. But when she entered the house, all was quiet.

Lee descended the stairs early the next morning. She doubted that she'd slept as well in years, probably since before a routine check-up had heralded Dana's final odyssey. Whether it was the fresh air or fatigue after the long drive, Lee was simply grateful for her renewed sense of energy.

The house was quiet, but it was barely seven o'clock, so Lee stepped outside for a smoke. On the porch, Lee lit up and inhaled deeply.

"I always used to enjoy that first one of the day, too."

Lee spun and saw Gaëlle sitting in a chair in the far corner. "Damn, I'm sorry. I'll just put this out."

"Not at all. At least don't do it for me. I finally managed to quit not long ago, but a couple of my brothers-in-law indulge now and then. There's a butt can in the corner."

Lee took up a position near the can, leaning one hip against the porch railing. She looked sheepishly at Gaëlle. “I do intend to quit again; I just haven’t quite gotten around to it.”

“When you don’t need the habit anymore, you’ll stop.”

“I wish it were that easy. My wife—” Lee stopped abruptly, inwardly cursing herself. It wasn’t that she was in deep cover, but she had no idea how her hostess would react to details of her personal life.

To Lee’s great relief, Gaëlle simply cocked her head curiously. “Your wife would what?”

“She’d kill me for starting up again. It took me almost a year to quit the first time, and Dana said I was as grouchy as a grizzly.”

“So why did you start again?”

Lee sighed and extinguished the cigarette. “Dana died, and nothing mattered anymore, not even the deplorable state of my lungs.”

“I’m sorry.”

Lee shifted uncomfortably, recalling that this woman had lost her husband and son many years before. “Me too. I mean about Dana and your family, too. Britten told me what happened.”

“Mmm. That was long, long ago now. Britten was only eight months old at the time.”

“Still, it had to be terribly difficult.”

“It was the worst day of my life.”

Lee and Gaëlle’s eyes met. Lee knew instantly that here was someone who understood, who had been through the same crucible but apparently emerged far more intact than Lee had.

Before she could say anything more, Gaëlle rose

and pulled her coat more tightly around herself. "Please excuse me. If you want breakfast, I left a pot of oatmeal on the stove. If that's not your pleasure, help yourself to anything you can find in the fridge or pantry. I'll be back in a while."

Lee watched Gaëlle walk down the stairs and follow a path around the house. When she could no longer see the woman, Lee went inside in search of the kitchen.

At the back of the house, overlooking an expansive deck, the large country kitchen was flooded with the first light of morning. A piece of paper sat next to a table setting. Noting her name at the top, Lee stopped to read it.

> *Lee,*
>
> *Britten will probably sleep well into the morning. There is coffee in the pot and oatmeal on the stove. Bread and English muffins are in the fridge, cold cereal in the pantry. Please help yourself to anything that strikes your fancy. I will be back about eight or so.*
>
> *Gaëlle*

"Oatmeal, eh? God, I haven't had that in years." Lee laughed aloud as she remembered how she'd had to bribe Eli to even try it, loading his bowl with raisins, brown sugar, and double cream. Even that hadn't been enough to make him like it. After finding what she needed, Lee sat down with a large bowl. "Yum. This is not instant, that's for sure."

True to her note, Gaëlle returned within the hour. Lee had washed her dishes and tidied the kitchen and was sitting in the living room, wondering how she was going to fill her time for whatever duration they would be there.

Gaëlle shrugged out of her coat and gloves and put them away in the closet. "She's still sleeping, is she?"

"I haven't heard a peep from upstairs yet."

"Enjoy the quiet while it lasts. Britten said last night that she was going to contact her old girlfriends and have them over today. They're a pretty shrill bunch when they're all together."

Lee hoped her face didn't reflect her dismay, but Gaëlle's amused expression indicated otherwise.

"I need to go into Donegal on a grocery run after I throw some laundry in. Care to come along?"

"I...I'd better stay here."

"Your call. In that case, would you like to make use of my library? I've got a decent selection of books that might break the monotony for you."

"Please, yes. I'd like that." More than anything else, Lee hated being bored. She would rather have gone with Gaëlle, but as unlikely as the need seemed, her client was paying for personal protection, and Lee didn't feel at liberty to leave.

The stairs to the basement were on the other side of the stairway to the second floor. Lee followed Gaëlle down the short flight to a door. Above the door hung a small sign with letters burned into the wood reading "*Momy's offis and libery*".

Gaëlle touched it like a talisman before opening the door. "Owen made this for me when he was seven. We'd given him a woodworking set for his birthday. He wasn't the world's best speller, but there's nothing I cherish more in this house."

Lee understood completely. For the past year, she had slept—when she slept—with a scarf Dana knitted her for their first Christmas together under her pillow. She'd rarely worn it while Dana was alive, but the love in each unskilled stitch comforted Lee in a way nothing else could.

Gaëlle turned on the light, illuminating a large room with bookshelves, battered filing cabinets, an old wooden desk, and a map of Africa that covered a third of one wall. Stickpins were scattered about the map, the majority of them in northwestern Africa. The small windows didn't admit much light, but any shadows were dispelled by the abundance of lamps and the powerful ceiling light. Three leather recliners formed a triangle in one corner, abutting a low table stacked with books.

In contrast to the elegant suite in which Lee had spent the night, this was a warm, restful, unpretentious room. It invited the user to relax with a good book or get some administrative work done in peace and quiet. Lee loved it.

"Stay as long as you like. Feel free to browse my library and borrow whatever interests you. I'll be back by noon. You won't hear anything down here as I had the ceiling padded for sound reduction years ago, so you might want to give Britten a wake-up call about eleven. She'll need time to put herself together before her friends arrive at one."

Lee was already lingering over the wide selection of books, so she nodded absently, barely noticing when Gaëlle left. *Maybe this won't be so bad after all.*

God, how bad is this going to get? Lee hunched in her corner chair, overwhelmed by the noise emanating from the six women and seven children. After the briefest of introductions, Britten ignored her completely in favour of her old friends, all of whom treated the ex-model as a returning celebrity and Lee as a non-entity.

Lee had briefed Britten before the gathering to caution her friends not to post anything on social media about her triumphant return. Because Britten was adamant that her mother not know the truth of her situation, they'd come up with a plausible cover story to justify the discretion, but Lee had also sent Willem another text requesting that he check for any cyber-leakage in the next few days.

Raucous laughter burst from the gaggle, and Lee briefly wondered what she'd missed. Given that not a word had been addressed to her all afternoon, she decided not to worry about it. However, a small boy with a runny nose that he wiped on his hand and then on Lee's knee was the last straw. She gently propelled the boy back in the direction of his oblivious mother, sidled around behind the women, and headed for the front door.

As Lee emerged into the crisp afternoon air, she felt as if she'd just surfaced after too much time underwater. She drew in great gulps of air and took out her pack of cigarettes. She was about to light up, when she stopped and stared at the pack for a long moment. *No time like the present.* Slowly, she slid the cigarette back into the pack and tucked it in her jacket pocket.

"Congratulations."

Bemused, Lee turned to face the far side of the porch where Gaëlle was sitting in a chair. "Are you always this quiet?"

"I only seem quiet in comparison to them." Gaëlle inclined her head toward the living room.

"They certainly are...excitable. I'm sure they're just glad to see your daughter again."

"Britten was queen bee when she lived here. Her friends all knew they would stay in the area, marry, and raise children, so when Britten went to Europe to be a model, they lived vicariously through her; they worshipped from afar. They're beside themselves that their idol has returned."

Lee was impressed by the calm, non-judgmental assessment. This was not a woman who would be easily fooled.

"Lee, what are you doing here?"

"Uh, I needed some time away from my life in Calgary, so I volunteered to keep Britten company on her trip home."

Lee was acutely conscious of Gaëlle studying her. Her heart dropped when Gaëlle slowly shook her head.

"I expect that's partially true, but you're no more a friend of Britten than a hawk is friend to a sparrow. Her sorts of friends have always been hapless, besotted boys and those types of women currently crowding my home. I would guess that you're a bodyguard of some sort. My daughter has gotten herself into trouble, and your job is to protect her—am I right?"

Lee absolutely did not want to lie to this woman, but she was also deeply conscious of her client's right to privacy. "Gaëlle...I..."

"No, it's not fair to broach you with this. All I ask is that you tell me how much trouble my daughter is in. Do I need to take steps to secure our home?"

Lee shook her head as she decided how much she could legitimately reveal. "I believe your daughter's situation has been somewhat overblown. I doubt it will go on for an extended period."

"I see. So I should relax and enjoy having her back for a little while, is that it?"

"That would be a good assessment."

"Thank you. For what it's worth, I think Britten's safety is in good hands."

Lee smiled her appreciation, grateful that Gaëlle was willing to leave it at that. "Can I ask you something?"

"Go ahead."

"Yesterday, you seemed to know we were coming. But I know Britten didn't call you, and you indicated that Eileen hadn't phoned ahead. So how did you know?"

"Wally told me last week. He wasn't specific about the date and time, but he was adamant that you'd be arriving by week's end."

"Wally? Wrong-Way Wally? The guy with the bike and all the ribbons?"

"My friend, Wally Woodson, yes. I don't call him Wrong-Way. I've never met a soul more intent on going the right way."

Stung by the mild admonition, Lee determined to never again refer to the man by his nickname. "Okay. So how did he know?"

"Wally often knows things that escape the average person. However, he has his own way of communicating, and few have the patience to wade through the dross to the diamonds."

"But you do."

"Wally and I go back a very long way."

"Britten mentioned you were born on the same day."

"We always have been."

Lee thought she had heard wrong and was about to pursue it when her attention was drawn by a vehicle turning into the driveway. Lee's muscles tensed, but she was reassured as Gaëlle rose with a smile on her face.

"Oh, it's Jill. She must have gotten off work early today. You'll get a chance to meet my other daughter, Lee. I don't see my grandsons with her, but she should have my enchanting granddaughter along."

I think I've had enough child-engendered enchantment for one day. But Lee couldn't hold on to her cynicism in the face of Gaëlle's obvious delight. She watched as Gaëlle hurried down the stairs and opened the passenger door almost before the truck stopped.

A dark-haired woman emerged from the driver's side. Lee could see the family resemblance, but it was clear that Britten had won the genetic jackpot. "We can only stay for a few minutes, Mom. Emmy has a dentist appointment in half an hour. But I just had to swing by and see if the rumours are true. Heather Ann is actually home?"

Gaëlle swung her giggling granddaughter in her arms and wrapped her in an enthusiastic hug. "Your sister is home, Jill. Go ahead in and say hi. Emmy and I will find some cookies."

"No cookies, Mom. Not this time. I just cleaned Emmy's teeth, and we don't want to spoil things for her appointment."

Gaëlle sighed. "None of Grandma's cookies today, squirt. But I'll save some for you, okay?"

"For Jamie too?"

"For Jamie and Nathan."

"Not Nathan."

"Why not Nathan? What did your brother do?"

Lee lost track of the conversation as Jill came up the stairs.

Jill stopped and looked at Lee. "Friend of my sister's?"

"Sort of."

Jill smiled. "Then welcome, sort-of-friend. I'm Jill, sort-of-sister."

"Lee."

"Nice to meet you, Lee. If you'll excuse me, I'm off to see the prodigal." Jill opened the door and went inside.

The shrill noise that emerged made Lee cringe as she retreated to the chair Gaëlle had occupied.

Gaëlle returned to the porch, granddaughter in her arms. "Lee, I'd like you to meet Emily Gaëlle Germaine-Hudson, or as we call her, Emmy G. Emmy, this is Ms. Glenn. Can you say hi?"

The child stared at Lee, then buried her face against her grandmother's shoulder.

Gaëlle shot Lee an apologetic look. "Sorry. Some days she's shyer than others."

"That's all right."

"Did you and Dana have any children?"

"Dana had a son, Eli. We raised him together from the time he was eight. He's engaged to a wonderful woman, and they're getting married in July."

"Ah, so you may have grandchildren yourself before too long."

"Eli says he's too young for kids yet, but one of these days he and Liz will make excellent parents." Lee hadn't thought much about it before, but she loved the notion that Dana's line would continue. She decided on the spot that she was going to be every bit as besotted a grandmother as Gaëlle evidently was.

The front door slammed open, and Jill rushed out with anger in every line of her body.

"Jill? What's the matter, sweetie?"

Jill sucked in a deep breath and reached for her daughter. "She hasn't changed a bit, Mom. Not one stinking bit. She's still the same b—"

"Jill!"

"Sorry, Mom. Look, Emmy G and I have to get going. Give me a call after Heather Ann leaves, okay?"

Gaëlle watched her daughter and granddaughter hurry down the stairs. She thrust her hands deep into her pockets as the truck flew down the driveway.

"Gaëlle? Are you okay?"

Gaëlle tried to smile at Lee. "I'd just hoped after all these years that things would be different."

"Sibling rivalry?"

"More like soul rivalry."

Before Lee could inquire further, Gaëlle left the porch and took the same path she'd taken early that morning.

"Huh. I wonder what that was all about."

CHAPTER 5

SHORTLY AFTER JILL'S DEPARTURE, LEE sat on her corner chair on the porch. She listened to snippets of conversation as Britten's friends poured out of the house and started loading children into their vehicles.

"Can you believe what she said? Poor Britten had to put up with that abuse all her life. No wonder she hasn't been back in since forever."

"I dunno, Tiff. I thought Jill had a point. If I'd ever treated my mom the way Britten treats hers, my dad would've tarred and feathered me."

"Yeah, but Brit doesn't have a dad. She's never had a dad. I think that explains so much."

"Jill didn't have her dad for long, either. She was only about seven when he died."

"Pam, why are you sticking up for her? Jill was just mean; she's always been mean to Brit. I remember in school when Jill stole Bobby away from Britten. I mean, how low can you get?"

"Uh-huh. Given that Jill and Bobby have been married for at least fifteen years, I don't think she exactly stole Bobby from Britten. Looked to me like Bobby was more than willing to swap one sister for the other."

"Well, I think Jill's just jealous. Britten got the looks, the glamorous career, the fabulously wealthy husband..."

Lee groaned inwardly, wondering exactly what Britten had told her friends about Saberi and also whether she had cautioned them not to post anything. The homecoming of a "glamorous" model was just the sort of news her old friends would be eager to spread around.

"I don't think Jill's jealous. My sister went to school with her, and she told me Jill was always far more popular than Britten. If anything, Britten was the tagalong."

"Hah. That was then; this is now. Jill should be jealous. What's *she* got in her life?"

"Gee, I don't know, Tiff. Husband, kids, job... kind of like the rest of us."

Lee snickered as doors slammed in near unison. Obviously, Pam's assessment was not universally appreciated. When the last of the vehicles had driven away, Lee went back inside.

"Aw, for crying out loud."

The living room was a disaster zone, and from what Lee could see, the kitchen wasn't much better. Britten was nowhere in sight. Lee shook her head in disgust and started cleaning up. "I'm telling Willem to add a surcharge to Britten's bill for cleaning and valet services. This is bloody ridiculous."

Lee had worked her way out to the kitchen by the time she saw Gaëlle returning from the fields behind the house. She stopped to watch her hostess. The look of fatigue on Gaëlle's face made Lee glad that she hadn't left the mess untouched.

Gaëlle entered the house through the kitchen door and stopped short as she saw the number of garbage bags Lee had filled and stacked in a corner. "Oh no, Lee. I'm so sorry. You didn't have to do that."

"I'm perfectly capable of helping out. After all, you're kind enough to offer hospitality; this is the least I can do."

"No, it's the least my daughter could do." Gaëlle shook her head as she gathered up dirty cups. "But I don't feel like fighting that battle again at the moment, so let me help, and then I'll get dinner started. Do you have any dietary restrictions?"

Lee chuckled. "Only those I imposed on myself this past year, and thankfully I'm well rid of them now. Anything you make would be appreciated. If I can help with dinner, I'd like to do so."

Gaëlle stopped loading the dishwasher and smiled at Lee. "If I hadn't known it before, I'd have no doubt that you're not one of Britten's set."

"I dunno. That Pam seemed pretty level-headed."

"True. Pam was always the one of Britten's friends I liked best."

"Did Britten like her best, too?"

"Sadly, no. Pam did not worship sufficiently."

Lee grimaced. The state of affairs between mother and daughter was frosty to say the least. She wondered if Gaëlle even liked her daughter.

"I love my daughter very much, but I recognize that she's a young soul. Sometimes I'm not sure I have the energy left to do the nurturing required. But I remind myself that we chose each other for a reason. I am very glad she came home, no matter how long she stays."

Lee was startled that Gaëlle had appeared to read her mind.

A loud clatter sounded from the second floor.

Lee dropped the garbage bag and bolted for the stairs. Within seconds, she threw open Britten's door, conscious that Gaëlle was right behind her. As Lee slipped inside, her eyes scanning the room for danger, she instinctively threw up an arm to block Gaëlle's entry.

Britten was sitting on her bed, sobbing. Pieces of a broken lamp lay near the far wall.

Taking a deep breath, Lee calmed herself.

Gaëlle peered under Lee's arm and took in the situation. "Are you all right?"

"I hate Jill! She ruins everything!"

Before Gaëlle could say anything further, Lee gently pushed her back into the hallway. In a low voice, she said, "Why don't you leave this to me? I need to talk to Britten anyway."

Gaëlle regarded her with a troubled expression.

"Please. Trust me?"

Gaëlle nodded. "All right. Call me if you need me; I'll be in the kitchen."

Lee returned to the bedroom and closed the door. She took a seat beside Britten, careful to leave some space between them. "Want to talk about it?"

"No!"

Lee smiled inwardly. This was how some of her most insightful conversations with a teenaged Eli had begun. She waited silently, not surprised when Britten burst forth with a litany of complaints, many dating back to childhood years.

"...and Mom always loved Jill best. Just because

I wouldn't go walk the stupid labyrinth with her and Jill would. Jill's such a suck-up. Now she's given Mom grandchildren, and I—"

Britten broke off in a torrent of renewed sobs, and Lee tried to puzzle out what she'd heard. She understood complaints about borrowed clothes not returned; homework supposedly sabotaged; Jill flaunting her athleticism; Jill who was stuck-up about being valedictorian; Jill who stole her boyfriend, then married him; the perceived unequal allotment of their mother's time and love; even the advantage of providing grandchildren; but she was completely lost with Britten's penultimate complaint.

Lee handed Britten some tissues. "Back up a little, will you? What do you mean 'walking the stupid labyrinth'?"

Britten blew her nose fiercely. "When we were little, Mom built this dumb labyrinth in the field next to the old barn. First it was just a design she tramped down in the summer grass, but then she made it so it was four seasons. Jill and Dale helped her, but it just bored me. I mean, what was the point? Jill and Dale would walk it with Mom some mornings, but I'd much rather sleep in. It was a huge relief when Mom stopped inviting me, but I know Jill used that time to fill Mom's head with bullshit about me. It made Mom much harder on me than on Jill. It still makes me mad. And Jill hasn't changed one bit. We were having a perfectly nice time this afternoon, and she had to come in and ruin it."

"How'd she do that?"

"Jill started ragging on me about not coming home years ago. Says I put Mom through hell. Like Mom even knows I'm gone. She's so damned wrapped up in her own world anyway. Well, I just told Jill that, unlike some people, I had a life—a busy, hectic, demanding life, and if she couldn't deal with that, then she could just shove it where the sun don't shine."

"I'm guessing that didn't go over well."

"She got all pissy. She slammed me in front of my friends, so I told her to get the hell out of there. I told her as far as I was concerned, she was no sister of mine and if I never saw her again, it would be too soon for me!"

"Okay, I get all that. So how did the lamp end up in a hundred pieces?"

"I was just so mad. This is all Michael's fault. If he hadn't been such an asshole, I wouldn't be here now; I'd be in Milan for the unveiling of the fall line-up. Arturo said I'd be perfect for a pre-fall, inter-seasonal show this spring. He'd have used me last year, but Michael didn't want me working. And I don't care what my stupid ex-agent said, an Arturo promise means something in the biz. I know it's not haute couture, but I was bored with that anyway. I'd much rather work with Arturo. His line is far more avant-garde than the major houses. He's going to be bigger than Dior and Versace combined some day."

"Okay, I understand that you're angry at Jill—"

"And Michael!"

"And Michael and pretty much the whole world right now—"

"Why does everything have to be so hard? Nothing ever goes right for me. Nothing ever has."

Britten's whining was suddenly too much for Lee to stomach. "I get it. Life sucks. Well, guess what. You're no different from anyone else, and it's damned well about time you realized that. Stop leaving your messes for someone else to clean up. Stop having temper tantrums and breaking innocent, immoveable objects. You're thirty-one—"

"Twenty-seven!" Britten snapped.

"Thirty-one...almost thirty-two, so grow the hell up. Yes, you've had a blip in your charmed life. I hate to break this to you, but no one gets everything they want; no one's life runs exactly according to plan. Stop wallowing in misery and get on with figuring out what you want from here on out. Once you've got that figured out, decide how you're going to go about getting it. But for God's sake, just stop and think about someone besides yourself for once!" Lee stood up and stalked toward the door.

"What do you know? I had it all! I was a star in Paris, New York, and Milan. Men fell at my feet every night. They'd give me anything I wanted, just so they could show up with me on their arms. I went to the best parties, drank the most expensive champagne, wore nothing but designer clothes. I flew all over the world in private jets. Now I'm stuck in Dogsville, and some two bit security hack thinks she can lecture me? What have you ever lost, bitch?"

"More than you could ever imagine."

As Lee closed the bedroom door behind her,

something distinctly breakable crashed against it.

Note to self, tell Willem to add a surcharge to the surcharge, this time for replacing our hostess' broken bric-a-brac.

Dinner was a quiet affair. Britten didn't come down, despite Gaëlle's efforts.

The third time Gaëlle returned from her fruitless trip upstairs, Lee said, "I'm sorry. I usually handle things much better than I did. I'm afraid I wasn't very diplomatic. Frankly, I'm surprised she hasn't fired me."

"Did you speak the truth to her?"

"As I saw it, yes."

"Then you have nothing to apologize for."

"I could've spoken it more gently."

Gaëlle shook her head and pushed the blueberry pie across the table. "If there's anything I remember about raising Britten, it's that subtlety never worked."

"What did?"

"Firmness, clarity; the usual tools. But she's an adult now and responsible for her own choices, including her emotional choices. She can wallow in misery, if she wishes, or she can adapt and find a way to enjoy her circumstances, even if they're not what she'd have wished for."

"Do you think she'd have come home eventually if this problem with her husband hadn't—"

"Husband? Heather Ann is married?"

"Um, yes. She didn't tell you?"

"No."

There was a world of pain packed into that syllable, and Lee didn't know how to respond. "Damn, I'm sorry."

Gaëlle swallowed several times before responding, "Don't be. My daughter has been ultra-secretive with me for as long as I can remember. I've often wondered..."

Lee waited out the long pause, then pressed gently. "What, Gaëlle? What have you wondered?"

Gaëlle looked at Lee sadly. "It shames me."

"I won't judge."

"I've often wondered if subconsciously I blamed my infant daughter for Hugh's and Owen's deaths. I know it wasn't her fault. I *know* that. Everything I've learned since the accident tells me that. But if, in those early months of grief and despair, I did blame her, maybe she picked up on that, even as a little girl. She was not an easy child to love, though I tried desperately to love all my children equally."

"Why would you blame Britten? Wasn't it a car accident?"

Gaëlle shook her head. "It's a long story."

"So I'll put on another pot of coffee."

Lee busied herself with making coffee as Gaëlle began her story.

"I have to back up a little. Hugh and I met at university. I know it's a cliché, but we were crazy about each other from the moment we met. I'd never met anyone with such a zest for life. It's as if Hugh was driven to live life on fast forward. With hindsight, that makes sense to me, but at the time... Well, let's just say my parents were less than pleased when I dropped out along with Hugh so that we could travel the world together. We had no plans and very little money. We went hungry many times, basically going where our hearts directed, but I've never regretted it for a moment."

Lee understood. She wouldn't have traded a single day with Dana, not even the times when news of Dana's medical setbacks plunged them into despair.

"When we came back to Canada and I was pregnant with Owen, my father was furious. When all was said and done, Hugh was a farm boy. That was not in Dad's plans for me at all, so they washed their hands of us and showed me the door. It hurt, but Hugh's family welcomed me with open arms. We got married immediately and moved into Hugh's great-grandfather's home. He started working with his older brothers in the family cattle business, and we began to raise our family."

"Sounds quite bucolic."

"It was, for many years. After Owen, we had Dale and Jill and thought we were done. Britten was a surprise, but we welcomed her too. Hugh joked that now we had a nicely balanced family—two of each. But even then I think he knew his time was running short. Owen's too."

"Why do you say that?"

"Because after the accident, I found out Hugh had taken out huge life insurance policies shortly after we found out I was pregnant with Britten. He must've had to struggle to meet the payments, but he never mentioned a word about them. Hugh was such a hard worker, and he was always taking on odd jobs to bring in extra income, even though the cattle business was pretty lucrative. He also worked like a fiend to update our home. I kept telling him to slow down, that we had lots of time to get things done, but he'd only laugh and keep doing whatever he was doing."

"He wanted to take care of you."

"Yes, that was Hugh's way."

"You said that he knew Owen's time was running out as well?"

"No, I didn't mean Hugh knew; I meant Owen did."

"How so?"

"The day before the accident, Owen came to me while I was nursing Britten. Owen was a loving boy, but not demonstrative. He was more of a show than tell sort of son. But he settled in at my feet and started to talk. I confess I only half-listened, because Britten was fussing, as usual. She'd had croup for weeks, and we were all exhausted, but I remember thinking later that Owen sounded like someone two decades older."

"What did he say?"

"He spoke of all the people he loved: me, his dad, his siblings, his grandmother, and his favourite cousin, Matty. He talked about school and his beloved math teacher, about hockey and how much he was looking forward to the weekend tournament. I remember I started to hum *My Favourite Things,* and he looked up at me and laughed. Then he said, 'Life is good, isn't it, Mom?' and he wandered off. A little while later, I heard him and Dale playing cards in the kitchen, and everything seemed normal."

"Maybe he did have a touch of precognition that day."

"It wasn't just that day. Normally, we all went to the boys' hockey tournaments. We'd make a family outing of it and have dinner at a restaurant, which was a big deal for us back then. But with Britten so sick, I told Hugh to take the boys and leave me at home. Fortunately, Jill had a cousin's birthday party on Saturday, so she had a sleepover at her Aunt Maggie's on Friday night. Because I wasn't going along, the boys fought over who got to ride shotgun in the front seat. Dale won a coin toss, but when it came time to leave at five a.m., Owen insisted that he get the front seat by virtue of his sibling seniority. Dale was terribly angry, especially when his dad didn't overrule Owen, because Hugh was always scrupulously fair with the boys. Banished to the back seat, Dale lay down and decided to sleep until they got to Saskatoon."

"And that saved his life?"

"That, and something else Owen did. Back then we had seatbelts in the old station wagon, but we rarely used them. But, as Dale told me later, about five minutes before the accident, Owen woke him up and told him to put his seatbelt on. He was so mad at his brother that he wasn't going to do it, but Hugh backed Owen up. Plus Dale said there was something in Owen's eyes that told him not to mess with his big brother. So he put on his seatbelt, and that did save his life."

Lee blinked. "God, that's incredible. But how was any of this Britten's fault?"

"Her crying had been keeping us all up at night for weeks. Hugh was so tired that I insisted that last night that he sleep in the girls' room, while

I kept Britten in with me. For a long time I was plagued by 'what ifs': what if the baby hadn't worn us all out; what if I'd been along as usual to help with the driving and keep Hugh focused; what if the temperature had been just a few degrees warmer or colder so there wasn't black ice; what if the boys hadn't won that last game that earned them a place in the tournament. What if, what if, what if..."

"You could drive yourself crazy that way."

Gaëlle chuckled, but there was no humour in the sound. "I did, and that's why I wonder if I unconsciously passed along the crazy to Britten. I was even angry with her that I didn't get to sleep with Hugh that last night, just to have felt him close one more time. It took me years to understand and accept that Hugh and Owen were here for a specific time, and nothing I did could've changed that. They'd chosen the terms of their life, and I'd agreed to them."

Lee shook her head. "You don't really believe that."

"I do. Souls stay until they complete their life goals, then they leave."

Lee had thought she was over her anger, but now she felt it escalate. "So you're telling me you think I agreed to Dana's early death? Are you fucking insane? I would never—"

Gaëlle looked at her calmly. "I wouldn't say these things to you if you hadn't come for this very reason. When the student is ready—"

Lee jumped up, knocking her chair over. "The only reason I'm here is to protect your dumbass daughter from her asshole husband, nothing else. It's pure coincidence; that's all."

"There are no coincidences."

Infuriated by the quiet words, Lee stormed out of the kitchen. Fortunately, the weather had warmed, as she didn't stop for a coat. Lee strode away from the house. "How can she say that? What kind of a lunatic is she, anyway! I agreed to Dana's death? Not in a million, billion years! I'd give anything to have her back, anything!"

Lee walked without direction. All she wanted was to get away from the house, from that infuriating woman. She stopped when she came to a field covered with an odd series of marker sticks. She stood studying it, but it didn't make sense.

Finally, Lee climbed a small wooded rise and looked back over the field. From that perspective, she realized what she was seeing. This was Gaëlle's labyrinth. The markers edged the paths of trampled grasses in a classic pattern. It didn't look difficult to navigate; there was a clear entrance and route to the centre where a stone bench was set. The bench was oriented north to south, so that a sitter could face east or west and view a sunrise or sunset as desired.

Her pique momentarily forgotten, Lee studied the structure. It was simple, yet elegant. There was an innate beauty to the design, even though it was composed of nothing but trodden grass and small, weather-beaten sticks. She wondered how many years Gaëlle had walked that ground and why. All she remembered about labyrinths was that they had some connection with Greek mythology.

Lee found a large stone and sat staring down at the labyrinth. A light breeze caressed her flushed face, bringing a tantalizing scent of the approaching spring. Slowly, her anger subsided, and she was left with sadness. She'd liked Gaëlle, much more than she liked Gaëlle's daughter. She'd felt they had something in common—a meeting of the minds, maybe even the hearts—given their shared experience of loss. She was saddened to discover that Gaëlle was simply a New Age nutcase.

Lost in thought, Lee didn't notice anyone approaching until Gaëlle draped a jacket around her shoulders and took a seat on the ground next to the rock. "I'm sorry, Lee. I only ever talk to Wally and Dale like that; I forget how I sound to non-initiates. I apologize."

"No, I apologize. You're entitled to your beliefs, even if—"

"Even if they're pretty far-fetched?"

"I was going to say even if they're not mine."

Gaëlle looked up at Lee. "What *do* you believe?"

"About what?"

"About life, about death, about where Dana is now."

"Life is hard; death sucks, and Dana is in Queen's Park Cemetery."

Gaëlle was quiet so long that Lee couldn't stand it any longer. "What?"

"What, what?"

Lee grimaced. "What are you thinking?"

"I'm feeling more than thinking."

"God, you can be so exasperating, woman. What are you feeling, then?"

"Sadness."

"For me? Why?"

Gaëlle leaned back on her hands and studied the sky. "I don't want to anger you."

"I don't want to be angry with you."

"Then let's just sit and enjoy the evening air for a bit."

Lee had the uneasy feeling she shouldn't leave it there, but she didn't want to fight or be angry or do anything but relax in the peacefulness of the spot.

They were quiet for a long time as dusk settled around them. Finally, Lee rose and extended a hand to Gaëlle. "We should probably get back to the house."

Gaëlle took her hand and rose smoothly to her feet. Side by side, they began the walk back to the house.

Lee asked, "Why did you build it?" The question had nagged at her since she first glimpsed Gaëlle's handiwork.

"The labyrinth?"

"Yes. It must've been a lot of work."

Gaëlle nodded. "It was. I started constructing it the fall after Hugh and Owen died. I'd get Dale and Jill off to school, bundle Britten up in a Snugli carrier, and come out here and tramp down the grass over and over."

"But why?"

"I could tell you that it was for exercise and fresh air."

Lee rolled her eyes. "You could, but I don't think that's the whole story."

"You're very perceptive. No, that's not the whole story, though it was what I told my in-laws when they thought I was going crazy. I'd actually stumbled across a book on labyrinths in the library. At the time I couldn't have told you why I even took it home. I certainly didn't have any previous interest in the subject, but once I started reading it, I couldn't put it down. I spent the summer reading many books on labyrinths and designing my own. By September, I was ready to build."

"Okay. So it sort of got your mind off Hugh and Owen?"

Gaëlle laughed. "Quite the contrary. It was how I *connected* with Hugh and Owen."

"Aw, hell. You're going to go all New-Agey on me again, aren't you?"

"You did ask."

Lee groaned. "Fair enough."

"Constructing the labyrinth gave me purpose in a time when every touchstone of my life seemed to have been ripped away. Using the labyrinth for meditation brought me a deep sense of calm and renewed hope. I'm years past the initial grief that almost broke me, so now I walk the labyrinth seeking spiritual understanding and growth."

"I guess I can understand that. Dana used to have an ex-minister friend of ours come in and pray with her when she was in the hospital."

"Did you join them?"

"No. I mean, I wanted Dana to do anything that gave her comfort, but me and the Church rejected each other long ago. I love David like a brother. It's our kids who are getting married this summer, and someday we'll be co-grandparents. But I never bought into his religion, even when he performed our wedding ceremony. Dana did, though, so I was happy he was there for her. He gave her something I couldn't. Religion, though, that's not my cup of tea."

"Mine either."

Lee stopped short and stared at Gaëlle. "What do you mean? What's all this stuff you've been talking about then?"

"Spirituality."

"What's the difference?"

"Someday you'll answer that for yourself, Lee."

Gaëlle refused to say any more on the subject. She also shooed Lee out of her kitchen when Lee tried to help clean up the dinner dishes. It was too early to go to bed, so Lee read for a while and finished the mystery she'd selected the previous day.

Lee returned to the basement, intent on finding another book to pass the hours. However, once down in the library, she was distracted by the large wall map. Was it to record Gaëlle's youthful travels with Hugh or perhaps places she wanted to visit in the future? If so, her hostess had odd taste, as many of the poorest, most unenticing spots on the Dark Continent were marked.

Lee supposed that she could ask Gaëlle. She wouldn't have been introduced to the library if the map held a big secret, but Lee decided to mull it over for a while. She'd always enjoyed solving mysteries, and her hostess was turning out to be quite the mistress of inscrutability.

"This could be fun. Sure beats watching Britten hold court."

Lee knew she should go talk to her client, but she couldn't face the thought. When she'd been reading in the living room, Gaëlle had passed her carrying a covered plate, heading upstairs. It bothered Lee to see Gaëlle catering to her daughter, but it also allowed her to justify not checking on the spoiled brat again this evening.

Lee chose another mystery and settled in a recliner to read. The story failed to hold her interest, however, and she soon found herself staring into space. Lee went over and over the odd conversation she'd had with Gaëlle, trying to reconcile her hostess' crazy beliefs with the woman she'd so quickly grown to like.

Maybe this Wally character has had too much influence on Gaëlle. Much as I don't care for Britten, she might be right about her mom and Wrong-Way. He might just be bad news.

CHAPTER 6

LEE WOKE EARLY THE NEXT morning, anxious and irritable. Her head was pounding. She felt the familiar nicotine withdrawal pangs, like worms moving under her skin. With a growl, Lee tossed back the duvet and leaped out of bed. She paced as she fought the craving.

"No, damn it. You can do this. You can at least go longer than twenty-four hours. Think of something else...anything else."

But all Lee could think of was how easy it would be to banish the physical misery. She tried to distract herself with a long, hot shower. It didn't work.

"Okay, go for a walk—a really long one. If you still want a cigarette when you get back...well, deal with it then."

Lee didn't care if she sounded crazy, talking to herself. Her hands shook while she dressed and tucked a packet of cigarettes in her jacket pocket. *Just in case.*

She bounded down the stairs, only to feel her irritation skyrocket as she opened the front door and saw Gaëlle sitting on the porch steps with Wrong-Way Wally. Their shoulders were touching.

Jesus Christ! Just what I don't need this morning.

The friends turned at Lee's approach. Wally stood up and sketched a small bow in Lee's direction.

Gaëlle pulled something out of her pocket and tossed it to Lee.

Lee caught it. It was a half-empty box of nicotine patches. "How did...?"

"Wally said you'd need them, and, as it happened, I had some left over from when I quit. Help yourself and keep the rest. I remember how rough it is at the start."

Lee felt more like hurling the box at the odd be-ribboned man, but good sense ruled. She nodded tersely, took out a patch, and rolled up her sleeve to apply it to her upper arm.

"Black, white, grey. Awake and stay. What say?"

Lee stared at Wally as she tried to decipher his words.

Gaëlle smiled at Wally. "Too soon, old friend."

"Okay." Wally grasped the bicycle and cart that were parked at the base of the stairs and pointed upstairs. "Gone song." He gave Gaëlle a look of profound compassion. "Best done. Best left. You know."

"I do, Wally. I know you're right, but it is hard."

"Hard, hard. Good hard. Bad hard. All hard. Worth hard." Wally bowed to both women, mounted his bike, and rode away.

"C'mere."

Lee was drawn from her fascination with Wally's fluttering ribbons by Gaëlle's command. "Pardon?"

"Come, sit." Gaëlle moved her feet and patted the stair below her. "I can help."

“Um, okay. Help with what?”

“With the withdrawal you’re suffering.”

Lee was already feeling some relief from the patch, but she was willing to see what Gaëlle had in mind, so she took her place on the step. Strong fingers began to massage her temples and forehead, and Lee groaned in relief. “Oh, my God, please don’t stop.”

Gaëlle laughed softly and worked her fingers through Lee’s hair to the base of her head.

Lee hastily shrugged off her jacket to provide better access and shivered with delight as Gaëlle’s hands dug into tense neck and shoulder muscles. “Where did you learn to do this?”

“When we were in Greece, Hugh decided he wanted to dive off a cliff. Stupid, really. He certainly wasn’t trained, but there was nothing he wouldn’t try, especially when we were young and dumb. He pulled some back muscles pretty badly, to the point where I thought we’d have to go home so he could be treated. But a woman where we were staying showed me the basics of massage, and it helped. Since Hugh’s back hurt for the rest of his life, I got pretty good at this.”

“Ughh, bless that Greek masseuse, then. And bless your hands. I’m actually starting to feel human again.”

“I suspect the patch can take most of that credit.”

“Maybe a little, but not ‘most’.”

Gaëlle worked steadily for another ten minutes, then pulled Lee’s jacket up and rested her hands on Lee’s shoulders.

“Thank you. Seriously, that felt fabulous. I feel

like I should be tipping about fifty per cent."

"Fifty per cent of no charge is zero, so we're square. You could keep me company on my walk, though."

"Fair enough, though I warn you that I'm so relaxed I may not be up to walking for too long."

"I'm only going as far as the old barn this morning, so you should be able to manage."

They walked around the side of the house toward the back fields. Lee was amazed at how much better she felt compared to when she'd woken up. She was relieved she could converse like a normal human being. "Can I ask you something?"

"Sure. What's on your mind?"

"Wally's ribbons. Do they hold some sort of symbolism for him? Or are they just an exotic decoration?"

"Actually, I guess I'm responsible for those."

"How so?"

"Wally and I were inseparable as children. Our families lived next door to each other in Donegal, and we went to the same school."

"Was Wally...um, different...even back then?"

"Yes, but not to the same degree. Still, he was shunned, and in fact my parents worried that the closeness of our friendship would stunt my social development and brand me as an outsider too. I discovered much later that was one of the reasons my dad took a job in Prince Albert when I was nine. When Wally and I were told we were going to be parted, we were inconsolable. The day the moving truck came, I went to his house, but he wasn't there. It didn't take me long to find him, though. I knew all his hiding spots, so I rode my bike to each one. When I finally caught up to him, he was crying so hard that it scared me. I didn't know what to say to make him feel better. I'd spent hours crying too, ever since my parents announced we were moving as soon as the school year ended."

"Poor Wally. And poor you."

"Second saddest day of my life. Anyway, I'd won a couple of blue ribbons in the year end track meet. I was so proud of them that I carried them around in my pocket all the time, just in case I ran into anybody who hadn't seen them yet."

"Was there anyone who hadn't?"

Gaëlle shot her a wry look. "No. But in my defence, Donegal was an even smaller town back then."

Lee laughed as she pictured the child Gaëlle flaunting her prizes. "So you gave Wally your ribbons?"

"I did. I know it sounds like a small thing, but I was so proud of those ribbons, and I really didn't want to give them up. I had this idea in the back of my head that winning a couple of races would make it easier for me at my new school; I wouldn't just be a nobody from a place hardly anyone had heard of. Silly, of course. Nothing was going to save me from being the new kid. I didn't even make the track team at the new school. The only thing my speed was good for was running away from bullies."

"So those track ribbons started Wally's penchant for coat ribbons?"

"Yes. When I gave Wally the ribbons, he was dumbstruck. Outside of his family, people rarely gave Wally anything, unless you count the finger or the back of a hand. He held them like they were the most precious gift he could imagine. Without saying a word, it became our thing, our way to stay connected. For years afterwards, I sent him postcards and ribbons. He kept every one of them."

"And what did he send you?"

"Oh, the occasional card or note, which always looked like it had been written in code. Wally isn't exactly a literate man. Even before I left, he'd been held back a couple of grades. In fact, he ended up in Hugh's class for a while. Wally told me years later that Hugh was one of the few boys who didn't torment him. Hugh told me that he was ashamed he hadn't been kinder, hadn't protected Wally more from the other kids."

"So you knew Hugh in Donegal? I thought you first met at university."

"In essence we did. Hugh was a couple of years younger, and I was so engrossed with Wally that I wasn't aware of Hugh's existence except as Scott's little brother. Scott and I were in the same grade through elementary. Then with moving away so young, it really was like meeting for the first time when we were older."

"It's an amazing coincidence how you ended up right back where you started."

Gaëlle smiled teasingly at Lee. "Not coincidence at all."

"What do you mean?"

"I mean that the plan all along was to end up back in Donegal."

"Yours and Hugh's plan, you mean? After you met up at university?"

"Not exactly. I mean it was in our soul plan, but also Wally's, Owen's, Dale's, Jill's, Britten's—"

"Aww, come on. We were having such a nice walk, too. Why'd you have to bring that hooey stuff into it?"

Gaëlle laughed. "Okay, no more 'hooey' stuff. We're here, anyway."

Lee stood at Gaëlle's side as they looked over the collapsed remains of the old fieldstone barn. "It really is a mess, isn't it?"

Gaëlle nodded. "It is, but the stone itself is still in good shape. I'll have to sort out the rotted lumber, but I plan to reuse the stone."

"What are you going to do with it?"

"Finish my labyrinth using the stones as pavers."

"Sort of like cobblestones, then."

"Exactly. I loved the cobblestoned streets Hugh and I found in older parts of Europe."

Lee tensed her shoulder muscles in sympathetic anticipation. "That's going to be a helluva job. Is anyone going to help you?"

"If need be, Dale or Wally can help with the heavier stuff, but for the most part, I'm content to work at my own pace. The labyrinth is just to the east of here. I'll use my garden cart to haul over a few stones at a time. "

As they surveyed the site, Lee pictured all the work involved with Gaëlle's project. *Glad it's not me.*

Finally, they started back to the house.

"Oh, before I forget, the TV that was in Dale's suite is now in Britten's room, if he's looking for it when he gets home."

"My daughter 'liberated' it, did she? Did she even ask you first?"

"No, but I don't mind. I'm quite enjoying your library."

"I'm glad. But if you want to watch anything, you're most welcome to make use of the TV in the living room."

"Thanks."

"Oh, and I should warn you that Britten told me last night that she intends to meet some friends at the Red Arrow on Friday."

"The Red Arrow?"

"One of Donegal's two pubs and not the nicer of the two."

"Thanks for the heads-up. I'll consider myself duly warned."

"I should also mention that the local Mounties keep a pretty close eye on drivers leaving the Red Arrow."

"Not a problem. I don't drink when I'm driving or on duty."

"Are you ever off duty?"

"Of course. I wouldn't be out here right now enjoying this walk—and the company—if I weren't off duty at the moment."

"And you're back on duty...?"

"When Britten wakes up."

Gaëlle smiled. "Then you should be good for another three or four hours. Feel like some breakfast?"

"If you'll allow me to provide it. Do you enjoy pancakes?"

"I do. So you're feeling better then?"

Lee considered the question carefully before answering. "You know, I am. I really am."

The day passed quietly. Britten rose in time for lunch, then spent the rest of the afternoon in her room with the TV blaring. Gaëlle disappeared to the basement after lunch, and Lee was left to her own devices. She went for a short walk, not straying far from the house, and returned to read for a few hours.

When she finished her book, Lee considered turning on the TV, but she decided instead that she had the perfect excuse to go down to Gaëlle's office.

The basement door stood ajar, so Lee called out before entering. "Hello? Is it okay if I get another book?"

"Come on in. Help yourself. You don't need to ask."

Lee pushed open the door.

Inside, Gaëlle was sorting through papers spread all over a large desk.

"I hope I'm not interrupting."

Gaëlle shook her head. "Not at all. I'm due for a break anyway. My eyes can only take so much of these spreadsheets at one time. Would you care for a cup of coffee?"

"I'd love one."

Gaëlle turned to the pot perched on top of a file cabinet. "This was fresh about half an hour ago. I think it's still okay, but if you'd like, I'd be happy to make another pot."

"No, that's fine. Trust me, after my assistant's coffee, I could drink ink and think it weak by comparison."

Gaëlle chuckled and filled two mugs.

Lee circled behind the desk to accept hers and nodded at the mound of paperwork. "Are you doing your taxes or something?"

"No. I received an e-mail from Dale overnight and was just summarizing some information he needs."

"Um, okay."

"Are you really interested in all this? I don't want to bore you if you're only being polite."

Was it only last week I wasn't interested in anything, including living? Damn, what a difference a few days make. "I really would like to know what you and Dale do, if you don't mind telling me."

"Not at all. I find it fascinating, but only Dale, Jill, and Wally really know the scope of this." Gaëlle led the way to the recliners. "Have a seat."

"What about Britten? Does she know what you do down here?"

"I doubt it. She's never expressed any interest. I don't think she's come down here more than a handful of times, even when she lived here."

"So do I need to be sworn to secrecy?"

"You tell me. Do you? For the most part it's a matter of public record, but you'd have to go digging to find those records. I'd certainly rather keep the full scale of this project quiet."

Lee was touched at the trust Gaëlle was displaying. "Then it goes no further. You have my word."

"That's more than good enough for me. Okay, this will just be an overview, but to give you the basics I need to go back in time again. I told you that Hugh took out massive life insurance policies a year before he died, right?"

Lee nodded.

"Because of the insurance and the fact that my brothers-in-law continued to pay me Hugh's share of the ranch profits, I never had any money worries while raising the kids. We were used to living frugally and continued to do so. I was fortunate enough to have a trusted and talented financial advisor, and the money grew to ridiculous amounts. I never spoke of it until one day a few years ago, when I was having coffee with one of my sisters-in-law, Nell, Scott's wife."

Gaëlle took a drink of her coffee. "We were talking about dreams, and Nell mentioned that she'd always wanted to start her own nursery specializing in native prairie plants. I asked why she didn't go for it, and she said that the banks wouldn't loan her money unless Scott co-signed. Because Scott co-owns the land with his brothers, he can't use it as collateral for a business loan without their permission. James and Peter would've been fine with it, but Andrew, who was going through a nasty divorce at the time, wasn't in a position to sign on."

"Let me guess—you loaned her the money."

"I did, yes. It was my first microloan, and Nell paid it back with interest. Her nursery has been a huge success in the years since. It got me thinking about women and entrepreneurship, but it wasn't until I read about Muhammad Yunus winning the Nobel Peace Prize in 2006 that my ideas started to gel."

Lee shook her head."I'm sorry—who?"

"Muhammad Yunus. He's the Bangladeshi economist who founded Grameen Bank in 1983.

It specializes in making micro-loans to poor people with no collateral. Amazingly, ninety-five per cent pay their loans back in full. But as I investigated, I found there were some issues that didn't get any publicity. It turned out that a lot of people using microfinance were doing so not to fuel entrepreneurship, but rather for consumption purposes, such as financing weddings and the like. That wasn't what I wanted to do, but I did want to help with more than just making charitable donations. Dale was utterly bored with his job as a government soil analyst, so the two of us started to brainstorm. We ended up taking a trip to Africa, talking to a lot of people and seeing things on the ground for ourselves."

"That must've been an incredible journey."

"It was. And what struck me, over and over again, was how perilous and fragile women's lives were. If their husbands died or were simply bad husbands, they were left without enough to feed and care for their children. There was no security net, and far too many of them ended up in prostitution just to put food on the table. With no money for education, even children with the most potential had no chance of advancing into the middle class."

"It sounds pretty hopeless."

"I know. I had to fight hard not to be overwhelmed with the sheer magnitude of need. Then one day we met an amazing woman in a tiny sweets shop in Guinea. Her name was Janjay. She was a Bassa tribeswoman from Sierra Leone who had been displaced to Guinea during the civil war. Her husband was killed, and her two eldest sons were taken for child soldiers. Her middle daughter was taken as a warlord's concubine when she was just eleven. Janjay herself had her hand cut off for daring to speak out against the warlords. Yet she had the most amazing spirit I've ever encountered."

Lee shuddered at a world where such atrocities were so common. "God, how did she stand it? Losing Dana almost killed me, and Janjay not only lost her husband, she lost two sons, a daughter and her hand. Just imagining what was happening to her children and knowing she couldn't save them from any of it... Jesus, I think I'd have hung myself from the nearest tree."

Gaëlle nodded grimly. "The horror is almost more than most of us can comprehend. But Janjay was determined that her family was not going to succumb to the devastation all around them, and she fought tooth and nail to make a better life. Even when they had to run from the soldiers, Janjay made sure to take along their precious few schoolbooks. She told me she used to keep them packed up in a bag when they weren't being used, so that if they had to flee, she could grab them on the way out of the hut. Janjay educated her children beside campfires and in refugee camps. I've never met such an inspirational soul. Because of her, we basically adopted her village. We built a school for both boys and girls and a clinic that serves villages within a fifty-mile radius. We educated Janjay's youngest son and a niece on the condition that they return to the village as doctors."

"Wow! Talk about making a difference."

"Janjay made the difference, Lee. Without

her insight and advice, Dale and I would've been a couple of wannabe philanthropists stumbling around in the dark, probably doing more harm than good. With her guidance, we've set up a foundation—the Huowen Foundation—and worked on making changes that will benefit people from the ground up. As we could afford it, we went farther afield from Janjay's village, but always with Janjay directing our efforts. Our latest project is solar panels. The electrical grid doesn't reach much beyond major cities throughout the continent, but with solar panels we can give rural people their own source of electricity. Janjay, who is now one of our directors, came up with the idea, and she's moved on it like a cheetah stalking a gazelle. Dale took a solar specialist with him on his most recent trip. He goes to Guinea frequently, and I sit back here, tracking where the money goes and how best to fund things."

"Do you pay for everything yourself?"

"Actually, we've gotten pretty good at getting government and UN grants for the bigger projects. God help the bureaucrat who tries to tell Janjay no when she's righteously fired up. I've seen that woman make dictators cry as she waves her stub of a hand in their face."

Lee looked around the basement room. "And you do all that from here?"

"Mostly Dale and Janjay do it from over there, but I help out where I can. I used to travel to Guinea fairly often too, but it wears me down. Dale's my good right arm, so I leave it up to him now."

"Amazing. Absolutely amazing. And most of your family has no idea?"

Gaëlle shrugged. "They know Dale frequently goes to Africa, but they're not exactly clear on why. I suspect they think he's still involved in soil analysis for the government. If they asked, I'd tell them. It's certainly not that I don't trust my family, but I also don't want to give them the impression that Dale and I think we're some kind of billionaire philanthropists like Bill and Melinda Gates. I'm a small-town girl, who by happenstance is in a position to help out a few people in Guinea. It wouldn't even have been possible if not for Hugh's foresight or Janjay's leadership, so I don't deserve any accolades for what we do. I just want to work quietly behind the scenes, which fortunately is what Dale wants as well. Besides, like most people, our relatives are mostly only concerned with their own lives and don't pay all that much attention to ours. Dale certainly isn't going to spill the beans. My son is as taciturn as his father was outgoing."

"Dale never married?"

"No, but he'd like to. He's crazy about Janjay's youngest daughter, Dechontee. Janjay and I joke together about what pretty babies they'll make, but Dechontee isn't about to jump into marriage at the expense of her dreams. She's got her mother's independence, and no man is going to sway her from her career ambitions. She's set on being a nurse practitioner, come hell or high water. I was Skyping with Janjay earlier, and she told me that she's starting to feel sorry for Dale, but it's Dechontee's choice, and she's not going to interfere."

"If she ever says yes, will Dale bring his bride back here?"

"She wouldn't come. Dechontee is as set as her mother is on improving conditions for their people."

"So Dale would stay there? Doesn't it upset you to think of Dale half a world away?"

"Well, I think it will take Dale a few years yet to persuade Dechontee that he'd make a good husband. If moving to Guinea to be with his beloved is in his soul's plan, I would never interfere or criticize. When Britten was set on going to Europe to pursue her dream, I supported her, even if her chosen career wasn't what I'd hoped for her."

"So it would be okay because Dale is doing something worthwhile?"

"It would be okay because it's Dale's choice, which he has an absolute right to make. I learned long ago that the only thing I can control in life is myself. So if my children choose to go far afield, I can control how I react to their absence, not the choice itself."

"Huh. That's very Zen of you."

Gaëlle laughed. "I'm no philosopher; I'm just me. And this 'me' better get back to work. Dale is waiting for those numbers, and I need to dig them up. We're trying to source the most economic supplier for a test run of solar panels."

Lee drained her mug and stood. She was upstairs, washing her cup at the kitchen sink, before she realized she'd entirely forgotten to select another book.

CHAPTER 7

LEE WAS STRETCHED OUT ON Dale's comfortable bed. "No, honest, Wil, it's been really quiet around here all week."

"Are you then bored enough to climb walls?"

"Nah, I'm actually enjoying myself, believe it or not."

"You're enjoying our client's company?"

Lee laughed aloud at the incredulity in Willem's voice. "No, not so much. In fact, I rarely see Britten. She sticks to her room most days, except for meals and the occasional shopping run into town. And, by the way, shopping in Donegal falls well short of Calgary standards."

"So, if it's not our client you're enjoying, or the shopping, what is there to recommend Donegal?"

"Fresh air. Big skies. Wonderful walks." *Gaëlle.*

"You sound so much better, Lee. I was obviously right to urge you to take this assignment."

"Geez, don't break your arm patting yourself on the back." Lee grinned at the sound of his chuckles. "But yes, you were right. I'll give you that. I like it here...a lot. It's like being back on my grandparents' ranch, minus the chores."

"Excellent. But back to business and the reason

I called. Barb found one cyber leak on Facebook. Some woman named Tiffany Howlick was apparently bragging about her close friendship with Britten. She extolled their grand reunion when Britten returned to Donegal from so many years away as a European supermodel."

"Damn it! I was afraid of that. What a feather-brained bunch."

"You insult our avian friends by the comparison. But don't worry; Barb jumped on it immediately, and that post is no longer visible. In fact, Barb disabled the woman's account. From what I'm told, it will take her weeks to get it sorted out. I'm certain Barb plugged the leak before any damage could be done. Nonetheless, I felt it imperative that you be told."

"Thanks, Wil. Britten is meeting a bunch of friends at a pub later tonight—oh joy, oh bliss—so I'll have my eyes peeled for any trouble. Hell, even without Tiffany's leak, this bar sounds like a venue for trouble, at least according to Gaëlle."

"Pardon? According to whom?"

"Gaëlle. Britten's mom. She said the Red Arrow is bad news any night of the week, but Fridays are the worst. So of course Britten wants to go on Friday."

"This Gaëlle is a trustworthy source? I would not imagine a mother of this client as being reputable."

"Then you'd imagine wrong. Gaëlle is as different from her daughter as day is from night. I'd trust anything she told me." *Well, almost anything. Still can't buy into the hooey.*

"Ah, so you have made a friend there."

Lee didn't hesitate. "I have."

"Then I am even more pleased. You can't see me, but I am polishing my fingernails on my lapel right now."

Lee rolled her eyes but couldn't help laughing. She knew exactly what Willem was doing. It was his trademark whenever he'd made, by his estimation, a brilliant call. She'd seen it often in their twenty-five years together. "Yeah, yeah. You're the greatest. Now go push some paper. I've got things to do."

Willem bade Lee goodbye, self-satisfaction clearly apparent in his voice.

Lee set down the cellphone and gazed at the ceiling. Contrary to what she'd told her partner, she really didn't have anything pressing to do. She'd been for the usual morning walk with Gaëlle and had passed the rest of a pleasant day doing small domestic chores and reading another good novel. Other than folding her laundry, Lee had nothing she needed to do until it was time to leave for the Red Arrow.

"I wonder what Gaëlle's doing." Lee swung her legs off the bed. "Think I'll go find out."

What a dive!

Lee followed Britten across the filthy floor to a corner table where several of her client's friends were gathered. Judging by the slurred exuberance of their greeting, they'd been there a while.

Lee was relieved to see that Pam was not among them. It would've lowered her estimation of the woman considerably. There was only one open chair at the table, and no one made a move to pull up another, so Lee quietly borrowed a chair from the next table and pulled it back against the wall. While she clearly wasn't a part of the celebration, she could see and hear everything that went on.

When a weary waitress with eyes far too old for her youthful face came by, Lee ordered a Coke and tipped heavily. Britten ordered wine and didn't tip at all.

The next two hours dragged by for Lee. Straight bars didn't hold any appeal, and watching the mating rituals all around her was depressing. *God, I don't want to ever do this again.* What did amuse her was the number of men who just *happened* to drift by the corner table, much to the hilarity of the women gathered there. They never spoke directly to Britten on first approach, but conversation with the other women inevitably led to offers to buy Britten a drink.

It was clear that Britten enjoyed the attention. She flirted madly with all her suitors, but skillfully never made any spoken or unspoken promises. Lee was relieved to see that Britten shared the freebies dropped on her table with her friends. Still, she consumed a quantity and variety of alcohol sufficient that Lee began to wonder if she'd have to carry Britten to the SUV at the end of the night.

It was after eleven when Tiffany's squeal snapped Lee out of her semi-somnolence.

"Oh, my God, Brit! Do you see who just walked in? It's Brian! You remember Brian, don't you?"

Britten's lascivious smile indicated she clearly remembered Brian...fondly. "Is he still married to that bitch? What was her name?"

"Rhonda. You remember Rhonda, Brit. She was always so jealous of you and Brian. The minute you left for Europe, she moved right in on him. Had a ring on his finger within the year."

Britten didn't look pleased at that. "A year? He forgot me in only a year?"

"God, no. But Rhonda got pregnant. I think she did it on purpose." There was a chorus of agreement among the friends. "So, Brian married her. It didn't last though. They got divorced five or six years later. Honestly, hon, I think he still pines for the one who got away."

Britten smiled seductively. She looked right past the man who had just bought her a Canadian Club and Seven-Up and who had his hand on her forearm.

Lee tensed at the look on the newcomer's face when he saw Britten. Brian had a smouldering aspect as he began making his way through the crowd toward his ex-girlfriend's table.

Uh oh. Lee didn't like the possessive manner in which Brian elbowed his way to Britten's side.

Neither did Mr. CC and Seven. "Hey, watch it, buddy."

"Go away, Junior. Me and the lady have some catching up to do."

The oblivious suitor protested. "Excuse me—"

"You're excused. Now beat it. I'm not telling you again."

"I was here first!"

"Like hell you were. She was mine a long time ago. Ain't that right, Heather Ann? You and me were doing the nasty before this boy could even grow a moustache."

"It's Britten now, Brian."

"So I heard. Well, *Britten*, why don't you tell this boy to take a hike? You and me are due a long stroll down memory lane."

Britten dropped her gaze, and her friends tittered.

Brian smiled lazily as he removed the rejected suitor's hand from Britten's arm. Mr. CC and Seven didn't take that well.

The first punch snapped Brian's head back but didn't drop him.

Mr. CC and Seven stepped back and stared at his hand as if he couldn't believe it had actually struck someone. Particularly someone twice his size.

Brian roared, charged, and bulldozed Mr. CC and Seven to the ground.

Screams and cheers erupted around them. Within moments, the entire bar boiled into a brawl.

Lee seized Britten's arm and pulled her toward the rear entrance.

Britten struggled to pull away. "What are you doing? Let go of me!"

Lee hung on grimly and dodged combatants as best she could. Pain blazed down the side of her cheek as glass sliced her and cold liquid drenched her. Gasping, Lee spun and saw Britten holding the remnants of the highball glass. Britten looked as stunned at what she'd done as Mr. CC and Seven had.

Lee was fed up. "God damn it!" She grabbed Britten more firmly and fought her way out the back exit. Britten obviously realized she had crossed a line; she said nothing. Lee didn't know where her client's friends were; she didn't care.

Lee pushed Britten into the passenger seat and hurried around to the driver's side. As they drove away, the fight spilled out of the bar into the parking lot. The sound of approaching sirens echoed through the night air.

Lee had just passed the Donegal town limit sign when she saw the whirling red and blue lights of an RCMP patrol car behind her. With a sigh, she pulled over and rolled down her window.

The Mountie strode up to the SUV and peered inside. "Did you just leave the Red Arrow?"

"Yes, I did."

"Licence and registration, please." The officer scanned the documents, looked at Lee sceptically, and wrinkled his nose. "Have you been drinking tonight, ma'am?"

Before Lee could answer, Britten yelled, "Yes! She's pissed as a rat! And she kidnapped me!"

"Please step out of the vehicle, ma'am."

After shooting her passenger a fierce look, Lee got out of the car.

"Are you injured, ma'am?"

Lee looked at the Mountie with puzzlement, then realized there was blood running down her cheek. "Just cut by flying glass."

The Mountie returned to his patrol car and came back with a field Breathalyzer.

Following his instructions, Lee blew hard and was vindicated when her blood alcohol numbers came up clear.

The Mountie leaned over and addressed Britten. "Are you genuinely claiming to be kidnapped, Miss? That's a very serious charge. I'll have to take you both back to the station if you're sticking with this allegation."

"I didn't mean it. I was just joking."

"You should probably think twice about your jokes, Miss. Particularly when you're making such a grave accusation to a police officer." Satisfied that the situation was under control, the Mountie handed back Lee's documents and gave her a sympathetic look. "You'd best have that cut looked at, ma'am. Drive safely."

Lee got back in the car and pulled slowly away as the Mountie made a U-turn and headed back toward Donegal. When Britten opened her mouth, Lee glared at her. "Not one fucking word, do you understand? Not one."

The ride back home was silent except for Britten's sullen mutterings, which Lee pointedly ignored.

When they arrived, Britten stormed into the house ahead of Lee and tried to slam the door in her face.

Lee caught the door and went inside to find Gaëlle staring at them. "My God! What happened?"

Britten stamped her foot and pointed at Lee. "What happened was she ruined my night! Everything would've been fine if she hadn't butted in and acted like a cave-dwelling dyke."

That was the last straw for Lee. "Look, lady, I don't give a good goddamn if you want to go home with some hayseed you once knew. It's no bloody skin off my nose who you have a booty call with. But I'm paid to keep your ass in one piece, and that's what I'm going to do."

"Not anymore. You're fired!" Britten ran up the stairs and slammed her bedroom door so hard it felt as if it made the whole house shake.

Lee closed her eyes and drew several deep breaths. A soft touch on her shoulder made her open her eyes.

"Let me look at that cut. You might need stitches." Gaëlle led Lee to the kitchen and sat her down at the table. She delicately dabbed at the cut with a clean, damp, soft cloth until Lee winced and pulled away. "Stay still. I'm not going to hurt you."

Lee submitted to Gaëlle's ministrations. Her head throbbed, and though she'd applied a fresh patch just before they left for the Red Arrow, she would have killed for a cigarette right at that moment.

"You're going to need a couple of stitches." When Lee shook her head, Gaëlle held up her hand. "No arguments. You're lucky you didn't lose an eye."

"I'm not going to the ER. Besides, they're probably overwhelmed with Red Arrow customers about now."

"You don't have to go anywhere. Wait here a minute. I need to make a call." Gaëlle left the room.

Lee leaned back and closed her eyes against the bright ceiling light.

When Gaëlle returned, she said, "My sister-in-law Wendy will be right over. She's an RN."

"She doesn't mind doing this?"

"She's used to stitching up family at all hours."

"I'm not family."

"No, but you're a friend of the family, and that counts too." Gaëlle wrinkled her nose as she tugged on Lee's shirt collar. "I thought you said you didn't drink on duty."

"I don't. And the local constabulary has the Breathalyzer results to prove it. I reek thanks to Britten's CC and Seven."

"Thanks to Britten's... My God. Lee, did Britten cut you?"

"Not on purpose. She just didn't appreciate me dragging her away from some guy named Brian. She'd been drinking pretty hard all night. Her resistance to dickwad behaviour was lower than it should've been." Lee was well aware that she was talking to Britten's mother, but she was tired, disgusted, and in pain. She was also fired, and the realization that she'd be packing to go in the morning was causing an unexpected and far more potent pain.

The doorbell rang.

"Oh, that must be Wendy. Thank goodness, she must've been close by. Wait here."

Lee heard Gaëlle open the door, the murmur of voices, then her name called in alarm. Instantly, Lee was out of her chair and running. Without stopping, she flew by Gaëlle and tackled the man in the doorway. A scream sounded from halfway up the stairs. Then Britten called out, "Michael!"

Lee pinned Saberi on the porch and yanked his arms behind him. Fists beat furiously at her back, and Lee tried to defend herself without letting Saberi free.

Gaëlle shouted, "Britten, stop that! Lee's protecting you!"

Britten screamed curses and clawed at Lee's shoulders as she tried to dislodge her.

Gaëlle wrapped her arms around her daughter and pulled her away. Another man hurried from a limousine toward the porch with his fists clenched.

"Enough. Stop this. Right now." A deep, authoritative voice rang out in the dark, freezing everyone in their tracks.

Wrong-Way Wally was in the yard, his arm impeding the man from the limousine. Wally repeated, "Enough."

Michael turned his head to Britten, who was still trapped within her mother's arms. "Darling, what's going on? Who are these people? Don't they know I'm your husband?"

Lee growled. "Being her husband doesn't give you the right to abuse her."

"Abuse her? What are you talking about? She called me two days ago to come pick her up. I am here by her request."

Lee looked at Britten. "Is that true?"

"Yes. He's my husband, and I want to go home."

"Aw, for Christ's sake. Just when I thought this night couldn't get any worse." Lee released Saberi and rolled to her feet.

Lee, Gaëlle, Britten, Michael, and his driver were gathered around the kitchen table. Wendy, who had arrived on the scene moments after the ceasefire was called, tended to cuts and bruises. Wally watched from the corner by the cabinets.

"So you were never in any danger?" Lee queried

Britten as Wendy gently cleaned her wound.

"Of course not. Michael would never hurt me." Britten hung on Michael's arm as if it was a life preserver.

"And the blood on your face in the hotel? He wasn't responsible for that?"

Michael blinked. "You thought I did that? I've never laid so much as a finger on my wife."

"So how did she get cut?"

"We had a...a little disagreement in our hotel room. My wife is as temperamental as she is beautiful. It was my fault, of course. It was a delicate issue that I should never have brought up. Poor Britten was so distraught that she threw a vase at me. I ducked and fell. The vase shattered; a piece of glass ricocheted and cut my wife. She ran out before I could regain my feet. By the time I got out to the hall, she had disappeared. Then I had to deal with hotel security, and... Well, you see it all just...how do you say it? Ah, yes. It all just snowballed out of control."

"You weren't tracking her?"

"Of course not. I know better than that. When these things happen, my wife just needs a little time to cool off. She always returns or calls me to come get her when she's ready." Michael beamed at Britten, who pouted and laid her head on his shoulder.

"What was the issue?"

Michael looked at Gaëlle. "Pardone, Madame?"

"What was the issue that caused my daughter to behave so poorly?" Gaëlle's voice was cool, but implacable.

"It was nothing, Mom."

"Now, darling, your mother has a right to know. We were discussing the best time to have children. Britten isn't quite ready to take such a major step, and I'm afraid I pushed too hard. I promise you, though, it won't happen again. My wife is a woman of tender feelings and deserves to be treated so. Don't you, darling?"

Michael and Britten nibbled on each other's lips, reconciliation obviously achieved.

Lee could see the magnitude of disappointment in Gaëlle's face. Her daughter's immaturity had caused problems for so many, and Lee was sure that no matter what she said, Gaëlle felt some sense of failure.

Lee found that despite the pain in her cheek as Wendy inserted three stitches, she held no animus for her flighty client. Ten days ago she had been mired so deep in her own misery that she couldn't see a way out. This past week, she had looked forward to waking up every morning. In a way, she owed Britten a debt.

Lee and the driver, who hadn't been introduced, sat uncomfortably across from each other in the living room. Wendy had departed, taking her little black bag with her. Britten and Michael were upstairs. Lee hoped they were packing, not taking their reunion to the next level.

Gaëlle and Wally were outside. Lee could see them talking on the front porch. They hugged each other and parted just as Britten and Michael descended the stairs.

“Ahmad, bring the luggage down to the car.”

Ahmad nodded at Michael’s instructions and hurried upstairs.

Lee briefly contemplated helping him with the excess of bags, then mentally shrugged. *I’m fired. Someone else can look after her things.*

Michael approached Lee, who regarded him warily. He looked a little more dishevelled than the suave, debonair bon vivant Lee had researched, but he smiled as he pulled a wallet from inside his suit coat and extracted a cheque. “I trust this will cover my wife’s expenses, Ms. Glenn. Thank you for taking such good care of my treasure. I tell you sincerely, I would not like to be your enemy.” He extended his hand, and Lee rose to take it, accepting the payment as she did so.

When Michael turned to address Gaëlle, Lee glanced at the cheque and raised an eyebrow at the generous amount. It would more than cover DeGroot and Glenn’s fee, with enough for staff bonuses all around.

“It was very good to meet my wife’s mother, Mrs. Germaine. I hope it will not be so long until the next visit.”

“That’s up to Britten.”

“Ah, well then. Perhaps we will have you to our home in Paris one day.”

“Perhaps.”

Britten offered her mother a self-conscious embrace.

Gaëlle held her daughter tightly before allowing Britten to pull away.

Ahmad descended the stairs with Britten’s bags

precariously balanced in one load. Gaëlle hastened to open the door, and Michael followed his man out.

Lee thought Britten was going to leave without another word, but surprisingly she turned to Lee. "Look, I'm sorry about all that—you know, what I said to the cop and all. I was just mad."

Lee nodded but didn't otherwise respond to the half-hearted apology.

Gaëlle followed Britten out to the porch and raised a hand in farewell as the limousine departed. She came back in and closed the door softly behind her. "That was quite the surprise, wasn't it? Can't say I expected all this drama when you set off for an evening at the Red Arrow. What did Britten mean with reference to her apology? Was that part of her throwing a drink on you and cutting your face?"

"Kind of the second act. I was pulled over shortly after I left the Red Arrow. Britten told the Mountie I'd been drinking and had kidnapped her. I imagine I looked the part, what with my face bleeding and my clothes stinking of Canadian Club, but I was able to persuade the officer that I was not guilty of either accusation."

"Oh, no. I can't believe Britten would cause such serious trouble."

"Fortunately the booze was all on the outside, not the inside. So after making me blow into a Breathalyzer, he let me go. No harm, no foul."

"Except for what my daughter did to you."

Lee shrugged. She wasn't going to make excuses for her former client.

Gaëlle sighed and patted the footstool. "Care for another head massage? I'll be very careful.

Maybe it will make up in a small way for Britten's misdeeds."

Lee took a seat on the footstool and closed her eyes as Gaëlle's hands began to work their magic. "It's not your responsibility. As you said, she's an adult, making her own choices."

"Mmm. Could be karmic debt by association, though. You can never be too careful with that hooey stuff."

Lee smiled at Gaëlle's teasing. She was going to miss this woman. Which reminded her...

"Would it be okay with you if I stay the night? It's kind of late, and I'll get out of your hair first thing in the morning."

Gaëlle was quiet.

"Or I could leave tonight. I saw a motel in Donegal."

"Shhh, don't be silly. Of course you're not going to leave tonight. In fact, I think that maybe you should stay on a few days. You know, until your face heals."

"Are you sure I wouldn't be in the way?"

"I'm sure."

Lee could've told Gaëlle about the time she drove through a near tornado with a broken leg, or how she'd once scaled the wall of an Algerian compound with a bullet in her side. The drive back to Calgary would not tax her unduly.

On the other hand, she wasn't as young as she once was. A few days of rest sounded good. "Okay, thanks. I'll stay for a day or two."

CHAPTER 8

LEE WAS STILL SLEEPING WHEN a loud knocking woke her up. She glanced blearily at the bedside clock and was surprised to see it was later than she was accustomed to rising. “Yes?”

“Are you coming with me this morning?”

Sleep in; walk with Gaëlle... “I’ll be ready in ten minutes.”

“Dress warmly. The wind is pretty raw, and I thought we’d walk as far as the lake today.”

Lee sat up and looked out the window. Gaëlle was right. It was grey and cloudy, and trees swayed in the wind. For a moment she looked back at her pillow, but it held less appeal than she’d have expected.

True to her word, Lee was dressed and downstairs within ten minutes.

Gaëlle handed her a trail bar and a tall travel cup. “I thought you might like something warm as we walk.”

“Thanks. That was very thoughtful.”

Lee was glad of the coffee. The wind signalled less a newly born spring and more a dying winter reluctant to release its hold on the land. “How far did you say we were walking today?”

“I thought we’d go to the lake, but we can cut it short if you’d rather.”

“How far is the lake?”

“About forty minutes each way. I was in the mood to see the geese return, but I can always go some other time.”

“No, that’s okay. I’m good.”

As they hiked, Lee became acclimated to the weather. She noted that Gaëlle seemed to enjoy the wind in her face, not bothering to zip her coat all the way closed as Lee had.

“Are we still on your land?”

“Not exactly, but we are still on Germaine land. I retain ownership to ten acres for personal use, but the family collectively has title to over twenty thousand hectares. About half of that is under cultivation—alfalfa and hay—and the rest is range.”

“So we could walk a long way and never leave your family’s land.”

“Indeed.”

“I grew up on my grandparents’ farm. They only had about seven hundred acres by the time they took me in, but it was enough to suit their needs. At one time my grandpa’s family was among the biggest ranchers in the province. My grandpa told me his mother ran a ranch in the foothills of Alberta that at its height was eighteen thousand hectares. But after she passed on, her family sold most of the land to developers. Grandpa Laird never left, though. He was such a homebody that he thought a day trip into Calgary was too far to go. He and my grandmother are buried in an old churchyard on the prairie. The town that was once there doesn’t exist anymore, but the church still stands as a heritage site."

"How was it that you grew up with your grandparents?"

"My parents were killed in a car accident when I was three. My paternal grandparents raised me."

Gaëlle touched Lee's arm. "I'm sorry."

"No, that's okay. I don't remember my parents, but I couldn't have asked for a better upbringing."

"I'm glad. May I ask how they took it when you told them you were gay?"

"For two people who were born in the last decade of the nineteenth century, amazingly well. Mind you, I didn't officially come out to them until I was in my twenties. I don't think they were surprised. And all they really said was that they wanted me to be happy."

"They sound like very evolved souls. Did they live long enough to meet Dana and Eli?"

"No. Unfortunately, they died before I met Dana. I know they'd have liked her, though. Everyone did."

They'd come to a wooden fence, and Lee drained the last of her coffee before following Gaëlle up and over. They climbed a small rise, and Lee could see water off to their left. "Is that the lake?"

"No, that's just a slough. It'll be dried up by late June. The lake is a little farther on. Are you doing okay?"

"Sure, no problem."

They fell into a companionable silence as they walked.

Soon Lee saw a small lake on the horizon. "That has to be it."

"It is. Welcome to Goose Lake, nesting and feeding ground to hundreds of birds, including my personal favourite, Canada geese."

"Why are they your favourites?"

"Because their call from overhead stirs something in my soul, and because their migrations are harbingers of the seasons."

"Huh." Lee shrugged. "They're kind of pests in Calgary. It's cute in the spring, when their fluffy, yellow goslings are running around, but at one point there were so many in Prince's Island Park that you couldn't walk around without getting goose grease on your feet."

Gaëlle lifted one rubber-booted foot. "Which is exactly why I wear Bog Boots that I can rinse off. Between cattle, horses, dogs, and geese, it's better not to think what's underfoot when you're walking Germaine land."

Goose Lake was a combination of grasslands, wetlands, and open water. It reminded Lee of a busy urban airport with flights continually arriving and departing.

Gaëlle stopped to watch a pair of Canada geese circle overhead and land on the shore.

Lee watched Gaëlle. "You really do love those birds, don't you?"

Gaëlle smiled at her. "I do. Sometimes I spend hours out here."

"By yourself?"

"Usually. Sometimes Wally comes with me."

"Did you bring the kids with you when they were young?"

"Not often. It was a bit far for little legs, and

when they were older, they were more interested in being with their friends than with their mother. But now and then I'd make a picnic, put Britten in her wagon, and Dale and Jill would keep me company." Gaëlle pointed at a single goose approaching the lake. "That's unusual. They're monogamous and mate for life, so either that one lost its mate to a hunter or it's young enough that it hasn't found its mate yet. It makes me sad to see them solo, though."

"You don't think they can live a satisfactory solo life? That's kind of depressing."

Gaëlle studied Lee. "Are we still talking about the Canada goose?"

"Yes. No. I don't know."

A stiff gust of wind sent a chill through Lee, and she shivered violently.

Gaëlle took her arm and turned her about.

"Come on. Let's start back. There will be warmer days for bird watching."

Lee could tell Gaëlle was deep in thought as they walked back. Finally, Lee broke the silence. "I didn't mean anything by what I said. I didn't mean to imply *your* life was depressing."

"It's all right, Lee. We're both in the same boat, aren't we? I've just been paddling for a lot longer, that's all."

"I didn't even try to paddle after Dana died; I just gave up."

"And yet here you are, so at some level you didn't give up completely."

Lee shook her head. "No, I gave up at every level. Eli told me he half-expected to come downstairs one day and find my body hanging from a rafter."

"Was he wrong to think that?"

"No, he wasn't. I thought about it. Hell, I thought of many ways I could end it all, but something always stopped me."

"What stopped you?"

"I don't know. Whenever I'd start thinking seriously about suicide, I'd get unbelievably tired, drained, you know? So I never had the energy to put any plan into motion. Even so, Eli said I was trying to kill myself when I'd ride my Suzuki during the winter. Maybe he's right, but if so, it wasn't conscious. I just felt free on my bike. For a little while I could focus on the ride and simply forget."

"And now?"

"Now? Now I'm relieved that I didn't do anything stupid. Well, anything stupider than what I did. Makes me wonder, though, how long I'd have gone on if my family and friends hadn't intervened."

"Then I'm very glad that they did."

"Me too. It was Dana's doing."

"It was? How so?"

"She set it up before she died. She wrote me a letter and left it with my friends. She told them to give it to me after a year, and if I wasn't getting on with my life, they should intervene and rescue me from myself."

"It must've been a magic letter."

Lee laughed. "No, it was just Dana being Dana. She always knew how to handle me; she combined equal measures of love and kick-ass. Basically, she told me to stop being an idiot, how much she loved me and that she always would. She said there were amazing things awaiting me, and it was time to seek them out, because I would dishonour our love if I gave up. She finished by telling me she'd always be around. I don't know if I believe that, though."

"I do."

"Why?"

"Because I've felt Hugh and Owen in my life throughout these past three decades."

"Seriously? You don't mean you hear them talking to you, do you?"

"That would be too hooey, eh?"

"Hell, yeah!" Lee gave Gaëlle a friendly elbow. "If you're going to tell me there are ghosts in that old farmhouse, I'm outta there tonight."

Gaëlle chuckled and shook her head. "No ghosts, I promise. Hugh and Owen didn't linger when they passed; they're not haunting me. They do, however, communicate in their own fashion."

"No way. How?"

"When Hugh was alive, he was always the first in the kitchen. I'd tend to the children while he made coffee. For months after he died, I couldn't make morning coffee because I'd break down. Then that fall, the day after I began to build the labyrinth, I woke to the smell of coffee."

"Dale learned how to make it?"

"No. There was no coffee on when I went to the kitchen. There was no coffee on down in the library, either. I checked. I assumed I must have dreamed it. But it happened again and again. Not every day, but regularly enough so that I knew I wasn't imagining it."

Lee tried to come up with a logical explanation but failed. "Okay, I guess I can see why you'd think that was a sign. What about Owen?"

"The last Christmas we shared in this life, Owen gave me a set of chimes. They weren't expensive or fancy, but he was so proud because he'd picked them out himself. I promised that, come spring, we'd hang them over the deck and enjoy their chimes together. He died before spring, and I couldn't bear to do anything with them all that summer. After I started smelling the coffee, I chanced across the chimes where I'd stuffed them in the back of the closet. On a whim, I put them up in my bedroom. One morning soon afterwards I woke to their soft sounds filling my room."

"A breeze from a window?"

"There weren't any windows open."

"Maybe a heating vent was blowing at them?"

"The furnace was shut off."

"Huh. And this has happened ever since they died?"

"After the first time, it happened consistently for about a year then it became more infrequent. It's rare now."

"Why would that be?"

"Because they know I've banished all my doubt. I don't need reassurance that they're alive and well; I know they are. So they'll pop by every now and then to say hi, but they've got their own concerns to tend to."

"You make it sound like...I don't know...like they're just in another town."

"In a way that's true. They're in a place where I can't touch them right now, but they're fully alive to me. I know I'll see them again one day."

A wave of anguish swept through Lee. "Why you? Why not me? Why hasn't Dana sent me some kind of sign? Do you know what I'd give to have that?"

"Yes, Lee, I do."

"Then why?"

"I'm conjecturing here, but from what little you've told me, you were so deep in mourning that you could barely function, yes?"

"Yeah. I was a mess."

"As was I the first eight months after the accident. Having to care for my kids was the only thing that kept me sane and barely sane at that. It wasn't until I pulled myself together enough to focus on something else—in this case, building the labyrinth—that Hugh and Owen were able to reach me. I think, like mine was, your grief has been too intense for Dana to make contact."

Lee considered that, amazed that she was lending *any* credence to such a thing.

Seeming to read Lee's mind, Gaëlle smiled. "I know—hooey. Still, if you open your heart and quiet your mind, I bet you find amazing things will happen. The other side is very subtle, though. You have to be aware of all that's around you."

"How do you know these aren't all coincidences? How can you be so sure?"

For the first time, Gaëlle was hesitant. "I've had other...experiences, which solidified my belief. Plus I'm not the only one Hugh's contacted."

"Who else?"

"His brother, Scott. Not that Scott will talk about it, because it shook him up so deeply. Nell told me about it in confidence years ago. Seven months after Hugh died, Scott had been working late baling hay. He'd almost lost the light by the time he quit and headed back to the barns. He told Nell that something off to the side caught his eye, and when he turned his head, he saw Hugh standing in a field, lit by the setting sun, smiling at him. It only lasted a moment, and then Hugh was gone."

"Do you think he really saw Hugh? I mean, he was tired after a long day's work. He might've been thinking about his brother and just imagined he saw him."

"Except Scott is the least imaginative person I know, and he told Nell that all he'd been thinking of at the time was having a cold beer. Nell certainly believes her husband saw Hugh. And of all the brothers, Hugh and Scott were the closest."

"Have you ever seen Hugh?"

"No, but I long ago reached the point where I can feel when he's around."

"Are you jealous that he would appear to his brother and not you?"

"Oddly, I'm not. I've never been uncertain of, or insecure about, Hugh's love for me and the kids, and that's only been reinforced since his death. But Scott is such a practical, no-nonsense sort of man that it would take something radical to make him believe. Seeing his brother's spirit was that something."

"Did it change him? Does your brother-in-law believe in all this...hooey now?"

"Not exactly, but I do think it planted a seed that's grown enough to crack open his closed mind. Thirty years later, Scott is still processing his experience, but he definitely hasn't forgotten or dismissed it."

As they walked and talked, they had reached the labyrinth. Lee stopped and stared at the trampled outline. "Do you think there's any chance...do you think Dana will ever contact me?"

"Are you open to that? Or would you find any excuse to dismiss the contact as imaginary?"

"I don't know, Gaëlle; I really don't. It all sounds so unlikely. But to feel Dana again, to know she's alive somewhere and still loves me...I can't think of anything that would mean more to me."

"It accelerates healing even more than the passage of time."

Lee turned to face Gaëlle and noted how ruddy her cheeks were from the wind. "Are you healed?" She was surprised when Gaëlle didn't respond with an automatic affirmative.

"Am I? Most days I think so. I'm certainly well past the devastation of that first couple of years. But there are still moments when the longing for Hugh's arms around me, the ache to hug my first-born son again, is almost more than I can bear. But those moments are few and far between now, and understanding that they're both alive in another form has helped me immensely."

Another gust of wind blew a loose tendril of hair across Gaëlle's face. Lee almost reached to tuck it back but caught herself. "Is that why you've stayed single all these years? Because you can't imagine anyone taking Hugh's place?"

Gaëlle looked past Lee at the labyrinth. "Hugh's place in my life and my soul are his own. His soul is not interchangeable with any other. That doesn't mean there isn't room in my life for another soul."

"But you haven't found that other soul?"

"Maybe I'm waiting to be found." Gaëlle started down the rise to the labyrinth. "Would you like to walk it with me today?"

"No, that's okay. I'll just wait."

Gaëlle glanced back over her shoulder. "Are you sure? There's great comfort to be found in walking the circuits."

Lee wasn't sure, but she shook her head. "You go ahead. I'll wait for you."

Gaëlle stopped at the entrance to the labyrinth and closed her eyes. After a few moments, she opened her eyes and began to walk at a measured pace, completing all the circuits until she arrived at the centre. There she stood, facing west into the wind, her eyes closed and her head tilted back.

Lee squatted on her haunches. She dangled the travel mug between her knees and scrutinized Gaëlle intently. *Meditation? Prayer?*

Gaëlle was a study in contrasts. On one hand she seemed like a grounded, sensible woman who balanced a difficult life with grace and courage; on the other hand...

Way too friggin' much hooey.

Lee was having trouble squaring the contrasts.

Finally, Gaëlle opened her eyes and started back to the entrance, which was also the exit.

Lee walked down the rise to meet her.

As Gaëlle completed the last circuit, her gaze focused on Lee.

Lee was struck not only by the serenity and peace

in Gaëlle's eyes, but also by the indefinable sense of power within the woman. Then Gaëlle emerged from the labyrinth, and was simply Gaëlle again.

They were quiet on their walk back to the house. Gaëlle seemed in no need of conversation, and Lee had far more on her mind than when they'd set out.

They'd almost reached the house when Wally intercepted them.

Wally addressed Gaëlle without preliminaries. "Boy man. Toy man. Song gone. Sad, sad. Too bad."

"Tonight?"

"Too right."

"Thanks for the heads-up, Wally. Did you get anything to eat this morning? Would you like to join us for lunch?"

"Lunch, brunch. No munch."

"Okay, but if you get hungry, you know where to come."

Wally's eyes cleared, and Lee was startled at the loving intelligence she saw there as he said, "Always." Then, as if realizing he'd exposed himself, Wally hurried away. He looked back once, perhaps to see if they were following.

Gaëlle raised a hand and nodded, and Wally flapped his fingers at her before disappearing around the side of the garage.

"Where on earth does that guy live? He seems to appear and disappear out of nowhere."

"Wally likes to stay outdoors when it's warm enough. Of course, his definition of 'warm enough' would shock most people. When it gets really cold, he beds down in his room for the night."

"So he has a room, somewhere to live? Where? In Donegal?"

Gaëlle pointed at the garage. "Right there. Ten years ago, after his sister died and he had no one left to care for him, I made him a place above the garage. I tried for a long time to convince him to stay in the house. I was going to convert part of the basement to a suite like Dale's, but Wally refused. My bedroom window faces his, so I can see when his light is on during the winter. It reassures me that he's safely indoors."

"Do you ever worry that he could die on an outdoor ramble where no one would know or find his body?"

"I might not find his body, but I'd know if he died. And whether his body was found or returned to the dust where he lay would be irrelevant to Wally. He doesn't care about cultural rituals. Never has."

"Huh. What a curious man. And what did he tell you? I couldn't follow that at all."

"He said that Brian would be by tonight, looking for Britten."

"He did? I would not have guessed that."

"It's easy once you master the key word. 'Song' is what he's always called Britten. So he was talking about an immature male who will be sad to find Britten gone. Simple deduction: Brian Nolan."

"Simple? You have an interesting definition of simple."

Gaëlle laughed as they mounted the stairs to the porch. "It helps if you know his code and the people around here."

"Is he always right in his predictions?"

"I've occasionally interpreted his words wrong, but, in hindsight, Wally was never in error."

Lee held the door open for Gaëlle. "He was certainly right about Britten coming home when you had no other way of knowing that."

Gaëlle paused before stepping through the doorway. "Wally wasn't talking about Britten, Lee; his prediction was about you. He told me *you* were coming."

CHAPTER 9

"He was talking about me? What...how—?"

The phone rang. Lee's questions went unanswered as Gaëlle grabbed the receiver. After she glanced at the caller ID, Gaëlle said, "I'm sorry. I have to take this, Lee."

Frustrated, Lee listened as Gaëlle answered the caller. She hoped it would be a quick conversation so she could solve the mystery of Gaëlle's cryptic comment.

"Hi, Dale. Yes, I was out for a walk. To Goose Lake today. No, go ahead. What's up? Janjay didn't like the bid? Why? Well, the Chinese bid was the lowest, but we can look at other sources if she feels that strongly about it." Gaëlle put her hand over the mouthpiece. "Go ahead and get something to eat, Lee. I think this will take a while." She went down to the basement, and the sound of her voice was cut off when the office door closed behind her.

Lee stared after Gaëlle. *But I don't want to eat. I want to talk.*

Though she longed to pursue Gaëlle and get some answers, Lee became aware that her cheek was throbbing. The cold wind had anesthetized it, but as she warmed up, she could feel Britten's handiwork again.

After taking some Aspirin she found in Dale's medicine cabinet, Lee lay down on her bed and stared at the ceiling. The pain slowly subsided as she considered Gaëlle's stunning disclosure.

How could Wally know I was coming? And when did he tell Gaëlle? I *didn't even know I was coming until a few hours before we left.*

Her thoughts churned without resolution. Finally, Lee grabbed the cellphone from the bedside table. She had to talk to someone.

"Hi, Marika, it's me."

"Lee! It's great to hear your voice. How's the protection detail going?"

"Well, let's see. My client fired me last night, then she left with her purportedly abusive husband, who had never actually abused her. Apparently, she fights and flees on a regular basis, and he caters to her every whim. Oh, and did I mention that she slashed my face with a bar glass and told a Mountie I'd kidnapped her when we were pulled over for a possible DUI?"

"Oh, my God! I don't know where to start. Are you all right? How bad is your face?"

"I'm going to have an interesting new facial feature, but it's only three stitches, so I'm not going to be mistaken for Scarface."

"And you were stopped for a DUI? Do you need a lawyer?"

Lee heard the worry in Marika's voice. "I hadn't been drinking. I passed the Breathalyzer with flying colours. I don't think the officer would've made me blow except that my idiot client cut me, dowsed me with Canadian Club, and told him I kidnapped her."

"She sounds like quite the handful."

"Hah. That's putting it mildly."

"Since you no longer have a client to protect, are you on your way home now?"

"Not exactly. Listen, do you have a few moments to talk? I'm not interrupting anything, am I?"

"Not at all. I'm doing some dreary paperwork, and Rhi took Marnie to 'Mommy and Me' swim classes about twenty minutes ago. They won't be back for at least an hour."

Lee grinned as she pictured her energetic goddaughter in a full-sized pool. "So do they have to refill the pool after Marnie's done?"

Marika laughed. "You'd think so, wouldn't you? Rhi says Marnie is actually so fascinated with the other kids in the class that she doesn't splash half as much as she does in the bathtub. Anyway, enough about our daughter. What's going on, and why aren't you halfway back to Calgary already?"

"It's a long story. There's a woman involved."

"*Really*?"

"No, not that way. It turns out that, as flaky as Britten is, her mom is...well, she's kind of hard to describe. I guess many people would say she's flaky, too, but she's not. It's just so weird."

"Okay, you've lost me. Let's back up a moment. What's the mother's name?"

"Gaëlle."

"All right. So how is she flaky? I take it not in the same homicidal vein as her daughter."

"No, not at all. And to be fair, Britten isn't homicidal. She's just a selfish brat who's been indulged far too much for her own good. Or as her mother calls her, she's a young soul."

"Interesting take. So the mother—Gaëlle—isn't hoodwinked by her daughter?"

"God, no. Gaëlle is the most clear-sighted person I've ever met."

"And yet you said some people would say Gaëlle's flaky too. Why?"

Lee sighed deeply. How to convey the essence of that fascinating, aggravating, contradictory woman? "I think I'd better start from the beginning. My first encounter with Gaëlle was actually an encounter with her dear friend, who is this eccentric called Wrong-Way Wally. He's apparently the Oracle of Donegal, but he speaks a language that only Gaëlle seems to understand..."

Lee spent the next half hour telling Marika everything that had happened since the night she'd arrived in Donegal, concluding with Gaëlle's revelation that Wally had predicted her arrival.

"It's baffling, Marika. Why would Wally tell Gaëlle about me coming here?"

"I would think the bigger question would be: how does Wally know these things?"

"Oh, trust me. After you've been here a while, accepting Wally's abilities isn't the strange part. The 'how' of it doesn't bother me, the 'why' of it does."

"Lee, you have no idea how odd this sounds."

"Hell, yes, I do. It's freakin' odd to me, too."

"No, you don't understand. I've known you what, about twenty years?"

"Give or take. Why?"

"Because in twenty years, I've never once known you to espouse anything paranormal. In fact, remember when Dana and Rhi dragged us to that psychic fair?"

Lee groaned. "I remember. Dana had to bribe me to go near the place."

"And you scoffed the whole time we were there, even when that psychic foretold that Rhi and I would have a baby girl. We weren't even thinking of a family at the time."

"Yeah, but you two were so obviously in love, *I* could've foretold babies in your future."

"You're making my point for me. You still mock the whole concept, yet here you are telling me about a man who can forecast the future and a woman who communicates with her dead husband and son. And you're telling me this as matter-of-factly as you'd say 'today is Saturday'. I'm not saying it's a bad thing; I'm just saying, what happened to change the old Lee?"

"I don't know. I really don't know. My head is whirling, and I haven't had anything stronger than Aspirin since I left Calgary. Hell, I even quit smoking again."

"That's wonderful. I'm so pleased. You had such a hard time quitting the last time that I wasn't sure you would even try it again."

"I'm on the patch. And Gaëlle helps. She gives these amazing head massages that make me forget everything else, including withdrawal pains."

"She does, does she? Interesting."

"Oh, don't go there."

"Why not?" Marika's voice softened from its teasing tone. "Sweetie, it's okay to develop feelings for someone else. Dana would not want you to become a nun for the rest of your life."

"It's much too soon. Besides, Gaëlle's as straight as they come."

"If you say so. But keep an open mind, because it sure sounds like she does."

"I...No, it's impossible."

"Is it? From what you've told me, Gaëlle and Wally are as close as two peas in a pod. If he told her you were coming, it was for a reason."

"Yeah, and can't you just imagine getting involved with someone who already has a crazy, smelly, omniscient significant other. There's a fucked-up triangle waiting to happen. Anyway, I don't think that's the reason, and that's what's driving me crazy. If Wally is right, and clearly, he's been right in the past, it would imply I'm here for a purpose. What purpose? And who decides that purpose? Damn it, Marika, you know me. I'm not one for all this hooey. I want two plus two to equal four, not be some metaphysical equation that only a few 'enlightened' people can decipher."

"You're right, old friend. You're a practical woman. Then let's look at this in practical terms. So what if Wally told Gaëlle you were coming? Didn't you tell me he predicted that Brian guy would be by tonight? I doubt that's going to be an earth-shaking event, even if he does actually show up. Maybe Wally was just passing along information so Gaëlle could have both rooms made up and ready for guests. Maybe it didn't mean anything more than an everyday weather forecast. Not all of his predictions are necessarily earth-shattering."

"I guess."

"You sound disappointed. You asked for logic."

“Not disappointed, exactly. I mean, you make a solid argument.”

“So all my years as a lawyer haven’t gone to waste, after all.”

Lee laughed at Marika’s dry tone. “No, you’ve always been able to argue black is white.”

“But I can tell you don’t want that from me. What do you want, Lee?”

“I don’t know. I wish I did.”

“Okay, let me throw this out. You said Gaëlle invited you to stay for a few days. So when Tuesday or Wednesday comes around, are you going to be happy to pack up your suitcase and hit the road? Or does part of you want to stay right where you are?”

“I can’t stay here. My job is done. I have no reason to stay here.”

“That wasn’t the question. How are you going to feel when you say goodbye to Gaëlle?”

Lee was silent.

“And that’s my point. Whether you buy into the notion that something otherworldly pulled you to Donegal, and Gaëlle, for a reason, you can’t deny that what you’ve found there intrigues you. Part of you doesn’t want to leave until your questions are answered.”

“You’re as down-to-earth as I am, Marika. Do you believe in all this hooey?”

“I believe in...magic.”

“What? No way!”

“I do. I believe there are things in life that simply can’t be explained, so I call them magic. You yourself said that Rhi and I were meant for each other. Yet were there ever two broken people more unlikely to meet and fall in love? You know how deeply damaged we were. Yet here we are, going into our second decade together and with a daughter we adore. I've never been happier. If that isn't magic, what is?"

"But that's different. Falling in love happens to people every day."

"That doesn't make it any less magic."

"Huh. Well, Gaëlle would say that the two of you planned on a soul level to meet."

"I could believe that. I've never given that aspect much thought, but on some level it appeals to me."

"Marika the Mystical."

Marika laughed loudly. "Just don't mention that to my partners. I'd be thrown out of the firm in a heartbeat."

"What do I do?"

"It's going to sound like a cliché, but do what your heart tells you to." Marika's voice was unexpectedly serious. "You have no idea how overjoyed I am that you're even wrestling with this. Two weeks ago I'd have thought it more likely I'd be attending your funeral than discussing matters of mysticism and metaphysics. Whatever you choose to do, know that all of us who love you are thrilled beyond words that you've re-engaged with life."

"Thanks to you guys."

"No, Lee. We may have played a part by carrying out our promise to Dana, but you're the one who made the decision to live again. You're the one who demonstrated the strength we all knew you had. You stepped out of the mire."

"I don't feel strong. I don't feel strong at all."

"That's okay. Baby steps. Relax and enjoy your stay. Enjoy Gaëlle's company. When you're ready to come home, we'll be delighted to see you whole again. That's what we've all wanted."

"You know, you're right. I'm just going to relax and see what happens."

"Excellent. And, Lee, something just occurred to me."

"What?"

"You told me that Gaëlle was the most clear-sighted person you'd ever met, right?"

"Yeah, so?"

"Did you know that clairvoyant means 'clear seeing'?"

"It does?"

"Uh-huh. Apropos of nothing, of course. Anyway, give me a call when you're on your way back to Calgary, okay? We'll have dinner when you get home."

"Will do. And thanks, Marika. I appreciate you listening."

"Anytime, Lee. Anytime."

It was late afternoon when the doorbell rang. Lee was in the living room. She hadn't seen Gaëlle since they'd returned from their walk that morning.

When Lee opened the door and saw Brian Nolan standing there with a sheepish grin on his face and flowers in his hand, she wasn't at all surprised.

"Uh, hi. Is Heather Ann—I mean Britten—here?"

Before Lee could answer, footsteps sounded behind her. Gaëlle stopped beside Lee and regarded

Brian with compassion. “Hi, Brian. No, I’m sorry, Britten isn’t here. She left with her husband last night. They were en route to their home in Europe.”

Brian’s face fell, and Lee couldn’t help feeling sorry for him.

“Her husband? But I thought...I mean, I didn’t know she was married.”

“I’m very sorry, Brian. My daughter should’ve told you.”

“It’s okay, Mrs. Germaine. It’s not your fault. Pretty stupid of me to think she’d come back for good, anyway. I even thought maybe she’d come back because... Dumb. Dumb, dumb, dumb. I guess I’d better go. Um, would you like these? I got no use for them.” Brian pushed the flowers at Gaëlle.

“Thank you, Brian. Are you sure you wouldn’t prefer to give them to someone else, perhaps your mother?”

“Nah. Mom would think I smashed her truck or something if I gave her flowers out of the blue. Better you take them.”

“Then thank you. They’re lovely.”

Brian turned away. His shoulders were slumped as he went down the stairs to his pickup.

Gaëlle watched him drive off, then closed the door. She looked at Lee apologetically over the multi-coloured carnations. “I’m sorry I was so busy today. I hope you weren’t bored.”

“Not at all. Looks like Wally was right, eh?”

“He always is. I’d best put these in water.”

Lee followed Gaëlle to the kitchen and wondered if she should bring up Wally’s other prediction. Instead, she decided to follow Marika’s advice.

"You must be hungry, Gaëlle. Would you allow me to take you out to dinner? As a thank-you for your wonderful hospitality. Is there any place in Donegal that is fancier than the Four Corners Café?"

"There is, but honestly the food at Four Corners is probably the best around."

"Then Four Corners it is."

An hour later, the women were seated in a booth at the café. Eileen was their waitress, and she filled their coffee cups the moment they sat down. "Hi there, hon. Heather Ann not with you tonight? Don't tell me she's hanging out with that no-brain, Brian. I heard he was prowling after Heather Ann last night at the Red Arrow, but that boy's no good. Never has been."

"Actually, Britten left last night. Her husband came to pick her up."

"Her husband? Heather Ann is married? Well, tie me in a knot and toss me off the boat! When the hell did she get married? And why didn't she tell any of us?"

"She got married about a year ago. Apparently, it was a spur-of-the-moment thing. They eloped while at an Italian villa on the Mediterranean. Britten said it was all very romantic."

"Yeah? Sounds like a Vegas quickie to me. Probably last about as long, too. Anyway, you want your usual?"

"That sounds good."

Eileen turned to Lee. "What about you, hon? And damn, what happened to your face? Did Heather Ann's husband throw a haymaker at you or something?"

"Just an accident. Could I have a moment with the menu first?"

"Okay. I'll be back in a few." Eileen moved on to another table.

Gaëlle lowered her voice. "She's wrong about Brian."

"How's that?"

"He's not unintelligent, nor is he 'no good'; he's just one those people who crested in high school. He was very good-looking and a jock. Girls swarmed around and boys wanted to hang out with him. Nothing that came after graduation was ever going to compare. Brian did some foolish things trying to recover his glory days, but he's more to be pitied than condemned. He's one who should've left the town that knew him too well, to start over in anonymity. I think if he had, he'd have become a very different man."

"From what I overheard last night, he and Britten were a couple before Britten left."

"They were. Dating Bobby had given Britten status because he was older, out of school, and working. When he broke up with Britten and started dating Jill, Britten decided she was going after the hottest guy in school. She got him, but more to flaunt her success in Jill's face than because she actually wanted Brian. Of course it didn't work out."

"Do you think Brian loved her?"

"To the best of his ability, yes. Sadly, Brian lacks self-love, which is a huge impediment to loving someone else."

"Really? I'd have said Brian was quite infatuated with himself. Certainly the way he strutted across the bar last night, he appeared to think he was God's gift to women."

"Infatuation isn't love, Lee. I think it will take a few more lifetimes before Brian learns to love himself."

Eileen's return forestalled Lee's response. "So, what'll you have, hon?"

Lee hadn't looked at the menu yet. "Um, I'll have what Gaëlle's having."

"Got it." Eileen jotted a note on her pad and trotted off.

Lee leaned across the table. "What did I just order?"

"The Saturday night special—liver and onions." Gaëlle laughed at Lee's horrified expression. "No, I'm just joking. Actually, you're having a lovely pasta dish with chicken and vegetables, and a side of garlic toast. You'll like it, I promise."

"Whew, you scared me there. Wil loves liver and onions, and it used to gross me out when he'd bring it for lunch. He'd reheat it in the microwave, and the whole office would stink for hours. Of course, that was back in the days when it was just Wil, me, and Ann in a one-room office."

"So that's Wil, as in Willem DeGroot of DeGroot and Glenn Security?"

"Yeah. You've heard of our company?"

"I confess that after Britten told me the firm she'd hired you from, I googled you. Your company has built an impressive record over the years."

"We've worked hard. It was Willem's initiative that had us expanding internationally. I'd have been happy for the two of us to keep gum-shoeing along in Calgary, but he had bigger dreams. Fortunately, he took me along for the ride."

"I suspect you underplay your role. But how did the two of you get started?"

"By accident, actually. I was a military policewoman for years. I'd just gotten out of the service and wasn't really sure what I was going to do. Willem's cousin had foolishly angered some rather nasty men. Wil asked one of his friends with policing experience what to do. That friend happened to be my ex-commanding officer. Since it wasn't a situation for official involvement, Marc put Willem in touch with me. I was able to negotiate an arrangement for Wil's cousin to make amends to the guys he'd pissed off."

"Amends?"

Lee laughed at Gaëlle's expression. "I don't mean he had to give up his first born or anything, but he did have to fork over some serious cash."

"Well, that's reassuring...I think, though I can't help wondering about your negotiating style."

"Aw, that was nothing. Remind me sometime to tell you about the time my best friend inadvertently got involved with a socialite slash snakehead boss. I ended up helping my friend and her later-to-be-wife go on the run from a Chinese assassin while I worked with my old military commander to bring down the head bitch's whole organization. It's a pretty good story."

Gaëlle's eyes widened. "You have lived a colourful life."

"Occasionally, yes. Anyway, when circumstance threw Willem and me together, he was a rising star in the corporate world. The trouble was that he found the corporate world dull as dishwater. So about a week after I got his cousin out of the jam, Wil asked me to meet him. I thought he was just going to express his gratitude by buying me a drink, but he actually had a business proposal. He'd been impressed with how I resolved his cousin's mess and wanted to go into business with me. He was willing to provide the start-up capital for what would become DeGroot and Glenn. He needed my policing expertise; I needed a job. The rest is history."

"It sounds so exciting."

"It can be, but most of the time it's pretty routine. I once overheard an air traffic controller describe his job as long stretches of tedium broken by moments of sheer terror. I always thought that was an apt description of my job, too."

"That would certainly describe guarding my daughter. Are you looking forward to the next assignment?"

"Actually, it was pretty unusual for me to take this one. We have extremely capable staff that usually handles personal protection details."

"That's very interesting. So why *did* you take this one?"

Lee shot Gaëlle a wry look. "There was nothing mystical about it. Wil suggested that after a year's inattention to our business, I get my feet wet slowly."

"So when you return, having gotten your feet wet, you won't take field work again? What will you be doing?"

Handling contracts, schmoozing with potential

clients, setting up branch offices, overseeing employees, and balancing budgets... God, Wil was right. That stuff bores me to death.

"Lee?"

"Oh, sorry. Just thinking of something Wil said when he was coaxing me into coming here."

Eileen returned and set their dinners in front of them. "Holler if you want anything else."

Lee inhaled the delicious scent.

"Better than liver and onions?"

"So much better." Lee dug into her food with relish.

Gaëlle followed suit at a slower pace. "You never did answer my question, Lee."

"Question?"

"Yes. Are you looking forward to returning to work?"

Lee shook her head. "Honestly? Not all that much. Our company has evolved to the point where everyone else gets to do the fun stuff."

"You don't like being the boss?"

"Not when it has me stuck behind a desk from eight to five. Willem eats up the admin side, but I always liked the nuts and bolts—solving people's problems, tripping up the bad guys, unravelling mysteries."

"Perhaps you should look at another field."

"That's what Wil said. He doesn't think I'm suited to the corporate grind. He says I need to find what gives me joy. I think he's just worried that I'll slip back into depression."

Gaëlle smiled. "He obviously cares very much for you."

"We care for each other. After twenty-five years together, he's like the brother I never had. If he thinks I should explore options, then I have to respect his insight. Problem is, I have no idea what options to explore. I figure I'll just keep doing what I'm doing until Eli's wedding and make some sort of decision after that."

"When is his wedding?"

"In July. I can't remember the exact date, but around the middle."

"So, a little over three months from now."

"Sounds about right."

"Lee, I have an idea. Would you hear me out before you say anything?"

"Sure. What's on your mind?"

Gaëlle set her cutlery aside and regarded Lee seriously. "From what you've said, it's your choice whether to continue on your current path or veer off, is that correct? Your company would not suffer from your absence?"

"No. Wil said it's running like a well-oiled machine. Not exactly stroking my ego, but he's right, and I get my partnership cut whether I'm there or not. This past year they learned to work very well without me. That's why he urged me to take some time and think about what I want to do with the rest of my life. As he said, I could easily afford to retire, but I don't really want to do that, either."

"Let me offer you an option. Stay with me until it's time to go home for the wedding. Help me finish my labyrinth. Look at it as an opportunity to do some contemplation on your direction, away from the distractions of the city and your business."

Lee realized that at some level she wasn't surprised at Gaëlle's offer, nor was it an unwelcome proposal. "Won't that be a huge imposition? What about when Dale gets home?"

Gaëlle reached across the table, patted Lee's hand, and chuckled. "Did you miss the part where I was going to put you to work hauling stone? I figure that's a fair trade for room and board in the luxurious Germaine resort. As for Dale, we'll move you to the other room so he can have his back. Problem solved."

"Yes."

Gaëlle smiled broadly. "As easy as that?"

"Well, we may have to negotiate my working conditions. Head massages will have to be part of the contract. But, yes, as easy as that."

CHAPTER 10

LEE STRAIGHTENED WITH A GROAN.

Gaëlle called from the other side of the rubble pile, "Are you okay, old woman?"

"Who you calling old, Ms. Soon-to-be-a-Senior-Citizen?" Lee twisted slowly and worked the kinks out of her lower back. "You know, I think we need to re-examine the terms of my contract."

"We do, eh? I don't know. It's a pretty iron-clad document."

"It's a napkin."

"But an iron-clad napkin."

Lee laughed and stretched. "Well, Eileen did witness it. I'll give you that."

"Lee, I found it!"

Lee looked across the remains of the old barn to see Gaëlle wrestling something out from under a broken tress. She quickly clambered across the debris. "What have you found?"

"The stone for the threshold. I knew there would be one in here somewhere."

In the last six weeks, Lee and Gaëlle had transported and laid enough of the old barn's fieldstone to pave five of the labyrinth's seven circuits. But Gaëlle had her heart set on finding what she deemed the perfect threshold, and nothing they'd found to date had measured up.

Lee eyed the stone dubiously. Aside from being much larger than most of the ones they'd transported, it didn't look particularly outstanding to her. As she had discovered, however, Gaëlle had a precise vision of her labyrinth, so if her friend said this was perfect, so be it. "Okay. Then let's see if we can get it on the cart."

Lee retrieved the odd-looking cart from where they'd been loading it. The first day they'd begun sorting, hauling, and laying stone, they'd used Gaëlle's garden cart, but they'd soon realized the sides were too high. Even working together, lifting fieldstones up over the sides had strained their muscles unnecessarily.

When they quit at the end of the first day and returned to the house, they found that Wally had solved their problem. He'd constructed a flat cart with a folding ramp. The cart ran on what appeared to be tricycle wheels. The cart bed was only six inches off the ground, so they didn't have to lift very far, and it trundled over the rough terrain without difficulty. The ramp allowed them to roll larger stones onto the cart rather than lifting them.

Lee had been amused when she recognized various pieces of their new cart as things she'd seen on Wally's junk wagon. But for a Rube Goldberg contraption, it served their purposes perfectly. They moved twice as many stones the next day and on subsequent days.

Lee rolled the cart into position and lowered the ramp, and they pushed, pulled, and rotated the stone into place for transport. Both were gasping for breath by the time they finished. Lee sank down on a pile of rubble and worked to catch her wind.

Gaëlle was bent at the waist, doing the same. "Damn, I'm glad I quit smoking."

"Me too."

They grinned at each other, and Lee stood up. "I think we've got enough of a load for another trip."

"Agreed."

They grasped the long handle together and started pulling. By now they knew every metre of their route, where to ease to the left or right to avoid gopher holes, and when to put their backs into it to get up a rise. Lee enjoyed how harmoniously they worked together without any direction needed.

"So, I was thinking."

Lee glanced at Gaëlle. "Yeah? About what?"

"I told you I need to go to Regina on Wednesday to meet Dale's flight, right?"

"Do you think he's really going to make it this time? He's postponed twice just since I've been here."

"I know. His heart is there, not here, but Dechontee told him last week that she needs to study for her exams and it was a good time for him to return to Canada."

Lee chuckled. "Basically she kicked him out of Guinea."

"Pretty much. The point being, he *will* be on the Wednesday flight. Why don't you come with me? We'll go down a day early and have a bit of a break. The hotel I always stay at has a wonderful spa. We'll treat ourselves royally—have a nice dinner, maybe take in a play or concert. We can even do some shopping if you like. You said you needed new work gloves and safety boots."

"I do, but I could just pop into the Donegal Co-op for those. Still, I like the idea of a respite from our labours. Someone's been working me like she's an overseer on the pyramids."

"I wasn't an overseer. I was a stonecutter."

Lee didn't even flinch. Over the past month and a half, she'd grown accustomed to the odd things that came out of Gaëlle's mouth. They'd long ceased to irritate or confuse her. Lee occasionally challenged Gaëlle, but mostly she simply accepted the statements for what they were—Gaëlle's unconventional beliefs.

"Dragging you back on topic, a trip to Regina sounds good."

Gaëlle clapped her hands in delight."Wonderful. I'm so looking forward to this."

"And, I imagine, to seeing Dale again."

"Absolutely. I always miss that boy of mine, even if we do talk every second day."

"I look forward to meeting him."

"You two will get along well. You're kindred spirits."

"You mean he's into hauling hundreds of kilos of rocks too?"

"Silly. No, I mean he's also a strong, solid, dependable soul. He's quieter than you, but you've both got the same staunch values, particularly love and loyalty toward friend and family."

"Sounds like he's a good man."

"And you're a good woman."

They'd arrived at the labyrinth, so Lee was relieved not to have to respond. Gaëlle was not one to hide her affection, and Lee wasn't always sure how to react.

Gaëlle was never flirtatious; she was simply straightforward. She was very fond of Lee and apparently saw no need to disguise that. Lee was accustomed to the love of her friends and family and returned it in great measure, but Gaëlle... Gaëlle didn't fit neatly into any slots. She wasn't lover or family, but she had rapidly become more than friend.

Lee banished the thoughts that had become her standard bedtime reverie and set to work helping grapple the threshold stone into place.

"A little to the left. That's it. Right there. Ease it down. There—good." Gaëlle stood back and admired their handiwork. "Is that not a superb fit?"

"I have to admit, you have a great eye. Well done."

Gaëlle extended her hand with a grin. "Congratulations."

"For what?"

"For a one-time overseer, you've certainly mastered working in the trenches."

Lee played along. "I was an overseer? Did I have a chariot?"

"No, but you had a whip, and you sure knew how to use it."

"Ouch. Did I use it on you?"

"Once or twice, but I was an excellent stonecutter, and you mostly left me alone." Gaëlle picked up another stone off the cart and carried it to the end of the circuit they were working on.

Lee watched Gaëlle carefully place her stone and shook her head. To listen to Gaëlle speak, millennia past were as real to her as last night's excursion to the Four Corners Café. The woman was a walking cryptogram. Lee doubted she'd ever break the code. She wasn't entirely sure she even wanted to try.

"Hey, did someone call a coffee break that I don't know about?"

The teasing words echoed across the labyrinth, and Lee picked up a stone. "Yeah, yeah. I'm coming." *I'm sure I liked it better when I was overseer!*

Lee and Gaëlle emerged from the spa into the late-afternoon sun.

Lee turned her face up and blinked at the bright sky. "Are you as blissed out as I am?"

"I'm way past bliss and well on the way to Nirvana. Wasn't that amazing?"

"It's hard to believe that this time yesterday we were hauling fieldstones."

"I don't think believing was hard for the manicurist. Did you see the disapproving way she looked at our hands?"

Lee laughed as she looked at her nails. She couldn't remember them ever being so shiny before. "No kidding. But at least you didn't freak out the esthetician with facial scars. I'm sure she thought I'd been in a gang fight."

Gaëlle linked her arm through Lee's as they walked down the street. "Oh well. So we're not their usual sort of clients. At least the masseuse was friendly."

"Mine wasn't unfriendly, but I could feel her looking askance at some of my old war wounds."

"Emblems of honour."

"Some are. Some are just reminders of youthful foolishness."

Gaëlle squeezed Lee's arm. "It's called living. None of us make it out completely unscathed."

"Not even you?"

"Of course not, though my marks are mostly the invisible kind."

Suddenly, Gaëlle was jerked violently and fell to the ground.

Lee grabbed for her. "Gaëlle!"

"I'm okay, Lee."

A man ran down the street with Gaëlle's purse.

"Hey! Stop him!" Lee took after the thief but came to a jolting halt when she heard Gaëlle call out, "Lee, stop. Come back."

It went against every one of Lee's ingrained instincts to let the thief escape, but she abandoned her pursuit and quickly ran back to Gaëlle's side. "Are you sure you're okay?"

"I'm fine. Really."

Lee helped Gaëlle to her feet. "Sonofabitch! I can't believe that happened in broad daylight. Where the hell are the police when you need them? And why didn't anyone stop him?" Lee glared at the people who had jumped out of the way of the fleeing thief rather than tripping him.

"Lee, it's okay."

"It's not okay! That fucking bastard got away with your purse. We need to call the police and also get your credit cards cancelled immediately. I hope you weren't carrying much cash. Jesus H. Christ!"

"Calm down."

"Calm down? Are you kidding me? You were just robbed. I was a foot away, and I didn't stop it. Some fucking protection detail I am."

"Look at me."

Lee swung her angry gaze from the hapless bystanders to Gaëlle.

"I know it's your nature, but it's not your job to protect me."

"Then whose job is it? Because they're not very damned good at it."

"Oh, I don't know."

"That prick got away with your purse!"

"All he got away with was a fifteen dollar purse, some tissues, a brush, and assorted sundries. Nothing valuable. Nothing irreplaceable."

Lee frowned.

Gaëlle reached into her front pants pocket and came out with a well-worn wallet. "See? Cash and cards still safe. Nothing to worry about."

"What the hell? Do you always carry your wallet separately?"

"No. When I was dressing after the massage, I got a nudge, so I transferred my wallet from my purse to my pocket."

"You got a what?"

"A nudge. Look, can we move along? I don't like being stared at." Gaëlle took Lee's arm and steered her in the direction they'd been walking.

By the time they reached the restaurant, Lee was still seething. For the first time in weeks, she ordered a drink, but when it was delivered, she merely toyed with it.

"Tell me what you're thinking, Lee."

"I'm mad."

"I know that. Why?"

"Because it isn't right. Maybe all he took was junk, but he hit you and he robbed you, and he got away with it."

"And you want to hit him."

"Damn right! I want to knock his fucking teeth down his throat."

"You've always hated injustice—"

"Don't. Don't go there. Not now."

Gaëlle sipped her wine quietly as Lee calmed.

Finally, Lee looked up to find Gaëlle regarding her serenely. "How can you do that?"

"Do what?"

Lee glared at Gaëlle. "How can you be so bloody peaceful about this?"

"I suffered no injury to person or purse. Why get angry?"

"Because...because...because he's a low-life bastard, and he won."

Gaëlle leaned forward and took Lee's hand. "What did he win? By wronging me, by wronging *us*, he added to his own bad karma; he didn't affect mine. Don't let him affect yours."

"I just can't look at it that way. I want him to pay for his crime in this life. I don't give a rat's ass about the next life. You're giving him a pass. What happens when he does this again, and he knocks down some old lady and breaks her hip? What if that old lady never has quality of life again because of what that punk did to her? What if I could've saved that old lady by catching the thief today?"

"Remember what I said about 'what ifs'?"

Lee scowled. "They can drive you crazy."

"Exactly. Don't do that to yourself."

The waiter came to take their order. Lee randomly picked something off the menu. When the waiter departed, she resumed their debate. "Don't you believe in evil?"

Gaëlle sighed. "I don't think that purse snatcher was evil. I think he was a young soul who has many lessons to learn, and he will have many lifetimes in which to learn them."

"That's not answering my question. Don't you believe in evil?"

"That's something I've wrestled with for years. I've gone from believing in absolute evil to absolutely rejecting it, even as I accepted that many souls do evil things. In recent years I've settled somewhere in the middle. I've had to reconcile my understanding that all souls emanate from the Source with the abundant evidence that many of those souls have wreaked horrendous evil on the world during their lifetimes. How can it possibly be that Hitler, Stalin, Pol Pot, Idi Amin, Gaddafi, Saddam Hussein, Robert Mugabe—the list, sadly, is endless—how can these men be sparks of the Divine just as the Master Jesus was, and yet their atrocities drip blood on the pages of history?"

"You mention Jesus. So you're a Christian? Do you believe in heaven and hell?"

"No and yes."

Lee shook her head in confusion.

Gaëlle smiled gently. "I'm not a Christian, because, by definition, Christianity excludes non-

Christians. I'm not an adherent of any formal religion, because they're all exclusionary. God...or the Divine...or the Source...or whatever term you're comfortable using, is the antithesis of exclusionary. His love is limitless and available to all. No religious door pass is needed."

"And heaven and hell?"

"They're just words to express concepts. All souls will go to an afterlife that we create for ourselves. Call it what you want—heaven, Nirvana, Summerland. The name doesn't matter."

"And hell? Do you think that thief today will go to hell?"

Gaëlle's face saddened. "He's in the process of determining where he'll go. Like pulls to like, so if he doesn't amend his ways, he'll find himself in the company of fellow ne'er-do-wells in a rather unpleasant place. But he doesn't have to stay there for eternity. There is always hope. There is always the potential for spiritual evolution. It's much better to achieve our personal evolution on this side, but we continue to work on it once we cross over. No soul is ever abandoned. Help is always available for the asking."

Lee scrubbed her arm across her eyes. "You're making my head hurt."

"I'm answering your questions based on what I've learned and what I've experienced, Lee. You're perfectly free to accept or reject my observations based on your own knowledge and experience."

"Fair enough. Well, right now my experience says I hope that bastard rots in hell."

Gaëlle's face tightened, but she said nothing.

Lee frowned. "What?"

"Nothing. Ah, here's dinner. Doesn't this look good?"

Lee knew an evasion when she heard one, but Gaëlle was right, dinner did look and smell great, so she let it go.

Later that night in the hotel room they'd decided to share, Lee lay awake in her bed, staring at the ceiling as Gaëlle finished up in the washroom.

"Okay to turn the light off?"

Lee grunted in response.

Gaëlle flipped the switch and made her way to her bed.

Lee listened as the sheets rustled and her roommate settled in. Lee quickly heard deep, steady breathing. She was surprised and somewhat envious of how rapidly Gaëlle fell asleep.

A few minutes later Gaëlle asked, "What's the matter, Lee? What's bothering you?"

Lee rolled onto her side. There was sufficient dim illumination in the room that she could tell Gaëlle was facing her. "I guess I just don't understand how you can simply move past being mugged. How can you not be angry? Or outraged? Or any of the many other emotions a normal human being would feel? Doesn't anything bother you?"

"Of course. Believe it or not, I am a normal human being."

There was a trace of hurt in Gaëlle's voice, and Lee instantly regretted her choice of words. "Hey, I didn't mean it that way. I just meant—well, it goes back to what I said earlier. It feels like you're giving this guy a pass for really bad behaviour."

Gaëlle sighed. "Have you ever read Victor Hugo's *Les Misérables*?"

"Geez, segue much? No, but Dana dragged me to see *Les Miz* on stage. Does that count?"

"Of course. I loved *Les Miz*, too." Gaëlle hummed a few bars of *I Dreamed a Dream*. "I took the kids to see it in Saskatoon in the late eighties. Afterwards, I bought the tape as soon as I could and played it endlessly until Britten begged me to stop. Given her loathing for that play, it rather amuses me that she ended up living in Paris, but I digress."

"That's okay. But what does *Les Miz* have to do with giving that mugger a pass?"

"Since you saw the show, you know that Jean Valjean was treated terribly for his original 'crime' of stealing bread to feed his sister's children."

"Yup, I remember that. Didn't he do twenty years or something?"

"Just about. He emerges from prison a deeply embittered man and is redeemed by another man's kindness."

"Okay, but I'm not seeing a correlation to our mugger. While he may well have spent time in prison, I doubt it was due to such an injustice."

"Patience, my friend, I'm coming to it. Despite Valjean's redemption and subsequent good deeds, he is pursued with a single-minded passion by Inspector Javert."

"I never really did get that. What was Javert's problem, anyway?"

"Well, in the book, Valjean isn't immediately redeemed. He rather mindlessly steals a small amount of money before he completely repents.

So there is a warrant out for his arrest. Plus he abandons the yellow passport all ex-convicts are required to carry. In Javert's eyes, this is more than enough to condemn him and justify years of pursuit."

Lee yawned. "Sorry, but you'd better cut to the condensed version. It's been a long day."

"Okay. So, had Valjean not been originally condemned for what was in reality not that great a crime—after all, he was just trying to keep innocent children from starving, and to my way of thinking that justifies stealing a loaf of bread—then events wouldn't have led to Javert's relentless pursuit and the fallout from his obsession."

"Would've made for a very short musical."

Gaëlle laughed. "True. But here's my point. Javert was a hardliner, what today we might call a far right-winger. He believed absolutely in the law, with no allowance for the fact that Valjean had suffered a grievous injustice. Javert didn't have a problem with a man being sentenced to five years in prison for stealing a loaf of bread or for fourteen more years for trying to escape his onerous fate. Javert was all black and white. No room for any shades of grey in his world view."

"I'm following so far, sort of."

"Today's mugger—what do we know about him?"

Lee snorted. "He's a thief, and he can run like hell."

"That's a pretty accurate summary. And it's also amazingly little to condemn a man on."

It was Lee's turn to be hurt. "So you're calling me Javert?"

"No, not at all. I'm simply making the point that judging someone else's journey isn't wise. Perhaps the mugger has also endured injustices. Perhaps everything in his life pointed him in the direction of being a criminal. Maybe there was never a kind bishop who gave him a chance to be anything else."

Lee kicked off her covers. "That doesn't give him a free pass to be a thief and prey on others."

"I'm not saying that society doesn't have the right to protect itself against such men. I'm saying that on an individual basis, we shouldn't judge."

"You mean without knowing the facts."

"No, Lee. I mean we shouldn't judge at all."

"Oh, c'mon. A few hours ago, you cited all the evil done by men like Hitler and Hussein. Granted the mugger isn't in that category, but you can't deny we have a duty to recognize evil and condemn it as such. To do otherwise is just freaking insane."

"If this life is the be-all and end-all, I'd agree. If, instead, you take the view that this life is merely a school, and that each soul is working its way through a particular course of lessons, with circumstances set up in the best way for them to learn those lessons, then who are we to judge another soul's progress?"

Lee shook her head. "No, no, no. You cannot claim to excuse murderers, rapists, thieves, and dictators just because they're working or, more likely, not working their karmic lessons. That's simply not right. You're inviting even more chaos into the world."

"No, I'm really not. I said that societies have the right to protect themselves against such people.

I'm certainly not advocating the overthrow of laws, police, or courts."

"Then I'm not getting it."

"I'm talking about your soul, my soul—our choices about how we react to the world around us. When we cross over, we'll judge ourselves on how *we* did. We don't get to judge other souls. So I choose—just for myself—to try and practice that now. I judge myself and how far I fall short of my own expectations. I'm not going to judge that mugger's soul."

"What if I had caught him and he was brought up on charges? Would you refuse to testify against him?"

"No, of course not. I live in this world, too. As you so astutely pointed out, who might he hurt next if he's not caught? I would certainly participate in the mechanics of our social justice; I just wouldn't condemn his soul to hell. That's not my right."

Lee recalled what she'd said in the heat of the moment. "Well, I didn't mean it literally. I was pissed off."

"I know. I also know this may well be semantics to you, but I genuinely believe that what we put out comes back to us. However satisfying it might feel in the instant, sending out such violent negativity is not healthy for a soul."

"I don't know. I don't think I can agree with you on this."

"That's okay. I won't judge you." Amusement was clear in Gaëlle's voice.

Lee grabbed a pillow and heaved it at the other bed.

Gaëlle laughed and batted it aside.

Lee rolled on her back and wriggled deeper under the covers. A few minutes later, she began to drift off. Suddenly, a pillow landed on her face, startling her awake. “Hey!”

“Negativity out, negativity in. I’m just saying.”

CHAPTER 11

"DALE! OH, LEE, THERE HE is."

Lee smiled at the excitement in Gaëlle's voice. All the while they'd been standing outside the gate, waiting for Dale, Gaëlle had been growing more anxious by the moment.

It wasn't difficult to pick out which arriving passenger was Gaëlle's son. There was a distinct family resemblance, though Dale had a much deeper tan, despite his mother's hours in the sun.

"Hi, Mom." Dale wrapped Gaëlle in an embrace that lifted her off her feet.

"You look so tired, sweetie."

"You know how it is. First a puddle jumper, then stops in Brussels, London, and Toronto. I feel like I've been on a plane since last week."

"At least you don't look like a scarecrow this time. I'll have to thank Dechontee for taking such good care of my boy."

Dale winked at his mother and planted a kiss on her cheek. "Best to thank Janjay, Mom. She's the one who kept filling my plate and insisting that I eat more. Obsessing over a dinner plate must be a universal maternal instinct."

Gaëlle slapped Dale's stomach, then tugged on

his arm. "Sweetie, I want you to meet a dear friend. This is Lee. Lee, this is my wandering son, Dale."

Lee stuck out her hand and got a firm shake in response. "It's nice to meet you."

"And you. My mom's told me a lot about you."

"Well, she hasn't stopped talking about you the whole time we've been on the labyrinth project."

"Aw, Mom, you're going to bore the poor woman."

"Oh, hush. I talk about all my kids."

Lee added, "Not to mention her grandkids."

"And speaking of grandchildren, any news about you and Dechontee?"

Dale slung his arm around his mother's shoulder and steered her in the direction of the luggage carousels. "Not the kind of news you're eager for, old busy-body of mine. Dechontee is studying like a madwoman and has no time for the likes of me."

Gaëlle sighed as she allowed her son to lead the way.

Lee grinned and walked behind them. In a few short moments, she already liked Dale. He reminded her a little of Eli, mostly in the affectionate way he treated his mother.

They collected the luggage and stowed it in Gaëlle's Jeep Liberty. Lee sat in the back seat so mother and son could catch up on the way home. She was content to listen to their animated chatter as they left the city and headed north.

When there was finally a lull in the conversation, Lee spoke up, "Thank you for the loan of your room the first week I was here. It's a beautiful suite, and your bed's exceptionally comfortable."

"You're more than welcome. Mom did a fabulous

job of renovating, though her room is even more impressive."

"Yeah? I haven't seen it, but the entire house looks amazing for a hundred-year-old building."

"She has the home and garden gift, all right. You know, you could've stayed in my room the whole time. I wouldn't have minded."

"Oh, I'm fine in your sister's room, thanks."

"Speaking of my sister, have you heard from Britten since she left, Mom?"

"Just a brief e-mail to tell me they arrived safely back in Paris."

"I can't believe she didn't even let you know that she was married. She has got to be the most inconsiderate—"

"Dale, stop. She is what she is. Asking her to be something other than that is useless. You know that."

"Yes, Mother, I know. You can't expect a kindergarten level soul to function as a university level soul."

Lee smirked. She apparently wasn't the only one who had been exposed to Gaëlle's metaphysical ruminations.

Gaëlle patted Dale's leg approvingly, and he chuckled.

The drive home passed quickly as Dale caught his mother up on the latest developments with their solar panel project. By the time they pulled into the Germaine driveway, Lee had learned all about solar power, Chinese labour practices, Guinea politics and village customs, and tariff protections.

The only subject that had been studiously

avoided was the purse snatching. Before they left for the airport, Gaëlle asked Lee not to mention it. They'd stopped to pick up a replacement purse, and Lee knew that as far as Gaëlle was concerned, that was the end of the matter. Her failure to catch the mugger left a bad taste in Lee's mouth, but she had decided not to obsess over the incident, no matter how great her misgivings about Gaëlle's reaction.

As Gaëlle pressed the remote to open the garage door, Wally peeked around the corner. When the Jeep stopped, Wally trotted up to Dale's door.

Dale climbed out with a big grin and punched Wally lightly on the shoulder. "How you doing, man?"

"Eaglet home. No roam. No more?"

"Not for a while, Wally. I'm not planning to leave for a few weeks at least."

"So good. Too good." Wally cocked his head for a moment as if listening to an inner voice, and a wide smile broke across his face. "Coal fly. High, high. My, my, my."

Gaëlle was at the back of the Jeep. She cocked her head at Wally's words, then shrugged and pulled Dale's luggage from the vehicle.

Dale hastily bundled Wally out of the garage and whispered in his ear.

Wally nodded his head enthusiastically and patted Dale's shoulder before trotting off.

Lee wondered what the curious exchange had been about but shrugged it off as Gaëlle beckoned to her for some help with their luggage.

The next morning when Lee got down to the kitchen, Dale was already finishing his breakfast.

"Good morning, Lee. Can I scramble you some eggs?"

"Thanks, but don't get up. I can do it." Lee busied herself with breakfast preparations. "I assume your mom's already gone out to the labyrinth?"

"Yes. She left about ten minutes ago. Was she supposed to wait for you?"

"No. I generally give her time to do her meditation before we meet up for the day's work."

"So you don't join her in walking the labyrinth?"

Avoiding Dale's gaze, Lee stirred the eggs vigorously. "No."

"Have you ever walked it on your own?"

"No." Lee poured the eggs into the pan. "No offence, but it's not really my thing, you know?"

"No offence taken, I assure you. As you've no doubt heard my mother say, every soul has the right to its own path. I would never assume anything about yours."

"It's just..." Lee fell silent. She had no idea how fully Dale bought into his mother's beliefs and didn't want to inadvertently insult either of them.

"It's just? I didn't mean to put you on the spot, believe me. I simply thought with you having worked with Mom for what—almost two months now—that maybe you were on the same wavelength, more or less. I apologize if I misread the situation."

Lee turned slowly at the stove to face Dale. "I think the world of your mom, but I sometimes have trouble with her...belief system. It's just so far from how I was raised and what I have always taken for granted about the world, about myself."

Dale smiled gently. "That's okay. You don't have to be in spiritual lockstep. If Mom didn't like you, if she didn't respect and appreciate you just as you are, you wouldn't be working on this project with her. Mom never pushes; she just opens doors in case people want to step through."

"What about you? Have you stepped through her doorway?"

"Actually, we pretty much stepped through together. She's probably told you about Dad and Owen."

"Yes, and I'm so sorry that you all had to go through that."

"And I'm very sorry that you lost your wife. I know it's only been a year or so for you. For us it's over thirty years, so our experience with grief has a much different emotional resonance these days. Now we can look back on it and appreciate that grief and loss are prime learning opportunities, spiritually speaking."

Dale got a faraway look in his eyes. "But as young as I was, I remember those early months. It was a brutal time. Mom did the best she could for me and my sisters, but she was suffering so much. I have no idea how she got through. Thank God for big families because ours couldn't have been more supportive. Grandma was here just about every day, making sure there was food in the fridge and things were ready to eat. My aunts were only a phone call away. One of them would drop over at least once a week to take the baby for an hour or two so my mom had a chance to rest. My uncles always made sure to include me and Jill on outings with our cousins."

Lee dished her scrambled eggs and brought them to the table. "Your family sounds great."

"They're the best. Which reminds me, I need to ask you a favour. Jill and I want to throw a big celebration for Mom's sixty-fifth birthday, which is in less than two months. We know she'll be expecting something on or around the actual date, so we decided the best way to surprise her is to do it early. It's up to me to figure out how to get her to Jill's place without arousing suspicions."

"That's where I come in?"

"Exactly. I thought maybe you could come up with some excuse to go out for dinner. Jill's going to have Emmy G leave her favourite dolly here earlier that day. Emmy G will call and beg Grandma to bring it home. You can offer to swing by Jill's on the way out to dinner. Et voila."

"Sounds like a good plan. I think I can help. We're going to be finishing the labyrinth about then. I'll tell your mom I'm taking her out for a celebratory dinner. She won't suspect a thing."

"Well, she won't as long as I warn Wally not to spill the beans."

"What was he on about at the garage yesterday? I've gotten a little better at deciphering Wally-speak, but even your mom was lost on that one."

"Wally just about gave away my big secret. Janjay and Dechontee are coming over to surprise Mom on her birthday. It's their first visit to Canada, and they're so excited about it."

"Okay, so 'coal' must be Janjay or Dechontee?"

"I think in context it's probably Dechontee, because their arrival is only half the secret. When they're here, Dechontee and I are going to ask our mothers for their blessing on our union."

"You're engaged? Man, your mother is going to be thrilled!"

"I know. Janjay will be too. I thought we could just announce our engagement at the party, but Dechontee is big on elder respect. She wants both of our mothers to learn about our engagement at the same time and to put their official stamp of approval on it."

"Congratulations, Dale. From all that your mom has said, you two make a terrific couple."

Dale beamed. "Thank you. I can hardly wait for the big day. Oh, and I'm even considering inviting my maternal grandparents for Mom's birthday."

"Gaëlle doesn't talk about them."

"No, they've been estranged for forty years. But they're getting on, and I'd really like to facilitate a reconciliation before they pass away. I've already touched base with them, just checking the lay of the land, as it were. I think they'd be open to accepting an invitation if I send them airline tickets."

"It's really nice of you to go to all this trouble."

"Are you kidding? You're the nice one. My part is easy. I'm not the one slinging old barn rocks just to make Mom happy."

"Believe it or not, I've really enjoyed it. And now I'd better get out there before your mom decides to convert her Cretan seven circuit to a Maltese eleven circuit."

Dale chuckled. "Sounds like Mom's been

educating you on labyrinths while you work."

"Your mom's been educating me on a whole lot of things, believe me." Lee rinsed her dishes and put them in the dishwasher. "See you later."

Dale waved goodbye and opened his newspaper. "Later."

Lee set aside her book and stretched luxuriantly. With the lengthening daylight, they'd been putting in extended hours. Lee doubted she'd ever been in better shape, but even with all her conditioning, she could still feel today's effects.

Gaëlle looked up from her laptop and smiled. "Calling it a night?"

"I think so. It was a long one today."

"It was, but isn't it exciting to be near completion? We've really accomplished something amazing, Lee. It's gorgeous."

"It is, and I'd like to celebrate. How about tomorrow I take you out for dinner? Jill told me of a place in North Battleford that sounds really nice. We'll get dressed up and go out on the town."

"Sounds lovely, but you know we don't have to go that far. I'm happy just to go to Four Corners."

"Nope, we do that all the time. This time we're celebrating somewhere special, and I'm not taking no for an answer."

Gaëlle laughed and surrendered. "Then I shall give a whole-hearted yes. But I think it's my turn to treat."

Lee shook her head. "My idea, my treat. You can get it next time."

"All right. Done deal. Have a good sleep, and I'll see you in the morning. Oh, if you hear noise in the middle of the night, it will be Dale. One of his old friends is getting married in a couple of weeks—I think for the third time—and the boys are having his stag party tonight."

"Thanks for the warning. I'll keep the earplugs near." Lee climbed the stairs to her room. As she undressed for bed, Lee noticed that her cellphone display showed a couple of missed calls. When she checked her voice mail, one was from Willem with a routine update. He'd made a point of keeping her in the loop during the months she'd been away. The other was from Marika, and that one she returned.

Rhiannon answered the phone. There was a muted commotion in the background.

"Hi, Rhi. How's it going?"

"At the moment, not well. Marnie had to have her shots today, and she is not a happy little camper. We put her down hours ago, but she just won't settle. It's Marika's turn to try persuading her to sleep. So, how are you doing?"

"Great. I was just returning Marika's call."

"She was probably phoning to beg for sanctuary."

Lee laughed at Rhiannon's droll tone. "Oh, c'mon, it can't be that bad."

"Oh yeah? Take a tempestuous two-year-old, add in hated inoculations and a bag of candy that Marnie somehow nicked without us noticing, and I give you our tornado of a daughter."

"Well, I won't keep you. Tell Marika I called, okay?"

"Will do. Hey, Lee? When are you coming home?"

"Soon. We're almost done. Just half a circuit to go, plus the centre."

"Are you looking forward to it?"

"What...finishing, or coming home?"

"Both."

"Sure, I guess. It's been a great experience. And I'm looking forward to seeing all of you again. I talked to Eli a couple of days ago, and it sounds like the final wedding preparations are going well. I need to buy a new suit when I get home, then I'll be ready."

A muffled wail erupted in the background.

"Go, Rhi. I'll catch up with you guys later."

"Thanks, Lee. See you soon."

With a smile, Lee set the phone aside and climbed into bed. She folded her hands behind her head and stared at the ceiling, considering Rhiannon's question. Was she looking forward to leaving?

Working with Gaëlle was meant to be only a temporary situation while she pondered her life's course. But Lee hadn't done much contemplating of what was to follow. Instead, she'd thrown herself into the work and their blossoming friendship and took great pleasure in both. She knew she'd stay in touch with Gaëlle, maybe even visit from time to time. But it would be difficult, if not impossible, to sustain the intimacy they'd developed.

Yawning again, Lee decided to set the issue aside. *One day at a time, right?* After she rolled over, Lee quickly drifted off.

Lee stared out from the shore over the brilliant green waters in front of her. She knew this place. Someone softly called her name, and she turned.

Dana sat on an ancient fallen tree, scoured white by wind and wave. She was sturdy and strong; her dark hair was lush and abundant—so different from Lee's last memory. Her clear eyes reflected a deep, abiding love. It felt like the most natural thing in the world to see her there.

"I miss you, Dana. God, I miss you so much."

"I know, sweetheart. But I am never absent from you."

Lee knelt in the sand at Dana's feet. They leaned forward until their foreheads touched.

"Stay? Please?"

"You know I can't, but I'll see you again. Take care of yourself. I love you. Cherish love, Lee. Always."

Their lips met. It was so familiar, so ordinary. So extraordinary...

Lee's eyes jerked open. Her heart pounded wildly, and her chest heaved. She sucked in deep gasps of air and fought for control of her breathing. Her whole body was frozen; her limbs wouldn't respond to her commands to move. Frantically, Lee's gaze flicked around, and she realized her eyesight was inexplicably acute. She could see the numbers on the alarm clock when normally they were a blur without her reading glasses.

3:33.

Within moments Lee's body returned to normal. Her breathing slowed; her heart resumed its normal rhythm; the clock's numbers grew blurry, and she rolled onto her back, wiping her face with her hands.

"What the hell was that?"

Dana! She'd been with Dana. It was so real...

Without thinking, Lee jumped out of bed and ran for the door. She had to share this experience.

Lee bounded down the hallway and up the short stairs to Gaëlle's attic suite. She hammered on the door and burst into the room without waiting to be bidden.

Gaëlle sat bolt upright. "Lee? What's wrong?" She fumbled for the bedside light.

Lee darted across the room to sit on the edge of the bed, one leg folded under her.

"Lee? What is it? What's going on?"

"I saw her, Gaëlle. I swear to you it wasn't a dream." Lee reached out and patted Gaëlle's arm. "She was as real as this. I touched her. I kissed her."

An understanding smile spread over Gaëlle's face. "You were out of body."

"What? No. I mean, I don't know."

"When this vision ended, what happened?"

"God, it was so freaky. I woke up, and my heart was racing. I couldn't breathe; I couldn't move. But I could see! I could see perfectly. My eyes haven't been that good since I was twenty."

Gaëlle laughed softly. "You've just described a classic case of astral travel. Your soul left your body and met Dana on the astral plane."

Lee's first impulse was to decry Gaëlle's explanation, but the power of what had just happened overwhelmed her with ecstasy. "I don't know what it was, but it was the most exhilarating thing I've ever experienced. Ever!" She seized Gaëlle's hands tightly as she remembered something. "I know where we were. The very spot I proposed to Dana on a trip to Emerald Lake years ago."

"She chose that deliberately. She knew you'd recognize it and remember the emotion attached to it. Do you remember what she said to you?"

"Yes, but it wasn't exactly talking. I understood what she said in words, but she wasn't really speaking."

"She was communicating soul to soul, Lee. Words aren't necessary on that level."

Lee released Gaëlle's hands. "This is just unbelievable. My God! Have you done this before?"

"Yes."

"Did you feel the same way...physically, I mean?"

"It depends on the particular journey. Sometimes I slip in and out of my body easily, with little effect. Sometimes I slam back into my body and feel everything that you felt. That's usually the case when I'm meant to remember an encounter or when something in the house or yard alerts my body and I'm instantly, prematurely pulled back, almost like an alarm sounded. One time I returned, hovered outside my body, and listened to it breathe. It was an odd, but not alarming sensation. I knew I was sleeping alone, so I tried to figure out if one of the children had come to sleep with me. Then I remembered my children were grown and realized that I was listening to myself."

"Now that's freaky."

"Not really. It was just part of my guides' agenda to prove to me that what I was experiencing was real. Tell me this, Lee. With the power of what happened to you tonight, do you now believe that Dana lives on? That her soul can communicate with yours?"

"I...I don't know. I guess so. It was real. It was so

real. She looked like she did fifteen years ago. Her lips felt just as soft, and her scent was identical. It was her. I know that with every fibre of my being."

"I'm so pleased for you. Dana gave you a gift tonight. That you were open to receiving that gift shows me how far you've come. That's beautiful."

"But what's with the vision thing?"

"I don't know the explanation, but I do know that every time I experience contact with the other side, whether through astral travel, meditation, or hypnosis, that's the way it is for me as well. Unfortunately it's not a permanent improvement, and my eyes soon return to their normal state."

Lee turned and planted her feet solidly on the floor. As she stared out the window on the opposite wall, she shook her head in wonder.

Gaëlle pushed back the covers, slid out to sit beside Lee, and slipped an arm around her back.

Lee tilted her head to rest against Gaëlle's and instantly had a sensory memory of touching foreheads with Dana. They sat for long minutes without speaking.

"I should go back to bed and let you get back to sleep."

But a few more minutes passed before either woman moved. Finally, Lee eased around and took Gaëlle in a gentle hug, which Gaëlle returned.

Lee whispered into Gaëlle's hair, "Thank you."

Gaëlle tightened her hug. "You're welcome." They released each other, and Lee rose to leave.

At the door, Lee turned and paused to look at Gaëlle. She realized she had never seen Gaëlle with her hair loose. It formed a wild silver nimbus around her head as she sat with one knee pulled up and watched her midnight visitor depart.

They exchanged smiles, and Lee closed the door.

While she descended the stairs, Lee heard a soft, faraway sound. She tried to isolate and identify it.

It was chimes.

CHAPTER 12

AFTER A SUBSTANTIAL BREAKFAST, LEE and Gaëlle briefly debated taking the day off but decided they preferred to put in a few hours on the labyrinth.

Gaëlle chose not to go by herself early for a meditation. They were on their way to the labyrinth when Wally darted out from a grove of poplar trees and flapped his hands at them.

"Wally, what's wrong?"

Wally jabbered unintelligibly.

Gaëlle took his arms firmly. "Slowly, Wally. You've got to slow down."

"Black back. Bad heart. Not smart. Go way, go way, go way."

Before Gaëlle could question Wally further, he broke from her grasp and scampered back into the trees.

"Wally!"

The fleeing man ignored Gaëlle's call and disappeared from view.

Gaëlle stared after Wally. "Now what was that all about?"

Lee shrugged. "If you don't know, I sure don't."

Gaëlle frowned as she shook her head. "I must

be losing my touch. I have no clue what he meant."

"It didn't sound good, whatever it was."

"He did sound upset, didn't he? I'll find him later and see if I can make some sense of it all."

Wally's odder than usual behaviour was quickly forgotten as they reached the labyrinth and stood surveying their progress. They were on the final circuit. The end was clearly in sight.

"I don't know whether to be happy or sad, Lee. It's been a lot of work, but I've enjoyed the company. I'm sure going to miss you."

It was the first time either of them had addressed the fact that Lee's stay was coming to an end.

"I'll miss you, too. Very much. But look at it this way. Even after I go home, we can still talk; we just won't have to move a mountain of stone while we do it."

"There is that." Gaëlle glanced at Lee, then lowered her eyes. "But I'll miss our mornings and evenings. I'll even miss having someone burst into my room in the middle of the night."

"I could arrange for Dale to do that every now and then, so you don't grow complacent."

Lee expected Gaëlle to chuckle at her jest. Instead Gaëlle turned and hugged Lee, holding her tightly.

Startled, Lee returned the embrace and felt a distinct shiver go through Gaëlle's thin body. "Hey, are you okay?"

Gaëlle pulled back and tried to grin. However, Lee saw the glistening in her eyes.

"Oh, don't mind me. I'm just being silly today. We should get to work."

Gaëlle took a step toward the wagon, but Lee caught her arm and gently pulled her back. Gaëlle laid her head on Lee's shoulder, and they rocked soundlessly together for long moments.

Lee had no desire to break away. She was content to stay exactly where she was, for as long as Gaëlle wished. Warmed from above by the late spring sunshine, Lee was also warmed to the core by the woman in her arms.

Finally, reluctantly, they disengaged and got back to work. An air of melancholy hung over them, though. They worked quietly until late morning, when they heard someone call out. Both straightened from their labours to see Jill and Emmy G approaching.

Emmy G ran headlong toward her grandmother, and Gaëlle quickly advanced to scoop up her granddaughter. "Whoa, squirt. Slow down. You don't want to trip over the stones." She smiled over Emmy's head at Jill. "What an unexpected delight."

"We're off to get groceries, and Emmy G insisted we stop and see Grandma on the way."

"I'm so glad you did. Why don't we go back to the house and get something cold to drink. I'm pretty sure I can scare up some cookies, too."

"Sounds good, Mom. But we can't stay too long. The boys are playing ball this morning. Bobby's working, so I'm delegated to retrieve them when they're done."

"All right. Then let's make tracks back to the house. Lee, are you coming?"

Lee shook her head. "No, that's okay. I think I'll keep working."

"Are you sure? Okay, then I'll bring you back a glass of something."

"And a cookie?"

"And a cookie." Gaëlle started walking with Emmy in her arms.

Jill winked at Lee, who returned the conspiratorial gesture.

All was going according to plan.

Lee knew that Dale had not been at a stag last night. In fact, he and Jill had spent the last three weeks working on their mother's surprise party. Lee was convinced that Gaëlle had no inkling what was to come and greatly anticipated the look on her friend's face.

As Lee worked, her thoughts wandered from last night's visitation and memories of Dana's kiss, to Gaëlle's unbound hair and the hugs they had shared in the last twenty-four hours.

Lee tried to analyze whether those hugs felt so good because she'd long been without the warmth of a woman in her arms, or if they felt fabulous because it was Gaëlle in her arms. She hadn't yet arrived at a conclusion when Wally walked up and squatted beside her.

Lee gave him her complete attention. He seemed to have calmed down since their earlier encounter. "Hey, Wally. How's tricks?"

He took a deep breath and spoke slowly, "Black heart. Pain gained. Blood bad."

Lee glanced at the farmhouse. "You're not talking about Janjay and Dechontee, are you?"

Wally shook his head vigorously. "Coal good. Coal great. Eaglet happy. Good, good. All good."

He laid his hand on Lee's forearm and repeated, "Black heart blood. Black heart blood. Past bad. Now bad. Cover star?"

"Cover star... Is Gaëlle 'star'?"

Wally's eyes lit up, and he bounced on his heels. "Star, yes! Bright star. Heart star."

"Okay, I got that. So, cover star...protect star? You're telling me Gaëlle needs protection from something?"

Wally closed his eyes and sighed in relief.

"What, Wally? What does she need to be protected from?"

"Blood's black heart."

"You're going to have to let me work on that one for a bit."

Wally nodded soberly. Then, as he had before, he tilted his head and listened. However, instead of the elation he'd displayed earlier, sorrow filled his eyes. "Choose, lose. Star, far. Sad, sad. Too bad." Shaking his head, he rose to his feet and trotted off.

"Ughh, I don't know how Gaëlle does it. Talking to that man is like trying to find a grain of sense in a wheat field."

Lee pondered the meaning of Wally's words as she worked. She understood that she needed to keep an eye on Gaëlle, but she couldn't decipher the nature of the danger or where it was coming from. For all she knew, it could be nothing more than Gaëlle tripping over a stone and wrenching her ankle, though that seemed unlikely.

Lee deliberated over telling Gaëlle of Wally's warning but decided against it. Whatever the future held, Wally seemed to think it would be up to Lee to protect Gaëlle. Lee felt as if she'd been deputized by the odd oracle, and she was determined to stay alert.

By the time Gaëlle returned, there were only three feet unpaved in the last circuit. Lee gratefully accepted the glass of cold lemonade and two oatmeal cookies.

"Sorry I took so long. It looks like you almost finished without me."

"Not quite. Besides, we've still got the centre to do. You haven't told me your plans for that."

Gaëlle cleared a patch of ground and picked up a stone to lay in place. "Mostly because I haven't settled on the design. Traditionally, the Cretan design doesn't even have a centre as such. The medieval twelve circuit does, but it's a six petal rosette that doesn't resonate with me. I've drawn on the classics, but altered the structure somewhat."

"Will it affect the labyrinth if you stray from tradition? You told me it's a sacred space."

"It is, but the power and the sanctity of it lay in the soul and intent of the walker. Essentially a labyrinth is a tool. The 180-degree turns from one circuit to the next are intended to help the walker turn off the left brain and shift into right brain focus. The deeper you can go within as you meander along your route to the centre, the more benefit you'll get from your walk. It's a calming discipline. There are no tricks to a labyrinth, unlike a maze."

"Very straightforward...sort of like you."

Gaëlle smiled and glanced over at Lee. "And here I was sure you were convinced I was just about the most baffling woman you'd ever met."

"Your beliefs baffle me at times—"

"Even after last night?"

Lee straightened and gazed reflectively over the labyrinth. "Last night...I still feel the power of last night. It's as clear and as real to me as this stone. But I don't know what to do with it."

"Then let it alone. Things of such magnitude are far better handled intuitively than by our rational left brains."

"I like my rational left brain."

Gaëlle laughed. "I've noticed."

Gaëlle and Lee worked until mid-afternoon and then quit for the day.

Lee decided to indulge herself in a bath before dressing for the party. While she luxuriated in the bubbles, she reflected on Wally's words but got no further in deducing his meaning. *Some mystery solver you are. You should turn in your Dick Tracy decoder ring.*

Whatever Wally meant, she doubted it would have anything to do with the party, since only Gaëlle's friends and family would be there. In the two months she'd been with Gaëlle, she was pretty sure she'd met all of her family and at least half the people of Donegal. None, in Lee's estimation, presented any kind of threat, though a few were mildly annoying.

Back in her room, Lee pawed through the closet and examined her meagre wardrobe. She'd had Eli send some additional clothes up the second week she'd been there, but still she lacked anything in the way of a formal outfit. She pulled out a pair of black slacks, a pressed white shirt, and a grey silk vest. They would have to do.

When Lee walked downstairs, Gaëlle was already waiting in a blue summer dress. The look of admiration in her eyes elevated Lee's mood.

"Well, aren't we the spiffy duo?"

"You clean up very nicely, Lee."

"You look great yourself. Are you ready to go?"

"I am. Do you mind if we swing by Jill's house? Emmy G left her favourite doll here, and she can't sleep without it. It'll just take a moment. I promise I won't stop and talk."

"Not a problem. We've got lots of time before our reservation."

"Oh, good. Emmy will be so happy to see her doll."

And hopefully Emmy's grandmother will be happy to see all her loved ones waiting to celebrate her. With a smile, Lee opened the front door for Gaëlle.

Gaëlle began to walk by, then stopped and sniffed. "Goodness, don't you smell wonderful."

"That's thanks to your daughter. Britten must've been in a hurry the night she left, because she forgot several scented soaps and bubble baths. I made an executive decision to accept them as a tip for my fine service."

"You mean when you tackled and hogtied her husband."

"That would be the service to which I was referring, yes."

They laughed together as they went out to the SUV.

They drove onto the dusty gravel road. Lee was glad for air conditioning so they could ride with the windows closed. She didn't want anything to diminish their finery.

"Did you see Dale at all today?"

"No. Why? Are you worried about your son?"

"No, he's a big boy. Perhaps the stag party is still going on."

"More likely he's recovering at one of his friends' houses."

"You're probably right. After all, he's not twenty anymore. Heavens, he's forty now. I doubt he can party the way he once did."

"You have a forty-year-old son? Wow, you are getting old, lady."

Lee got a punch on the shoulder for that.

She laughed and turned onto the main road, which would take them to Jill's house. Jill and her family also lived in the country, about five kilometres from her mother's place. Lee had sent Dale a text just before going downstairs, so she was confident that everyone would be well hidden by the time they arrived. When Lee pulled into the shaded yard, they saw only Dale's vehicle parked to the side of the driveway.

"So that's where he's been."

"Relieved, Mama Hen?"

"Of course. I don't think you ever stop worrying about them, no matter how old they get. Don't you still worry about Eli?"

Lee was silent. The sad truth was that because of his mother's illness and the traumatic aftermath, Eli had slipped far down her list of concerns. Lee regretted that more than she'd ever be able to tell her son.

Gaëlle was distracted as Emmy G came out the front door. "Oh, good. This won't take long, then." She climbed out of the car with doll in hand.

Lee followed, wondering how they'd dealt with the guests' cars, because there wasn't a hint of any other vehicles around.

"Hey, squirt. I found Miss Jelly Belly for you. You left her in the bathroom. She's been missing you."

As Gaëlle knelt to give the doll to Emmy G, people suddenly appeared from everywhere, shouting, "Surprise!"

Gaëlle's mouth dropped as family and friends swarmed her with hugs and kisses. "Oh, my God!" Gaëlle shot an inquiring look at Lee.

"Don't look at me. I'm just your chauffeur for the evening. You can thank Jill and Dale for this shindig."

The miscreants in question descended the front stairs, laughing at their mother's expression.

Two men quickly strung a banner across the front porch that read "Happy Birthday, Gaëlle".

Children of all ages danced around the adults, their shrieks of joy elevating the noise level.

Dale reached his mother's side and urged her to follow him. "Mom, we've got some special guests waiting to see you. Come with me."

Lee followed, alongside Jill and her husband, Bobby.

When they rounded the corner, Lee gave a low whistle. There were white linen covered tables set in a large circle around the deck and lawn.

Eileen and her daughters tended a buffet line. Party lanterns were strung from trees overhead, and flaming citronella stakes ringed the dining area. Lee estimated over a hundred guests were mingling about.

"Jill, how did all these people get here without vehicles?"

"They all parked at Rick and Janet's place, one concession over, and Janet drove them here in a school bus."

"You two have done brilliantly. This is an amazing set-up." Lee looked around and dropped her voice. "Did Janjay and Dechontee make it?"

"Yes, but they've been staying with my cousin Matty, and he got a flat tire on the way over. He called to say they'd be here in twenty minutes."

"So the special guests are..."

"My grandparents. They flew in yesterday and have been staying with me. It's been kind of weird, actually. As far as I can remember, I've never met them, so it's like having two elderly strangers in the house. Still, they seem nice enough, and I'm glad Dale arranged for them to be here. I'm sure Mom will be thrilled."

Lee was doubtful. From her vantage point, she could see Gaëlle's face as Dale brought his grandparents out from the kitchen. There was utter shock in her expression. Lee suddenly felt an urge to reach Gaëlle's side, and she wormed her way through the crowd and up to the elevated deck.

As Lee came behind Gaëlle, her friend exchanged a stiff hug with her mother and a handshake with her father. Dale stood to the side, a mildly confused look on his face.

"Hey, Gaëlle."

Gaëlle turned to Lee with relief in her eyes. "Hey, yourself. I wondered where you'd gotten to. Come and meet my parents." She pulled Lee to her side. "Mom, Dad, this is a dear friend of mine, Lee Glenn. Lee, this is my mother, Sue Revkin, and my father, Allan Revkin."

Lee extended her hand first to Gaëlle's mom, who shook it limply, then to her father. She was startled to see distaste in Allan Revkin's eyes, but his voice was neutral as they exchanged pleasantries.

Lee stood with Gaëlle, her parents, Dale, Jill, and Bobby and made small talk as people came and went, offering congratulations to the woman of the evening.

The longer she stood there, the more an instinctive dislike for Allan grew within her. Lee couldn't have said why. He did nothing overtly offensive, but Lee's long-honed people instincts had her hackles raised.

Suddenly Lee recalled Wally's words. *Blood's black heart. Blood...as in relative? Was that what he meant? He was warning me to guard Gaëlle from her father?*

It hadn't escaped Lee's notice that Gaëlle still clung to her arm. It was highly unusual behaviour from the normally confident, outgoing woman. But before she could give it any further thought, Dale's face beamed as he looked past them.

"Mom, you're going to want to turn around. Your parents aren't the only special guests tonight."

Lee turned as Gaëlle did.

Two African women in colourful clothes mounted

the steps. The older woman leading the way wore a vivid red and yellow caftan. A necklace of coral and amber beads hung round her neck. The younger woman wore a gorgeous orange and green skirt with a short black fitted jacket and a head wrap that matched her skirt.

"Janjay? Dechontee? Oh, my God! I can't believe you're here!" Gaëlle rushed to embrace the two newcomers.

Janjay and Dechontee grinned broadly, their smiles a brilliant contrast to their ebony skin.

Dale sidled up next to the trio, his smile as big as theirs. "So, did we surprise you, Mom?"

"Surprise me? Oh, my sweet Jesus, did you ever! Brat! I can't believe you didn't tell me." Gaëlle was laughing and crying at the same time, clearly exhilarated that her friends were there.

Lee stole a look at Gaëlle's parents. This time Allan's distaste wasn't restricted to his eyes. His countenance radiated revulsion. Lee overheard him mutter to his wife, "Nothing's changed. We should never have come."

Sue nervously patted her husband's arm, and he led her away from the joyful scene to chairs at the far side of the deck.

I think you nailed this guy, Wally. He definitely bears watching.

Lee was about to take up a position near the entry to the kitchen, where she could keep an eye on the Revkins, but Gaëlle was suddenly at her side and tugged her over to meet the newcomers.

"Lee, you have got to meet our friends."

Laughing, Lee allowed herself to be rushed

across the deck. She found herself standing in front of Janjay, whose shrewd eyes quickly assessed her. Lee offered her hand and got a left-handed shake in return.

Janjay smiled and turned to Gaëlle. "This one is all right, my friend."

Gaëlle shot an affectionate look at Lee. "I kind of thought so."

Dale had his arm around Dechontee, and he gently steered her to face Lee. "Lee, this is my... this is Dechontee."

"It is indeed good to meet you. I've heard so much about the work you and your mother are doing. It's quite amazing what you've accomplished."

"Thank you very much. Perhaps later we can talk about this."

"It would be my pleasure."

With all the special guests now in attendance, the party took off with a vengeance. Two of Hugh's brothers and a niece and a nephew dug out musical instruments. When they weren't eating, people danced to the sounds of guitars, a fiddle, and an accordion.

Lee stuck close to Gaëlle, who, except for the occasional dutiful chat with her parents, remained near Janjay. Dale and Dechontee danced until Lee was sure their feet would fall off.

"Do you dance, Lee?"

Lee looked over to see Janjay's eyes sparkling with mischief. "Well, ma'am, I've been accused of being hard on my partner's feet, but I do enjoy it. Would you care to take your chances with me?"

"Eh, eh, eh. Not me. My ancient feet are all

danced out. But you take this one out there." Janjay pushed Gaëlle toward Lee.

Gaëlle laughed and cocked her head. "Shall we do as we're bidden?"

Allan Revkin was in Lee's line of sight. For a moment, she thought he was going to erupt at Janjay's suggestion, but he visibly restrained himself.

"Sure. I should warn you, though, that Dana wore steel-toed cowboy boots when we went dancing."

"I'll take my chances."

Lee decided that either her dancing had improved over the years, or Gaëlle's avoidance skills were far superior to Dana's. They enjoyed three rapid dances without a single injury to Gaëlle's toes, then breathlessly returned to the deck, arm in arm.

Gaëlle nudged Lee as they climbed the stairs. "That was so much fun. Promise we'll do that again later?"

"Absolutely."

Lee settled Gaëlle back in the chair next to Janjay and went to find them something cold to drink. Snagging a couple of bottles out of one of the numerous ice chests, she noticed Dale and Dechontee approaching their mothers.

Lee grinned. *This is it. The big announcement.* As pre-arranged, she put her fingers to her mouth and gave a piercing wolf whistle.

The music stumbled to a halt, and heads swivelled in her direction.

"If I could get you to direct your attention to the deck, Dale and Dechontee have something to say."

With all eyes on them, Dale and Dechontee knelt in front of their mothers, who began to beam with anticipation.

"Mom, Janjay, Dechontee and I would like to ask for your blessing. We want to get married as soon as—"

Before Dale could go any further, Allan leaped to his feet. "No! This is an abomination. No grandson of mine is going to marry the likes of her." He spat the words out to the night sky as a multitude of shocked faces snapped toward him.

Lee dropped the bottles and sprang forward. Seizing Allan's arm, she hissed, "You and I are going to have a word, Mr. Revkin. Inside. Now!" Lee hustled the protesting man past the kneeling couple and their distressed mothers.

Sue Revkin, in tears, followed close behind.

Inside the house, Lee kept on going until they reached the living room. "Sit."

Allan looked as if he was going to ignore Lee's order, but her flashing eyes apparently changed his mind. He dropped into the nearest chair.

"I don't know what your problem is, Mr. Revkin." *Blood's black heart.* "I have no idea why you'd fly all this way just to make trouble, but—"

"*Me* make trouble?" Revkin's voice trembled with indignation.

"Yes, you. That was a tender scene between two people who love each other deeply, and you thought you had the right to interrupt? Who the hell do you think you are?"

"That man's grandfather. And I was trying to stop him from making a terrible mistake, just like his mother made forty years ago."

Lee snorted and scowled at the man. "The only mistake here tonight was Dale thinking he could bring you back into the circle of a loving family." *Black heart, black heart.*

"I will not sit here and be lectured by the likes of you."

"The likes of me, eh? I see you're an equal opportunity bigot. Race, sexuality—is there nothing your intolerance doesn't cover?"

"Sue, go pack our things. We are leaving this instant."

"Yeah, you are. In fact, I'm driving you to North Battleford. You can get a hotel there and take a bus to any airport you choose in the morning. The only thing I care about is getting your poison away from a whole lot of great human beings, who don't deserve to be exposed to such filth."

Sue scuttled from the room, and Allan followed.

Lee sought to calm herself as she paced. When Jill joined her, Lee explained what had happened.

"Thank you, Lee. I didn't know what to do. I'm ashamed that they're my blood."

"Don't be. As your mom would say, they alone are responsible for their actions."

Jill gave Lee a quick hug and then left the room.

A few minutes later, Gaëlle came in with tears in her eyes. Reacting instinctively, Lee opened her arms, and Gaëlle hurried into her embrace.

"I can't believe they did that. That was even worse than when Hugh and I..."

"Shhh, it's okay. I'm going to take them away from here."

"I know. Jill told me. Thank you, Lee. I hate to have you miss the party, but I just can't deal with him. I've never been able to."

"No worries. I'll be back by midnight. You'll probably all still be partying."

"If he hasn't put a permanent damper on things."

Lee took Gaëlle's face in her hands. "Don't let him, okay?"

"Okay."

Lee brushed Gaëlle's tears aside. "Promise?"

"Promise."

"That a girl." Lee planted a soft kiss on Gaëlle's forehead, only to hear an outraged hiss come from behind.

"I should've known! Sodomite! Whore!"

"Oh, for crying out loud. Gaëlle, go back to your guests. Celebrate your birthday, the engagement, and have a good time. I'm going to take out the trash." Lee kissed Gaëlle's cheek and turned to the Revkins. "C'mon, you nasty old bugger. It's time you left this party."

CHAPTER 13

Driving Mr. and Mrs. Revkin to North Battleford felt like one of the longest hours of Lee's life. Sue hadn't stopped weeping since they left Jill's house, but even that was more tolerable than listening to Allan rant about his daughter's shortcomings.

Mile after mile, Lee grimly resisted the urge to toss the old bigot out and leave him on the side of the road. She tried cranking up the radio, but reception was poor and the crackling was almost harder to listen to than Revkin.

Finally, Lee had enough. "Shut the fuck up!" The full-volume bellow stopped Revkin in mid-rave. "No more, do you hear me? I'll kick you out and let you find your own way back to civilization; don't think I won't. You're slandering the most decent human being I've ever had the pleasure to meet. I can't believe she's actually your daughter, because you've got to be the nastiest human being I've ever encountered."

"She's not my daughter."

Lee rolled her eyes. "I'm sure Gaëlle will be absolutely crushed to learn you're going to disown her."

"That woman is no blood of mine. Never has been; never will be."

Lee looked in her rear-view mirror at her two passengers.

Sue had her face buried in her hands. Unexpectedly, the look on Allan's face appeared to be one of triumph.

"Come again?"

"Ask my wife. Ask her about fornication with the adulterer Adam Woodson, which produced the devil's issue. I raised the child up right, but blood tells. Blood always tells!"

"So you're saying that Gaëlle is your wife's daughter..."

"But not mine. No legitimate daughter of mine would allow her son to marry a spawn of Africa. No rightful daughter of mine would have relations with another woman."

"Not that it's any business of yours, but your daughter and I are just friends. End of story."

"Don't insult my intelligence. I know what you are, and I know what I saw."

"What you saw was one friend comforting another. But I doubt you know much about friendship or compassion."

"I know the word of God, and I know a sinner when I see one."

Lee twisted her mirror until it showed him his own reflection. "Then take a close look, Revkin. It won't be long before you're answering for a life's worth of nastiness. Frankly, I wouldn't want to be you on that day."

"Hell-bound bitch! You and my wife's daughter

can keep each other company in the lakes of fire."

"Cool. I'd much rather be wherever she is than wherever you end up. Now shut up, or get out. Your choice."

Revkin looked as if he'd bitten into a lemon, but he was silent for the remainder of the ride.

Lee pulled into the parking lot at the first hotel she came to in North Battleford. After confirming that they had a vacancy, she dumped her passengers' luggage at the front door. When she looked in her rear-view mirror, Allan Revkin had already gone inside while Sue Revkin struggled with their bags.

Lee felt a moment of sympathy for the woman. She couldn't imagine a lifetime married to such a tyrannical man. "I guess your daughter would say you chose your life circumstances for a reason, Sue. I hope you learned whatever lessons you set out for yourself and don't have to go around with that son of a bitch again."

Lee shuddered. It might have been her imagination, but she could almost feel the negativity the Revkins had left behind. "I'm going to have to cleanse my car with burning sage."

When Lee realized what she had muttered, she laughed until tears ran down her cheeks. "Damn, old girl, she's getting to you."

But when she wiped her eyes dry and drove into the night, Lee did feel as if the atmosphere had lightened.

By the time Lee arrived back at Jill's, it was nearing midnight. The party was still going on, though more than half of the guests had departed. There were far fewer dancers, and they now swayed to the sounds of recorded music. Some young children napped in their parents' arms, and older children congregated near the food table.

Lee passed a steady trickle of people leaving, exchanging goodnights as she went.

Off to one side, she spotted Dale and Dechontee leaning against a tree with their arms around each other. She smiled, relieved that Revkin had not inflicted any perceptible damage.

As she rounded the corner of the house, Lee saw Gaëlle and Janjay deep in conversation on the deck. She hesitated, but Gaëlle spotted her.

"Lee!" Gaëlle jumped to her feet and met Lee at the top of the stairs. "Did you get them to a hotel?"

"I did."

"Come sit with us. Eileen and the girls just put out midnight snacks. Let me get you a plate."

Lee was going to refuse, but Gaëlle was already down the stairs and moving toward the buffet table. Lee took a seat facing Janjay. She rubbed her face wearily and sighed.

"It was not a pleasant drive, I'm thinking."

Lee shook her head. "No, it wasn't. They are not pleasant people...well, he isn't, anyway. I'm afraid I wasn't exactly diplomatic. I may have ruined any future chance of reconciliation."

"Do not worry about that. I believe that Gaëlle has no such desire in any case. Poor Dale has apologized over and over since that ill-bred man's outburst. But it was not Dale's fault. He thought he was doing a good thing for his mother. He is a good son."

"He'll make a good son-in-law, eh?"

"He will. I am very pleased with my daughter's choice, though I confess I am somewhat worried about having that nasty man's DNA transmitted to my future grandchildren. It is so hard to believe that my dear friend has a father like that."

"She doesn't, actually. At least not according to the sonofabitch himself."

"What?"

When she heard Gaëlle's exclamation behind her, Lee whirled around, belatedly realizing what she had just disclosed. "Shit. Shit. Shit. I'm so sorry, Gaëlle. I didn't mean to tell you like that."

Gaëlle set the plate she'd filled on a side table. "What did you mean?"

"Your...Revkin said a lot of things on the way to North Battleford."

"I imagine he did. Dad's never been shy about expressing his opinions, no matter how outrageous."

"Yeah, well, one of the things he said...he accused your mom of...he said that someone else was your biological father."

Janjay raised her hand to the sky. "Praise God!"

"Someone else? He's not my father?" Gaëlle sank into a chair. "My God. I never knew."

"You never suspected?"

Gaëlle shot Lee a wry look. "That my mother would cheat on my father? Did you meet my mother?"

Lee nodded her understanding. It was hard to imagine the woman doing anything to cross her husband.

"If you'll excuse me, I need a few minutes to think. I'll be back shortly, I promise."

Lee watched Gaëlle descend the stairs and walk

toward a gate on the east side of the yard. Lee's gaze never left Gaëlle as she disappeared into the darkness of a grove of trees beyond the yard.

"Why are you still sitting here?"

Lee turned back to Janjay. "Pardon?"

"Why are you sitting here when she's out there? Go to her."

"Um, she said that she wanted some alone time."

Janjay made shooing motions. "Phstt. Gaëlle wants time away from this crowd, not from you. Go find her."

"Are you sure?"

Janjay grimaced, and Lee had no trouble deciphering her opinion.

Lee jumped to her feet. She took two steps before looking back at Janjay. "How will I find her? It's pretty dark out there."

Janjay touched her chest. "But light in here. Listen within, Lee. You won't get lost if you do."

Lee grinned. "You're as crazy as she is. Okay, call in the search team if we're not back in an hour. Or you could wait for the ransom note from the gophers and see what their demands are."

Janjay burst out laughing. It was a deep, rolling sound that carried Lee like a wave, off the deck and across the yard.

Lee left the yard behind her and reached the trees. It was difficult to see beyond the edge of the grove, and she had no idea which direction to take. "It's all well and good to tell me to listen within, but how the hell do I do that?"

Lee took a deep breath and tried to quiet her mind. She found it impossible to do—Gaëlle filled her thoughts. Finally, exasperated, she said, "I don't know who I'm asking, I don't know if there's even anyone there to ask, but if you are there, please help me find her."

She stood still for a moment, then, without thinking, angled to her left and plunged into the copse of trees. She was glad that enough of the tree trunks were light-coloured that she could find a path through them. After a few minutes of walking, she could see the far edge of the grove and the dark prairie stretching out beyond it.

"Gaëlle? Are you here?"

A shadow detached itself from a tree ahead of her. "Lee?"

"Well, I'll be damned. That works better than a GPS." Lee quickly joined Gaëlle. "Hey."

"Hey, yourself. What are you doing out here? You could've gotten lost."

"Apparently not, at least not according to Janjay. As for what I'm doing here, I was worried about you. Are you all right?"

"I was just thinking."

"About?"

"Questions and answers."

"Okay. That's a little cryptic. Darn near Wally-speak, in fact. Care to expand? I'd like to know what you're thinking."

Gaëlle held out her hand. "Walk with me?"

Lee took her hand, and they walked north along the edge of the grove. "I'm sorry I opened my big mouth. I never meant to hurt you."

"You didn't. In fact, you gave me answers to questions that have plagued me all my life."

"Questions such as?"

"Why didn't my parents love me like Wally's parents loved him and his sister? As hard as I would try to please, my dad never seemed to even like me. And for some reason it got much worse after we moved from Donegal. My mom was afraid to love me. If my dad was away on business, things would be great between Mom and me. But the moment he walked back in the door, she would be terrified to show me the least bit of overt affection. Now I know why."

"Damn, that's a hard way to grow up."

"It was bearable until we moved away. Wally's parents were wonderful to me, and Wally gave me unconditional love. I don't know what I'd have done without him. I'm so grateful that he decided to come back again. He didn't have to, you know."

"You lost me."

"About Wally?"

"Yeah. What do you mean 'he didn't have to'? Didn't have to come back to Donegal? Was he away somewhere?"

Gaëlle chuckled. "You could say that. I meant that Wally's soul is so evolved that he didn't have to reincarnate this time. He did it for me, because I still had much to learn. Because I chose such a difficult situation to be born into, Wally chose to be born nearby to love and support me."

"Why would you choose such a rotten situation? Why not choose to be born into...I dunno, Wally's family? Then you could've grown up with all the love that he did and have had him as a brother. Seems to me that would've been a win-win situation."

"Not in a karmic sense."

Lee sighed. "No, of course not."

"Seriously, contrast what I learned with what I couldn't have learned as part of Wally's family."

"Definitely lost now."

"One of my karmic lessons is to learn self-love and self-reliance. By being part of a family that didn't give me much love, I was forced to turn to myself to learn those things. It wasn't fun, and it took a long time, but I finally mastered that lesson. Remember what I was saying about Brian and how difficult it actually is to learn to love yourself?"

"I still say he loves himself plenty."

"No, Lee, he really doesn't. No matter how frequently he swaggers into a bar or how many women agree to go home with him, come morning when Brian looks in the mirror, he sees someone who has failed repeatedly. He has a broken marriage; he has worked at a series of low paying jobs, and he has trouble making his child support payments. His good looks are beginning to ebb, abetted by years of self-indulgence and far too many nights in the Red Arrow. Soon he won't even get reassurance from the weekend women who say yes. Yet Brian came from a very loving family. His soul plan was probably to build on that solid foundation, but he strayed off course."

"Say you're right. Why would he be allowed to stray? Why wouldn't...whoever...keep him on the straight and narrow so he could achieve exactly what he wanted to?"

"Two answers really. The first is that we all have free will. Brian can choose to work on his growth or slack off for this lifetime and not make much progress. It's his call. That said, his soul isn't going to be very happy between lives, because he wasted some great opportunities and he'll have to plan another set of circumstances to try and learn that same lesson the next time around."

"And the second answer?"

"We don't value or retain what comes too easily."

"You lost me again."

"We don't have to incarnate, Lee. No one forces us to do anything against our will. However, our guides and teachers will certainly try gentle persuasion if they feel it's in our best spiritual interests. I imagine there are souls who are so gravely damaged by a life's experiences that they refuse to return for another go-around. That doesn't mean they have to stop learning and evolving, but they won't make progress as quickly on the other side."

"Why not? If you're right, and the 'between lives' is so wonderful, why the hell would anyone choose to leave?"

"Because if you never experience the dark, how can you value the light?"

Lee stopped walking. "Well, damn. That actually makes sense to me. You're saying that because your parents didn't love you, which would be the dark part, then when you encountered real love, you didn't take it lightly."

"Exactly. I cherished Wally's love and, years later, fell so deeply in love with Hugh that being with him did feel like heaven. My dad didn't stand a chance when he tried to separate us." Gaëlle stood at Lee's side, gazing up at the star-filled night sky. "You know I can't help feeling sorry for Dad. He's accumulated an awful lot of bad karma in this lifetime."

"Um, Gaëlle?"

"Mmmm?"

"I kind of said some not very nice things to your dad."

"What did you say?"

"I told him he was going to have to answer for all his meanness."

"You're not wrong, though the only one he has to answer to is himself."

"Won't he give himself a pass? He seems pretty sure he's on the side of the angels."

"We can't lie to ourselves when it comes to reviewing our lives. Dad will have to face up to the consequences of his actions by experiencing the pain he caused others."

"Huh. Does that mean he'll lose brownie points for condemning you and me to lakes of hellfire?"

Gaëlle chuckled and squeezed Lee's hand. "He did that, did he?"

"Yup."

"Do I dare imagine what you said in response?"

"I said I'd much rather be with you swimming amidst the flames than wherever he's going to end up."

"I'm sure that went over well."

"Not exactly, but it did shut him up. I just...if you wanted to reconcile some day, I hope I didn't ruin things for you."

Even in the scant moonlight, Lee could see the open affection on Gaëlle's face.

"Don't give it another thought. I'm very sorry for my mom, though. I spent a lot of years wishing I could rescue her until I finally understood that she, too, chose her circumstances for a particular reason. As for my dad, I don't think there's any going back, but then, there was very little to go back to. And I'm okay with that. I just—"

When Gaëlle hesitated, Lee pulled her closer. "You just what?"

"I wonder who my real father is, that's all. Not that it matters now. I'm only curious."

"Oh, I can answer that. Your dad said it was some guy named Adam Woodson." As soon as she said the name aloud, it struck Lee. "Oh, my God. Woodson. Is that—?"

"Wally's dad."

They stared at each other. "Wally's your brother?"

"Wally's my brother. Wow! The Woodsons were our neighbours the whole time we lived in Donegal. But I just can't imagine Mr. Woodson and my mom..."

"I can't imagine your father continuing to live next to the man who cuckolded him."

Gaëlle shook her head. "There's no way his pride would've allowed that. He must not have known until after they moved away."

"Do you think Wally knows?"

"If he does, he's never said anything to me."

"That you understood, anyway."

"True. My comprehension isn't one hundred per cent. Wally...my brother. Wow!"

"Are you happy...sad...confused?"

"Happy, I guess. Not that it would be possible to feel closer to him than I already do. But it's kind of reassuring, actually."

"How so?"

"Because if I am his sister, then I have legal standing to help him on more than an ad hoc basis. I've always worried that Wally might get to a state where the authorities would step in and confine him somewhere. That would kill him quicker than a bullet to the brain."

"So you're going to follow up, take whatever steps are needed to prove kinship?"

"I am, but I'll wait until after Janjay and Dechontee go home."

"Are Dale and Dechontee getting married here or in Guinea?"

"Both places. We're going to have a family wedding here as quickly as we can arrange it, then Dale will return to Guinea with Dechontee and Janjay. Jill and I will fly over later for their local celebration."

"With Eli getting married too, it's a summer to celebrate."

"It certainly is. And speaking of Janjay and Dechontee, they've been staying with my nephew Matty and his wife so as not to spoil my birthday surprise, but I'd like to bring them back to the house tonight."

Lee understood immediately. "Of course. If you've got an air mattress, I'll sleep down in the library so they can have my room. Or I can just crash on the living room couch. We'll be done with the labyrinth in a few days anyway, and then I'll get out of your hair."

Gaëlle shook her head. "No, that's not what I had in mind." She gently pulled her hands from Lee's grasp and slipped them around Lee's waist.

Lee's breath shortened as she felt the warmth of Gaëlle's body against hers. She rested her hands lightly on Gaëlle's back. "What did you have in mind?"

"I want you to share my room...my bed."

"Are you asking...do you know what you're asking?"

Gaëlle answered wordlessly.

Lee lost herself in Gaëlle's kiss, in desire for the body pressed so firmly against her own. She tightened their embrace fiercely, setting fire to what had smouldered between them for weeks.

Finally, Gaëlle eased away. "If we don't stop, I'm going to fall down. I feel as shaky as a newborn calf."

"And this is a bad thing?"

"Definitely not. I'd really like to collect our guests, go home, and pick up where we're leaving off."

Home. Yes. "Mmm, you're right. We should go back." But Lee couldn't make her arms let go, and Gaëlle didn't seem to mind. After another longer bout of kissing, they drew slightly apart.

Lee couldn't believe she was going to say it, but she had to ask. "Are you sure about this? I didn't get the sense that you've ever been interested in another woman."

Gaëlle nibbled at Lee's neck, then reluctantly pulled back enough to look Lee in the eyes. "You're right, I haven't. But then you hadn't come along yet, so why would I? I've been waiting for you for a long time."

"You have? For me...for a woman?"

"I had no idea what body you'd show up in. I was a little surprised the night you arrived with Britten, not that it mattered; it was still you. Wally was right about that."

"You confuse the hell out of me sometimes, but it doesn't matter. I've fallen in love with you, Gaëlle." Lee shook her head in amazement. *Teach me never to say never.*

Gaëlle took Lee's face in her hands. "Is that so bad? To have fallen in love with me? You have to know I love you, too."

Lee kissed Gaëlle softly before answering, "Not bad at all. I just...I never thought after Dana's death...I never planned to fall in love again."

"Actually you did. You just didn't remember it."

"So you're saying if my soul had shown up wearing a hulking, hairy, rotund old man's body, you'd still have fallen for me?"

"Your soul knew I'd fall for exactly the body you came in." Gaëlle trailed her hands lightly over Lee's chest. "It's a very sensible soul, when all is said and done."

Lee grinned. "You know, I'm having a hard time picturing Britten as Cupid."

Gaëlle chuckled and took Lee's hand to lead them back to the house. "She did love to dress up as fairy princesses for Halloween."

"Close enough."

It took twice as long for them to get back to the house because they kept stopping to kiss and touch each other. Finally, though, they could see the lights through the trees.

Lee let go of Gaëlle's hand.

Gaëlle immediately took Lee's hand back.

"Are you sure? Your family—"

Gaëlle gave her a reassuring squeeze. "Will accept us or they won't. I'm not going to lie to them or pretend that I'm not madly in love with you. But I also have a lot of faith in them. I'm making this lifetime's journey with an amazing group of souls. I'm not worried."

Lee pulled Gaëlle in for one more embrace and murmured into her hair, "Is there any way to send my soul flowers for having the remarkable good sense to choose you?"

They returned to the deck and found a cleanup underway. People were bustling around, picking up dishes, filling trash bags, and breaking down tables.

Dale smiled at them as they passed him and Dechontee carrying tables to stack against the side of the house.

Jill, in full command of the clean-up operations, didn't bat an eye as her mother and Lee mounted the steps to the deck, hand-in-hand.

Janjay waved to them, a big grin on her face.

"Why don't we help out, then we can get going."

Jill overheard and shook her head. "No way, Mom. You're the guest of honour tonight; you're not lifting a finger to clean up. But when Dale and Dechontee get married, be prepared to work, because that party's going to be twice as radical as this one."

Lee steered a mildly protesting Gaëlle to Janjay's side. "Go, sit, and do what your daughter tells you. I'm going to make a quick pit stop, and then we can leave."

As Lee walked to the kitchen door, she could hear Janjay happily pressing Gaëlle for information. She grinned to herself. She knew her friends and family would be just as eager for details when she told them about Gaëlle.

Gaëlle. A shiver of delight and anticipation ran through Lee's body. She greeted the ladies in the kitchen, who were washing, drying, and stacking dishes, but her mind was far away.

While a part of her was shocked at what had happened so rapidly between her and Gaëlle, a much deeper part acknowledged that it felt destined.

When Lee emerged from the washroom, Jill was trying to open a hutch to put away a large stack of serving dishes. Lee hastened to help, taking the dishes from Jill so she could put them away a few at a time.

"Thanks. We may have to consider a caterer for the wedding. Preparation is fun; cleanup is not."

Lee scanned the family photos on the hutch while Jill re-ordered stacks to work the dishes back into place. She smiled as she saw one of Gaëlle and Emmy G laughing together on the lawn. It had clearly been taken a few years ago, as Emmy G was a toddler in the picture. "Your daughter sure is a cutie."

Jill followed Lee's gaze and smiled. "That's one of my favourite photos."

She took the last bowls, and Lee picked up the picture to admire it. "Your mom's lost a lot of weight since then, eh?"

"Yeah, that was taken before the second go-round. The first time, Mom bounced back from chemo and radiation like nothing had happened, but the second time, not so much. I was concerned, but her doctor assured us that it wasn't uncommon. He and Mom finally convinced me I was just being a worrywart, but then I already mistakenly thought she'd beaten it the first time, so I didn't think a little worrying was out of line." Jill stood up and closed the hutch doors. "There. That should do it."

Lee's hands shook so badly that the picture frame rattled.

"Hey, are you okay?"

Jill's face blurred, and Lee struggled to catch her breath.

"Whoa, Lee. You'd better sit down. I'll go get Mom."

"No! I just...I just need some fresh air." Lee stumbled toward the front door, ignoring Jill's worried voice trailing behind her. Gasping, Lee sprinted down the stairs to her SUV. There was no one in the front parking spot when she hastily spun in a circle and accelerated out of the yard. Stones spat from underneath the tires as Lee raced down the gravel road toward Gaëlle's house.

When Lee reached the house, she jumped out before the engine had fully shuddered to a stop. Running as if the hounds of hell were after her, Lee took the stairs three at a time. She burst into her bedroom, grabbed her suitcase out of the closet, and jammed clothes in. What wouldn't fit, she threw into the laundry basket. Lee flew down the stairs, in too much of a panic to stop for the shirt that tumbled out of the basket.

She dashed back to the SUV and threw the

suitcase and basket into the trunk. But when she slammed the hatch shut and hurried around to the driver's door, she found her way blocked.

Wally stood, his back pressed against the door, shaking his head. "Far star. No go. Far star. Cry, die."

Tears streamed down Lee's face. "I can't, Wally. I can't go through it again. I just can't."

He glared at her fiercely, tears in his eyes too. "No go. No go. Sad, sad."

Desperate to get away, Lee yanked Wally away from the door and accidentally ripped two of his ribbons off. "I'm sorry. I'm sorry. I'm sorry. Tell her, Wally. Tell her I'm sorry, but I can't. Not again." Lee jumped into the vehicle and started it up. She hit the gas and backed away, careful only to avoid Wally.

As Lee roared down the driveway, the disconsolate man clutched his torn ribbons and stared after her through a swirling cloud of dust.

CHAPTER 14

HARD AT WORK AT HER desk, Lee barely noticed when the office door opened.

"Lee, do you have a few minutes?"

Lee looked up from her computer and waved Willem in. "Sure."

Willem took one of the chairs opposite Lee. He leaned back and studied her for a long moment.

Lee took off her reading glasses and ran a hand over her eyes. "What's up? What's on your mind?"

"You."

"Me? Why? My production lagging?"

"Of course not. Since you returned from Saskatchewan, you've been working insanely long hours."

"Then is my work not up to snuff?"

Willem blew a raspberry, and Lee couldn't help smiling. It was such an undignified sound to be coming from a man of exceeding mental and physical substance.

"Okay, then what's got your tail in a knot, Wil?"

"I'm worried about you."

"No need, old friend. I've done a complete one eighty. I'm eating properly, working out, seeing friends. Just last weekend I took my goddaughter to the zoo so Marika and Rhi could have a day off. Eli and I have been working on my bike in the evenings. I'm excited about his wedding this weekend, and weekend after next I'm going with Terry and Jan to a softball tournament in Edmonton. My hermit days are over. All's well. Honest."

"I can see the improvement. Your eyes are clear. You don't stink of smoke or booze. You're obviously healthy and in extremely good shape. But—"

Lee shook her head impatiently. "No 'buts', Wil. I've done everything you all wanted of me. What more can you ask?"

"That you be happy."

Lee was shocked at the rush of tears that filled her eyes. She hastily turned away and fished a tissue out of a drawer. She blew her nose loudly. "Damn allergies."

"Lee, next to my wife and children, you mean more to me than anyone else in the world. So, you're fired."

Lee laughed through the tears. "You can't fire me; we both own exactly fifty per cent of DeGroot and Glenn. Why on earth would you say that I'm fired?"

"Because I don't know any other way to make it better. You were happy for a while. I could hear it in your voice when I talked to you in Donegal. You were excited about a silly old pile of rocks. You could hardly wait to wake up every morning. Now..." Willem shook his head and frowned. "Now you put all your energy into a job that gives you little joy. When I'm actually here late enough to see you go home first, it's like watching a dried-up husk of a human being trudge down the hall to the elevators."

"Jesus, Wil. Sugar-coat it, why don't you?"

"I can't stand what you're doing to yourself. This is even worse than before the intervention. At least then I had hopes that you would eventually pull yourself together and be the old Lee. Now you've pulled yourself together splendidly. You're a healthy, engaged, fully functioning member of society...and day by day, piece by piece, it's killing what makes you, you."

Lee was startled to see Willem pull a handkerchief out of his pocket and blow his nose. She could count on one hand the number of times she'd seen him get visibly emotional in all their years together.

"Damn allergies."

Lee smiled at Willem's gruff disclaimer. "Aw, Wil... Maybe it's just a matter of time, eh? Grief doesn't evaporate on a schedule, you know? Maybe I just need a little more time."

"If you were still grieving for Dana, I would agree with you, but I don't get the sense that this is what consumes you." Wil held up a hand to halt Lee's protestation. "Perhaps I am wrong. You know you can take all the time you want. But let me ask you a hypothetical question, yes?"

"Sure, go ahead."

"Eventually you'll retire. Me, they'll have to take out feet first because I'm not leaving that desk, but you should have a life outside of DeGroot and Glenn. Years from now we'll have a party, present you with a new motorcycle helmet, and send you off to enjoy your golden years. Who do you think should move into this wonderful office of yours?"

"That's easy. Ann. No question about it. She's been with us since the start. She's as well versed in the business as we are, and God knows she's proven her loyalty a million times over."

Willem heaved himself to his feet. "An excellent choice. I agree completely. Of course, Ann is only several years younger than us. We wouldn't get much time from her before she would retire as well. Still, for a brief while it would certainly let her know how deeply we esteem her and all she's done for our company. You're right, Lee. When the day comes, we'll definitely promote Ann to your office. I'm glad that's settled. Now, if you'll excuse me, I have a meeting in ten minutes. Meena and I will see you at Eli's wedding on Saturday." Willem left the office and closed the door behind him.

You old fraud. As if I didn't know exactly what you were doing.

But to Lee's chagrin, the seed Willem planted took root. She found her thoughts repeatedly drifting back to his scenario during the day. Willem might not have played fair, but he'd certainly targeted her altruism. *Is it fair to fill a job Ann would love when I hate it?*

About mid-afternoon, Ann rang from the outer office to let Lee know she had an unscheduled visitor. "Reverend Ross is here to see you."

Lee smiled. David had left the Anglican ministry years earlier, but as far as Ann was concerned, once a priest, always a priest. "Send him in. Thank you." Lee rounded her desk to greet David with a hug.

David had a garment bag over his shoulder.

"Thought I'd save you a trip. I stopped by the tailor and picked up our suits."

"Thanks. I'll just hang that up. Do you have time for a cup of coffee?"

"If I'm not interrupting anything."

"Not at all. In fact, I was just staring out the window, woolgathering really."

David took a chair and looked out at the distant mountains. "I can hardly blame you. With a view like that, I don't think I'd get any work done at all."

Lee poured two cups of coffee from the office pot. "I made fresh about an hour ago. Hopefully, it's still all right. Black, right?"

"Yes, thanks. Trust me, after the swill we brew at the foundation's offices, anything would taste great."

Lee handed David a cup and returned to her seat. "How's it going at the foundation these days?"

"Some days good; some days not so good. Unfortunately, having one of our clients attack someone with a knife on a downtown street, like last weekend, throws a bad light on all of us."

"Don't worry, David. It'll be news for five minutes and then forgotten. I really admire what you're doing. There was a time I didn't get it. I figured if you put homeless street people into decent apartments without ensuring they'd first beaten their addictions, they'd just ruin their nice new homes. I've been amazed that it's worked out so well."

"It has, but it's not only my doing, of course. I'm working with a wonderful bunch of people to get this done. Because the community got behind us with fifty per cent of funding, we finally secured government backing for a second facility."

"That's wonderful."

David beamed with a father's pride. "Liz was instrumental. She was like a bulldog. Even while planning for the wedding, she practically camped out on the Human Services minister's doorstep. Personally, I think he finally agreed to her proposal just to make her go away."

"She is an amazing woman. I'm very pleased that she's going to be my daughter-in-law."

"Liz thinks you're going to be a fabulous mother-in-law, too."

"I know it would've been better if Dana—"

David shot Lee a stern look. "Don't even go there. We all wish Dana had lived to dance at their wedding, too, but don't imagine for a moment that Liz and Eli wish that you'd died instead."

"I know, I know. It's just, Dana was so much better at this kind of thing. I'm only hoping not to screw up my part."

"You won't. I have faith. And I have to tell you, Liz is over the moon about your wedding gift to the two of them. That was incredibly generous."

"I'm glad it makes them happy. I was surprised when they chose China for their honeymoon trip, though. I thought they'd go for a destination a little more conventional."

"Are you kidding? Liz has been fascinated with all things Chinese since she was a little girl. She's never had the money to go there, so a honeymoon in China is a dream come true."

"Maybe her most recent incarnation was in

China." Lee stopped abruptly as she realized what she'd said. "Uh, sorry. I didn't mean to give offence."

David waved a dismissive hand. "Don't worry. I'm actually quite taken with the concept of reincarnation and have done quite a bit of reading on it."

"But I thought you being a former priest and all, you wouldn't buy into such hooey."

"Hooey?"

"A term I used with a friend who believed in all that crazy stuff." As Lee had done for weeks, she ignored the agony ignited by every thought of Gaëlle.

"Well, your friend is certainly not alone in her beliefs. It's really not that radical a concept. Christianity is one of the few religions that doesn't acknowledge and accept reincarnation as one of its tenets, but there was a time that it did."

"Really?"

"Really. Early church fathers believed fully in reincarnation. In the third century an esteemed theologian named Origen taught the very New Age concepts that we are all, including Jesus, sparks of the Divine, and that the soul evolves through many lifetimes until it reunites with God. Emperor Constantine had references to reincarnation deleted from the New Testament in the fourth century, and in the sixth century, the Second Council of Constantinople officially declared belief in reincarnation a heresy. Of course that was a lively little council. Emperor Justinian had ordered Pope Vigilius, who proclaimed that reincarnation was consistent with Christ's message, to denounce reincarnation. When he refused, he was arrested. He escaped, but under pressure Vigilius later recanted and signed off on the new doctrine."

"What was their problem with reincarnation? I kind of like the idea. Not only do we get many more lives with the souls we love, we get more chances to get things right. If you screw up in one life, you're going to get other chances to get a 'Get out of Hell Free' card. Who wouldn't appreciate that?"

"The Catholic Church. Think of the impact if the masses knew that Jesus' message was actually of our shared divinity, and that we were all working our way back to the Godhead through many lifetimes. Then add in the notion that a soul didn't actually need anyone's intercession to achieve reunion with the Source. In that case, why would people accept the Church's authority? If, however, they believed they only had one lifetime and submission to official church doctrine and church prelates was the only way to salvation, they were far more likely to fall in line and behave as the Church intended. So the Church struck out the heretical passages from the Gospels and instigated the concept of a single Judgment Day. Worked very well for them, though the Inquisition had to get a little nasty in suppressing Christian sects like the Cathars, which did hold to reincarnation well into the Middle Ages."

"So Gaëlle's maybe not so crazy after all."

"Pardon?"

"Oh, sorry, David. I was just thinking of my friend who believes strongly in reincarnation. She was even convinced that... Well, it doesn't matter now."

David eyed Lee keenly. “Is this your friend in Donegal?”

“Yes.”

“She sounds like an interesting woman. Will she be coming to Liz and Eli’s wedding?”

“No. Her son is getting married too.”

“This weekend? Oh, that’s unfortunate. Just bad timing, I guess.”

Lee stared at her hands, unable to meet David’s eyes. “Truthfully, I don’t know if Dale’s wedding is this weekend or not. I haven’t talked to Gaëlle since I left.”

“Why not? I thought you two became great friends.”

To Lee’s dismay, the tears started again. She hastily grabbed for the ever-present tissues.

David was quiet while she composed herself.

“Do you want to talk about it, Lee?”

“No, I’m good. You can put your pastoral hat away, thanks.” *Damn eyes. Stop this bawling.*

“I wasn’t donning it. I was offering a friend’s ear.”

Lee was certain when she opened her mouth that she was going to forestall any such discussion once and for all. Instead the words erupted. “I fucked up so badly. I just ran like a goddamned coward. I took off into the night without even giving her a chance. I was just so scared. I couldn’t do it again. It almost killed me the first time. I couldn’t...I just couldn’t.”

“What couldn’t you do?”

“I couldn’t take a chance on loving Gaëlle, not when she has cancer. I couldn’t watch another woman I love die on me. But I should’ve talked to her. I should've explained why I couldn't stay. I'm so ashamed of myself."

"Gaëlle is battling cancer presently?"

"No. Her daughter said Gaëlle's in remission—for a second time. But we thought Dana had beaten it the first time, too, and look what happened to her. Maybe Gaëlle has beaten it back twice. What happens the next time?"

"You don't know that there will be a next time, Lee."

"And you don't know that there won't."

"You're right. Tell me, did you ever confess your love to her?"

"Yes. The night I ran."

Lee felt the ever-present despair of going from the thrill and expectation of new love to disappearing without a word. She had spent countless hours brooding over the pain she'd inflicted on Gaëlle. "She didn't deserve that."

"She didn't deserve what?"

"One minute we're in love, kissing and looking forward to the future...*the near future*...and the next minute, poof! I'm out the door and down the road."

"And you haven't called? Has she called you?"

Lee hung her head. "I haven't taken any of her calls since I left."

"Tell me, my friend, if Gaëlle walked in the door right now, what would you say to her?"

"I'd fall to my knees and beg for forgiveness for being such a mean-spirited bitch."

"Would you ask her to take you back? To give your love a chance?"

"No. That I couldn't do."

"Let me play Devil's Advocate for a moment. You and Dana were a couple for many years. You raised a son together, built a home and a life, all the while believing it would never change. It was understandable that you were devastated by her loss." David leaned forward, his gaze kind, but insistent. "You've only known this other woman a few months. Why do you assume that you would suffer to the same degree? Perhaps if her cancer did return, you would be able to handle it with far greater equanimity, albeit sadness, of course."

Lee's laugh was painful to hear. "Because with Gaëlle, it would be all or nothing."

"She is not one to be a casual romance?"

"No. No, she sure isn't. She's brilliant, passionate, intense, and I know when she loves, she loves without escape hatches. Anyone who dares love her couldn't help but do so in the same way."

"So you chose nothing."

"I chose nothing."

David was silent for several long moments. "It's your choice to make, but I wouldn't have made the same one."

Lee was quick to protest. "You can't say that until you've walked in my shoes."

"Perhaps. You know I met my wife at her brother's funeral, right? I'd gone to B.C. to officiate at Conor's funeral, and it was there I met Camille. We were brought together through shared grief, but I've always believed there was a greater hand in our meeting. From what I've gleaned from Eli and Rhi, you and Gaëlle bonded over shared grief as well. Perhaps the same hand was at work?"

"Her grief is much older."

"My point being that she understood what initially took you north to Donegal. I imagine that if she is all you claim, she understands what drove you into the night as well."

"You're saying I should go back?"

David shrugged. "That's your call, Lee. I'm just saying that I doubt the door you shut is as firmly closed as you think."

Lee smiled at Eli as they finished their dance. "Go dance with your bride, son. At least your feet will be safe."

Eli glanced over to where Liz had concluded her dance with David. "Thanks, Lee. And thanks again for your wonderful toast. It was beautiful. I could almost feel Mom here with us. "

"I know I was speaking for both of us." Lee hugged her son and walked off the dance floor as Eli went to claim Liz. Rather than rejoin the head table, she navigated through the throng to the table at the edge of the dance floor, where her friends were sitting.

"Hey, Lee. Pull up a chair."

"Thanks, Rhi. Marika, Terry, Jan...are you guys having a good time?"

A chorus of yeses answered.

Lee snagged an unused chair from another table and sat down.

Marika threw an arm over Lee's shoulder. "Kudos, my friend. It's been a terrific wedding and reception. Eli and Liz look so happy."

"Thanks. Yeah, the kids did us all proud."

"And you did them proud. That toast made me cry." Jan's eyes sparkled.

Lee grinned to herself. She suspected her friends had been enjoying multiple toasts at their table. "Thanks, Jan. I wanted Eli to know how proud of him Dana always was."

Terry nodded towards Eli and Liz as they danced past their table. "He certainly knows now, if he didn't before."

Lee smiled at Terry and changed the subject. "I imagine you're all enjoying a night out without the little ones, eh?"

She then sat back and quietly listened as the four mothers plunged into what had apparently been an ongoing discussion of the difficulties in finding reliable babysitters. It wasn't long before her mind drifted. A bump against her arm recalled Lee to the present. She blinked at Rhiannon. "You elbowed?"

"I did. My wife asked you if you wanted to dance, and you were a million miles away."

"Oh, sorry, Marika. Sure, I'd love to dance."

Marika led Lee to the floor for a slow turn. "So where were you, old friend?"

"Sorry?"

Marika chuckled. "I think you're still there. You're being very quiet tonight. Everything all right?"

"Sure. Just thinking, I guess."

"About?"

"Dana. Wil. This and that."

"Mmm. Did you ever consider asking 'this and that' to the wedding?"

"I couldn't. Too much water under the bridge."

Marika stopped dancing and led Lee out of the hall, past a group of smokers, and into the fresh air. Marika stopped at a bench and took a seat. "Okay, Lee. The only thing you told us when you got home was that you'd decided you needed to resume your real life and get back to work. Rhi and I knew there was more to it, but we figured we'd let you have some time. Time is now officially up, so spill it. What happened in Donegal?"

"I fell in love."

"That's not surprising. I could sense it coming on when I talked to you. I'm sorry. We all know the dangers of falling for a straight woman who can't love us back."

"No, you don't understand. She made the first move. She loves...she loved me, too."

"But that's wonderful! Then why isn't she here meeting all of us tonight?"

"It's a long story."

Marika patted the bench beside her. "Sit; tell me."

Lee repeated the story she'd told David that afternoon. Her sense of shame hadn't diminished with the telling, but Marika withheld judgment as she listened.

"We were an hour away from becoming lovers, and I threw it all away. The most amazing woman I've met since...well, since Dana...and I treated her so badly that *I'd* never forgive me."

"You do have a problem with self-forgiveness."

Lee laughed bitterly. "Gaëlle would probably say that's one of my karmic lessons."

"She really sounds like a fascinating woman. Are you sure—?"

Lee didn't give Marika a chance to finish that thought. "I'm sure. I'm not going to put myself in that position again."

"Sweetie, I hate to tell you this, but at some point, each of us will die. It's the human condition. Some day you are again going to be in a position to watch someone you love die. There's just no getting around it."

"Almost everyone I love is younger than me. Maybe I'll get lucky."

"So you're really determined not to ever fall in love again?"

"I'm determined I'm going to stack the odds in my favour by not falling in love with someone who's had cancer twice."

"Oh, Lee. You know there are no guarantees. You know that. God forbid, but as young as she is, even Marnie could develop cancer. Life simply doesn't come with assurances of health and longevity. You deal with whatever arises to the best of your ability. I know you know that. It's the way you always lived before. What you don't do is give up before you even take the field of battle. That's so not you. You've lived large all your life. I hate to see you living small now out of fear."

"Can I tell you something I've never told anyone?"

"Not even Gaëlle?"

"No one. It's my greatest shame."

Marika put a comforting arm around Lee's shoulders. "Go ahead. It's not going to change the way I feel about our friendship."

"At the end, I just wanted Dana to die. And it wasn't to release her from her suffering. It was to stop *my* suffering."

"Aw, sweetie, that's pretty natural. You were utterly exhausted. It wasn't like Dana had any chance of recovery. We all knew it was just a matter of time."

"But I should've treasured every second with her. I should've held on tooth and nail until she couldn't hold on any longer."

"You did. You held on, you treasured your time with her, you did everything possible to make her last days as rich as they could be."

Lee mumbled something.

"Pardon?"

Lee raised her head. "That last day...I told her she could go."

"That was a kindness, not a cruelty. She was probably waiting for that."

"But maybe she needed more time with us, or Eli needed more time with her. Maybe she left prematurely because of what I said."

"That's what's been haunting you? Oh, Lee, no. You did nothing wrong. It was a terrible disease, and nothing you said or didn't say made any difference. When it was Dana's time to go, she left. That's all."

"I keep picturing Gaëlle in that hospital room, dying. I just don't think I could be there for her the way I tried to be there for Dana. I think...I *know* I'd run, just like I ran from Donegal. I'm such a chicken-shit."

"Lee Glenn, you stop that right now. You are no such thing. No, I don't think leaving Donegal was your finest hour. I think you were in shock, and you made a bad decision. That doesn't mean you'd make the same decision again."

"I might."

"True, you might. But given how hard you've been on yourself for the mistakes you have made, I think you've inoculated yourself against making them again. Let me ask you something. Say you're right. Say that your worst fears were realized and Gaëlle succumbed to a third bout with cancer."

Lee shuddered and shook her head.

"It could be a year or five or ten down the road. By rejecting her now to protect yourself, you not only deny the both of you potentially years of joy you could share by loving each other, you also deny her the chance to have you with her should the cancer return. Would you want a woman you love to endure her toughest trials without you?"

"She has family. She wouldn't be alone."

"No, she wouldn't. But think how Dana would've felt without you. We'd all have been there for her. No question. But the one person who loved her above all else, who knew her more intimately than any living human being, would've been missing." Marika slid a comforting hand up Lee's back and through her hair.

Lee's head dropped lower. Her voice was a whisper. "It's agonizing to even contemplate it."

Memory of Gaëlle's touch overwhelmed Lee, and her tears began to flow.

Marika handed Lee a couple of tissues.

Lee sat upright, wiped her eyes, and blew her nose. Then she looked at Marika's sleek, form-fitting dress in amazement. "Where on earth were you carrying tissues?"

"Don't ask. I have a two-year-old, remember? I've gotten very creative about such things."

Lee began to laugh and found it hard to stop. Marika joined in, and the two were still chuckling when Rhiannon found them.

"Hey! I didn't think you guys were going to vanish on me. What's so funny?"

Lee stood and pulled Marika up with her. She slung an arm around each of her friends as they walked back to the hall. "Just life, Rhi. Just life."

It was almost midnight when Lee dropped Marika and Rhiannon off at their home. They exited her SUV, arguing about who had to drive the babysitter home.

Lee was smiling as she drove home. Despite her earlier meltdown, she'd enjoyed the rest of the reception. There had been a bittersweet moment when Eli and Liz left the hall. Lee felt like a big part of her life had abruptly ended, but the melancholy passed swiftly. She'd danced and socialized and behaved like any other mother of the groom.

Lee pulled into her garage and got out with the suit jacket slung over her arm. She lingered in the doorway and enjoyed the cool night air. Even with air conditioning, it had gotten very hot in the crowded hall.

By the time Lee turned to go inside, the automatic light was off and the garage was in darkness. As she went around her vehicle, Lee bumped into the old

Suzuki she and Eli had spent hours tinkering with. Lee grabbed the bike so it didn't fall off its stand.

"Geez, and I didn't even have a drink tonight."

She rested her fingers on the familiar curves of the cool metal. It had been a long time since she'd taken it for a drive.

"Tomorrow. How about you and I go for a drive out to the mountains tomorrow?"

Lee patted the bike and moved toward the door. She hit the remote on the wall to close the door. The garage was again dimly illuminated by the automatic light.

She turned in the doorway. Her gaze fixed on her bike, then moved to her riding leathers hanging on the wall over her boots.

"I'm certifiably insane to even think about it."

She stood for a few moments more and then tossed her jacket to the floor just inside the house. Lee pulled out her cellphone and hit Willem's number. It went directly to voice mail.

"Wil, hi, it's me. Give Ann the promotion and my office. I'll be in touch, and we'll figure out how to work the financial stuff later. Love you, man. I'm out of here."

Within moments, Lee had pulled her leathers on and donned her boots and helmet. She smacked the remote to open the garage door and backed the motorcycle out. Lee closed the door, started the bike, and rolled out of the driveway.

The old Suzuki sped down the street as laughter hung on the night air.

CHAPTER 15

THE SUMMER DAWN FOUND LEE closing in on Donegal. She knew she should be exhausted, but a deep, pervasive peace had filled her from the moment she left the city limits and pointed the bike north. That peace had carried her through the night hours.

Lee had no idea what she would say to Gaëlle. She wasn't sure whether Gaëlle would even see her. It didn't matter. This wasn't a trip simply to make amends.

She didn't fill the long night hours with plans or projections, wishes or fears. Lee's mind dwelled on memories—recent memories of Gaëlle and their hours working on the labyrinth and more distant memories of her life with Dana. With every mile that rolled beneath her tires, the bitter faded and the sweet remained.

By the time Lee drove through Donegal, slowed, and made the turn onto the gravel road that would take her to Gaëlle, she was in a state of meditative calm.

What happens, will happen. All Lee knew for certain was that, this time, she would not run.

It occurred to Lee that the first time she'd made this trip, it had been dusk.

Today, it was dawn.

Just when Lee was due to take the last turn before reaching Gaëlle's driveway, she noticed something ahead on the side of the road. She smiled and slowed as she recognized Wally's cart.

Lee spotted Wally stooped over to pick up something in the ditch. She coasted to a stop and saw him straighten with an empty beer bottle in his hand.

Wally dropped the bottle into a bag tied to the side of the cart and then ambled toward her. Lee turned off the bike and removed her helmet.

Wally beamed. "Roam, home."

"That's right. I'm home. At least I hope I am. Is she okay?"

Wally sobered. "Star, bad sad. Cry, cry."

Lee hung her head, then looked up with renewed determination. "I made a mistake. I regret that more than I can ever say, but I'm going to forgive myself for my fear and weakness, and I hope she will forgive me, too."

Wally nodded vigorously. "Forgive, give. Heart, star. Over moon, soon."

"I wanted to apologize to you, too, Wally. I'm very sorry for manhandling you the night I left."

A thought struck Lee, and she unzipped her leather jacket. She still wore her formal shirt and vest beneath. Inside the vest pocket was the wedding favour she'd snagged off the table before leaving with Marika and Rhiannon. She'd meant to give it to them to pass along to Marnie, but it had slipped her mind.

Lee offered Wally the candies wrapped in lace

net and tied with an elegant black and white ribbon. "These are from my son's wedding last night."

Wally accepted the gift and cradled the small package in his hands. He grinned at Lee. "Wacky wombat."

"Oh, great. Gaëlle gets to be a star. I get to be a wombat."

Wally reacted to Lee's teasing with a hiccupping laugh, then he quieted and delicately untied the ribbon. He dropped the candies in his pocket, turned so his right sleeve was toward Lee, and held out the ribbon.

Lee saw where several small pins were attached to an open space on the sleeve. Shreds of ribbon still hung from two of the pins, and she realized it was where she'd accidentally torn Wally's ribbons when making her escape.

With great solemnity, Lee accepted the ribbon and pinned it to his sleeve. When the small ceremony was completed, she rested her hands on his shoulders and looked into his intense, pale eyes. "I promise this, my friend. If she can overlook my flaws and give me another chance, I'll never let her down again. If she can't, I'll understand and I'll leave. I'm not sure where I'd go, but I do know it's time for a new life."

Wally's expression softened, and he patted Lee's arms affectionately. "Rebirth, mirth. Go home. Go home."

"You're absolutely right. It's time to go home." She gave Wally a quick hug and walked back to her bike.

Lee eased her bike around Wally's cart, careful

not to spray gravel. She raised a hand in response to his enthusiastic waves and then steadied the bike for the remainder of her journey.

As she turned into Gaëlle's driveway, Lee throttled down and idled to a full stop. She removed her helmet and sat on her bike. It was quiet. There was no sign of light or life.

Lee hesitated. *She's probably still asleep.* Lee decided she should wait on the porch until someone woke up. She didn't want to compound the boorishness of her drastic departure with a rude return.

Suddenly, the more than twenty-two hours of wakefulness hit Lee, and she wearily closed her eyes. Then, just as abruptly, a surge of energy swept over her, and her eyes snapped open.

Lee dismounted and put the bike on the stand. She stripped off her jacket and tossed it across the seat. Without hesitation, she began walking, past the house and out to the back fields on a route she could've walked in her sleep.

Long before she reached the labyrinth, Lee could see Gaëlle standing in the centre, facing the rising sun with her head thrown back. Her hair was loose, and the wind lifted and tossed silver strands, the movement in stark contrast to Gaëlle's absolute stillness.

Lee stopped at the threshold stone and waited.

Within seconds Gaëlle began to slowly turn, like a compass needle seeking north. Her legs pressed against the stone bench, and Lee could see that her eyes were still closed.

Gaëlle's eyes opened. She looked directly at Lee.

Her expression was calm, neither welcoming nor rejecting. She waited.

Lee stepped onto the threshold stone and closed her eyes. She had seen Gaëlle take this walk many times. Now, it was her turn.

Lee took a deep breath and reached for an elusive freedom from thought. Without a word, she opened her eyes and began to pace at a deliberate speed. She focused on the stone beneath her feet, the fields that stretched to the horizon, the grey clouds that filtered the early morning sunshine, and the gusts that cooled her face.

As she made the first turn onto the second circuit, Lee heard the distant call of a Canada goose. Grateful for the blithe omen, she sent an acknowledgement to the Universe.

With each step along the path, Lee found it easier to stay in a contemplative state. She didn't focus on the centre and the woman waiting there; she stayed in the moment, deeply conscious of the grace growing within.

By the time Lee stepped onto the seventh circuit, she experienced connection: with the world she walked; with the universe that surrounded her; and with each step closer, with the woman at the centre of the labyrinth.

Lee stopped at the edge of the centre and locked gazes with Gaëlle.

Now Lee was close enough to see the joy that filled Gaëlle's eyes and the tears that trickled down her cheeks. She took the final step and entered the heart of the labyrinth. "I'm sorry, Gaëlle. Every moment since that night I ran, I've regretted my cowardice. I know I can never make it up to you—"

Gaëlle crossed the short space between them. "No, stop. I was just as much to blame. I should've told you."

"Why didn't you? We talked about so many things, but that never came up." Lee wasn't angry; she was curious. For a woman of such integrity, it seemed like a curious lapse.

"You may find this hard to believe, but it's not something I ever dwell on. It happened. I dealt with it. I moved on. I was so consumed with the joy of what was growing between us that until Jill told me how you reacted, it never occurred to me that you deserved to know."

"It could happen again. The cancer could recur."

"It could. I don't think it will, but, yes, it's a possibility."

"I couldn't face the thought of loving you and then losing you."

"And yet, here you are."

"Here I am."

"I'm so very glad, Lee. I've missed you terribly."

"I should've taken your calls. I should've explained why—"

Gaëlle laid soft fingers against Lee's lips. "I knew why."

"Did you know I'd come back? Did Wally tell you?"

"No. He didn't know one way or another. He reminded me that you loved me, but there was no knowing what you'd ultimately decide to do."

"Free will, eh?"

"Yes."

"Then I freely choose to do this." Lee reached for Gaëlle. Their lips met, softly at first as they re-established their connection, then with a growing hunger as they celebrated their reunion.

When they broke apart, Gaëlle mumbled breathlessly, "Give me your keys."

"Why?"

"Because you are not leaving this time until we finish this."

Lee laughed and held Gaëlle closer. "No worries, my love. I'll stay as long as you'll have me."

Gaëlle leaned back in Lee's arms, her expression suddenly sober. "Seriously? You're going to stay? Because if you leave it open-ended, I'll want to keep you here for the rest of your life."

"That's fine with me."

"What about your job, your company?"

Lee grinned. "Wil fired me. I'm footloose and fancy-free."

"What? How could he—?"

"I'm just kidding. About the fired part, not about staying here." Lee led Gaëlle to the stone bench. She sat astride on an edge.

Gaëlle promptly straddled Lee's legs with her own.

Lee locked her hands behind Gaëlle's back, enjoying the gentle touch that traced her face.

Gaëlle asked, "You truly are serious? You're going to stay?"

"I've got a lot of loose threads to tie up at home, including resolving finances with Wil. I don't plan to sell out, and I know Wil wants to keep both our names on the business, but we'll figure it out. Oh, and I only have the clothes on my back. But, yes, if you'll have me, I want to stay."

Lee abruptly found herself lying back on the bench, with Gaëlle on top. She laughed and cried as she smothered Lee with kisses.

"If I'll have you? Are you kidding? After I waited all these years, I'm not letting you out of my sight."

"Fine by me."

Gaëlle snuggled into Lee and idly toyed with the buttons on her shirt.

Lee considered that although she was lying on a stone bench and her body ached from the long ride, she was remarkably comfortable. But she soon decided there was a much better place they could be. "Are Dale, Dechontee, and Janjay still at the house?"

"No, they went back to Guinea two days ago."

"So Dale and Dechontee have married?"

"Yes, last weekend. We all worked like madwomen to pull it together in such a short time. I was glad to be so busy. It kept my mind off..."

"Me."

"Your absence."

"I'm sorry I missed Dale's wedding. And I wish you could've been with me last night for Eli's."

Gaëlle unbuttoned the top half of Lee's shirt and slipped a hand inside. "I'd have liked that. I look forward to meeting your family and friends soon."

"I suspect your family will be far less happy to see me than my family will be to meet you."

"Please don't worry about that. I explained the situation, and they understood. They won't blame you."

"Even Janjay?"

"Even Janjay, and considering the cultural taboos in her country, her and Dechontee's accepting attitudes are pretty remarkable."

"I take it Guinea is not fond of its LGBT population?"

"No, though it's not as bad as in some African countries. There are laws against homosexuality, but they're not as radical as some places. We wouldn't be put to death for holding hands, but we could be thrown in jail for a few months."

"Mmm. So when we go over there, we probably shouldn't do what you're doing at the moment."

Gaëlle's hand stilled, and she chuckled. "No, we'll definitely have to be more discreet. Does that mean you'll come with me when Jill and I go to Dale's and Dechontee's ceremony?"

"Where you go, I go...if you want me along."

"I thought we'd settled that."

As Lee rolled upright, she carried Gaëlle with her. "We have. Right now I'd really like to settle in some place a little softer, if that's okay with you. I haven't taken such a long ride in many years, and I think my body is going to pay for it."

Gaëlle wriggled off Lee's lap and stood up. "You rode your bike all the way here? You must be exhausted. C'mon. Let's go back to the house. I think a hot bath and a soft bed are in your future."

Lee pulled Gaëlle in for another kiss. "As long as you're in my future, that's all I care about."

When they left, Lee turned to look at the centre of the labyrinth. A symbol resembling a sideways figure eight was done in lighter stone that was surrounded by darker stone.

"I see you settled on a design."

"I did. The night you left, I didn't sleep much. Toward morning I thought of the infinity symbol, and I knew that's what I had to use. It was two days before I had time to get back to the labyrinth. By the time I did, Wally had piled up all the stone I'd need to carry out my concept."

"What does it mean to you?"

"The loops are an endless configuration. For me, it signals the infinite nature of love and the soul as opposed to the finite nature of physical life."

They walked the circuits, Lee following Gaëlle as she considered that. "Love outlives death."

Gaëlle smiled over her shoulder. "Exactly. To quote the poet Phillip Larkin, 'What will survive of us is love.'"

"That can be pretty cold comfort."

"I know. When the warmth and nearness of the one you love has been ripped from you, it's hard to believe that love does endure, in both the physical and metaphysical sense."

"Do you think Hugh, Owen, and Dana miss us the way we miss them?"

"No, not really. They can be with us anytime they want. That's not to say that they don't feel and empathize with the depth of our distress, but they're well aware that they're still alive and will be with us again. No matter how strong our beliefs, it's difficult to get beyond the barrier of sorrow to a place of acceptance."

"That's what I couldn't get past—the potential sorrow of losing you."

"I know, love. And I admire your courage in taking that chance."

They'd reached the threshold stone. Gaëlle stopped and closed her eyes. Lee stepped up next to her. She knew Gaëlle always concluded a labyrinth meditation this way, and she waited quietly.

After a moment, Gaëlle reached for her hand, and they began the walk to the house.

"I'm not really courageous, you know. It still terrifies me to think of your cancer coming back."

"And the thought of you riding your bike all through the night scares me. Bikes aren't that safe to begin with, and you probably hadn't slept since the previous night."

"True. So if I'd been killed in an accident..."

"I'd have grieved deeply for you, but in time I'd remember that our love survived, and that I'd be with you when my turn came."

"Okay, I have a question. You loved Hugh, and now you love me. I loved Dana, and now I love you. Who will we be with when we cross over? Old spouse or new?"

Gaëlle laughed and squeezed Lee's hand to her chest. "Trust you to come up with a question like that."

"And it's not like you to dodge a question."

"I'm not dodging. We're surrounded by loved ones when we initially cross, but eventually we sort ourselves out and rejoin our soul groups. That doesn't mean we can't be with souls from other groups. Not at all. But there are different levels to the afterlife, and you'll congregate with souls at the same level."

"What you were saying to Dale about kindergarten and university level souls?"

"Exactly."

"We're probably not on the same level, are we?"

Gaëlle shrugged cheerfully. "No idea, and it doesn't matter one bit. We all evolve at our own speed. Look at my children. Dale is more spiritually advanced than Britten, but I love my youngest deeply, too. I'll be there for her when she crosses, and I'll never stop loving her. Owen was the oldest soul of all of us, except for Wally. Owen only spent twelve years on this earth and has been gone thirty. But I know when I see him again, I'll feel the same love I did the last time I hugged him."

"So I won't have to compete with Hugh for your attention when I cross?"

"You won't need to be competitive, Lee. When love abounds, you don't have to fight over scraps."

"And on this side? Do I have to compete with Wally and Dale and Emmy G and Janjay and—"

"Dear one, your place in my heart is unique. But love isn't rationed. My heart simply expands to encompass all whom I love."

"I can't help feeling a little jealous."

Gaëlle stopped walking and faced Lee. "Why? Should I be jealous of Eli or Willem or your best friend, Marika?"

"No, of course not."

"And why not?"

"Because I sure don't want to do this with them." Lee kissed Gaëlle with exquisite tenderness. They lingered until they were both breathless.

Gaëlle wrapped her arms around Lee's neck. "I am very, very glad of that."

They laughed together and embraced for a long moment before resuming their walk.

"I forgot to tell you that I ran into Wally on my way here."

"Did you stop to talk to him?"

"I did. He seemed happy to see me. He called me a wacky wombat. What I want to know is why you get to be a heavenly body and I'm relegated to being an Australian marsupial."

"Hey, don't ask me. I'm not responsible for my brother's language choices."

"Which reminds me, did you ever tell Wally what we found out about your common biological father?"

"I did. He was rather excited about the whole idea. I ordered DNA kits online. They should be here next week."

"Cool."

They walked in silence for a few minutes. Lee's mind drifted wearily over all they'd spoken of. "Does the pain ever completely disappear?"

"Pain?"

"Of losing someone. I can think of Dana now and not feel the desperation and agony I first felt. I know that's in large part because of you...not only because I fell in love with you, but also because of what I've learned from you. But I wonder sometimes if I'll ever stop being haunted by the way she died, the terrible pain she suffered through. Does the way that Hugh and Owen died still affect you?"

"It did for a long time, but I came to understand that the method of departure really doesn't matter. Cancer, car accident—the way our loved ones leave is simply the vehicle they use for stepping from this life to the next."

"But you told me that Hugh and Owen were

killed instantly. Dana spent months slowly dying. Surely that's far worse."

"I understand your reasoning, but didn't Dana's slow death give you two an opportunity to say everything you needed to say? Wasn't it, in that sense, a gift in disguise?"

"A gift of thorns."

"Life is often thorns, but there are roses to be found among them."

"I do remember one afternoon almost at the end. Dana had been moved to a hospice. I was the only one there at the time. She asked me to hold her. I was afraid to do it because I didn't want to hurt her, but she insisted. As carefully as I could, I moved onto the bed and cradled her. We talked a little, but mostly Dana just rested. She was down to less than ninety pounds and felt unbearably light as she reclined against me. I think at some level I knew it would be the last time I would hold her like that. I thought my heart would literally break. Now I think about how much you would've given to hold Hugh and Owen once more, even knowing they were about to leave you for good. I guess what I had *was* sort of a blessing."

"It was."

They walked into the yard and entered Gaëlle's house.

Lee looked up the stairs to the second floor. The fatigue that had vanished while she walked the labyrinth returned in full force. Lee grasped the rail, and Gaëlle took her arm. They trudged up and paused at the base of the stairs to the attic suite.

"Maybe I should just crash in my old room for a

few hours. It's not like I'm going to have any energy for anything else anyway."

Gaëlle smiled and rubbed Lee's back soothingly. "Don't worry. I won't try to take advantage of you in your depleted state. But it'll be worth your while to go up one more flight."

"Promise?"

"I do."

Lee summoned the last of her reserves and climbed.

Inside the suite, Gaëlle directed her to a recliner and gave her a gentle push. "Sit here. I'm going to start the bath. I'll be right back."

Lee nodded; she was too tired to respond. Gaëlle disappeared through a door, and Lee stared at the bed longingly. It took a few moments to sink in, but Lee eventually realized she was looking at something familiar.

Gaëlle returned and knelt at Lee's feet to unlace her boots.

"Hey, that's my shirt, isn't it?"

"It is. You dropped it when you left."

"I remember now. So why is it on your bed?"

"It makes a very good nightshirt."

"It does, eh?"

Gaëlle pulled Lee to her feet and steered her in the direction of the bathroom. When Lee entered, she whistled. By any standard, this was a luxurious set-up. White and silver marble tiles lined the walls and floor. A huge jetted bathtub was rapidly filling with sweetly scented bubbles. It faced a picture window that looked out over the prairies, north to the labyrinth.

Lee grinned. "I did not know about this side of you."

Gaëlle finished unbuttoning Lee's shirt and pants. "I admit it, I'm a hedonist. I love this tub. But it's not purely physical. I also find being immersed in water is a fabulous way to meditate."

"Right now, all I care about is the physical." Ably assisted, Lee hurriedly threw off her clothes and slipped into the water. She moaned with delight. "Oh, my God, this is heavenly."

Gaëlle laughed as she picked up Lee's clothes and draped them over a chair. "I thought you might like it. Soak as long as you like."

"You know, there appears to be room enough in here for two."

"I thought you were exhausted."

"I am, but it doesn't take a lot of energy to share a bath."

Gaëlle smiled and began to undress. She tossed her pants aside, then hesitated for just a moment before she allowed her shirt to slip from her shoulders and turned to face Lee.

Lee met Gaëlle's gaze steadily, a refusal to flinch from the clear evidence of Gaëlle's battle with cancer.

Lee extended her hand.

Gaëlle took it and stood motionless beside the bath as they regarded each other.

Lee drew Gaëlle's hand to her mouth and kissed it gently. "Join me, my love."

Gaëlle brushed her hands over her eyes and stepped carefully into the bath.

For just a moment, Lee wished that she was

twenty again. As a youngster, she could go on a forty-eight-hour field exercise and still have the energy for lovemaking when she returned to base.

Now...not so much.

Gaëlle slipped into the water and settled back into Lee's arms.

Lee revelled once again in the blissful sensation of a lover's naked body in her arms.

They rested together in the hot water and watched the clouds build up over the land.

"Storm's building."

"I'm glad I got here before it did."

Gaëlle rolled slowly to face Lee. "So am I." Her body rested on Lee's as she began to trace her fingertips lightly over Lee's face. When they lingered on Lee's lips, Lee took them gently between her teeth.

Gaëlle smiled as she withdrew her fingers and replaced them with her lips. They lost themselves in each other for a long time. Finally, Gaëlle lowered her head to Lee's shoulder and slid her arms around the lean body. Lee's hands, which had been leisurely exploring Gaëlle's back, stilled, and she simply held her.

Lee felt no urgency to explore the burgeoning desire between them. She felt no need to talk, either. There was absolutely nothing she could say that would be more evocative than the way their bodies slid together—scarred, imperfect, aging—yet as if each had been created for the other and for this moment.

Lee knew there would be time to make amends and time to make love. There would be time to heal the self-inflicted wounds. There would be time for so many things she thought had died with Dana.

Would she and Gaëlle have all the time in the world? Lee didn't know. She couldn't know. But it no longer mattered.

She would take whatever time was given them and be grateful for every second.

Lee floated in that ephemeral space between conscious and unconscious and reflected on love... specifically, the abundance of love in her life. She felt infinitely blessed in the journey she'd been on with Dana, Eli, and all her friends. Their steadfast love had saved her.

Gaëlle.

Gaëlle had only just begun to teach Lee about the magnitude and dimensions of Love. Lee knew she had much to learn.

Her mind drifted to the land they'd walked and the labyrinth they'd built. In this place, she could learn; she would learn. There would be thorns, but there would also be roses.

Lee felt no impatience. She had all the time she needed.

Letting the water and the woman heal wounds and provide balm to her soul, she settled deeper into the soothing bath, closed her eyes, and listened to the sounds of Gaëlle's breathing so close to her ear as she contemplated the last few months.

The Universe was fragile and enduring, mystical and miraculous. It could spin from joy to despair, from desolation to delight in the blink of an eye.

Lee had forgotten its magic for a while; she wouldn't forget it again. Having Gaëlle in her life, having a love she thought could never be hers again, would remind her of life's potential every day.

Lee didn't know what the future held, but uncertainty did not matter. All that mattered now was the woman who rested so peacefully in her arms. All else she would take on faith.

###

ABOUT LOIS CLOAREC HART

Born and raised in British Columbia, Canada, Lois Cloarec Hart grew up as an avid reader but didn't begin writing until much later in life. Several years after joining the Canadian Armed Forces, she received a degree in Honours History from Royal Military College and on graduation switched occupations from air traffic control to military intelligence. Having married a CAF fighter pilot while in college, Lois went on to spend another five years as an Intelligence Officer before leaving the military to care for her husband, who was ill with chronic progressive Multiple Sclerosis and passed away in 2001. She began writing while caring for her husband in his final years and had her first book, Coming Home, published in 2001. It was through that initial publishing process that Lois met the woman she would marry in April 2007. She now commutes annually between her northern home in Calgary and her wife's southern home in Atlanta.

Lois is the author of three novels, *Coming Home, Broken Faith, Kicker's Journey*, and a collection of short stories, *Assorted Flavours*. Her most recent novel, Kicker's Journey, won the 2010 Independent Publisher Book Awards "IPPY" bronze medal, 2010 Golden Crown Literary Awards best historical winner, 2010 Rainbow Romance Writer's Award for Excellence - first place win in the historical category, and 2009 Lesbian Fiction Readers Choice Award for historical fiction.

Visit her website: www.loiscloarechart.com

E-mail Lois at eljae1@shaw.ca

OTHER BOOKS FROM YLVA PUBLISHING

http://www.ylva-publishing.com

SOMETHING IN THE WINE

Jae

ISBN: 978-3-95533-005-7
393 pages

All her life, Annie Prideaux has suffered through her brother's constant practical jokes only he thinks are funny. But Jake's last joke is one too many, she decides when he sets her up on a blind date with his friend Drew Corbin—neglecting to tell his straight sister one tiny detail: her date is not a man, but a lesbian.

Annie and Drew decide it's time to turn the tables on Jake by pretending to fall in love with each other.

At first glance, they have nothing in common. Disillusioned with love, Annie focuses on books, her cat, and her work as an accountant while Drew, more confident and outgoing, owns a dog and spends most of her time working in her beloved vineyard.

Only their common goal to take revenge on Jake unites them. But what starts as a table-turning game soon turns Annie's and Drew's lives upside down as the lines between pretending and reality begin to blur.

Something in the Wine is a story about love, friendship, and coming to terms with what it means to be yourself.

L.A. METRO
Second Edition

RJ Nolan

ISBN 978-3-95533-041-5
349 pages

Dr. Kimberly Donovan's life is in shambles. After her medical ethics are questioned, first her family, then her closeted lover, the Chief of the ER, betray her. Determined to make a fresh start, she flees to California and L.A. Metropolitan Hospital.

Dr. Jess McKenna, L.A. Metro's Chief of the ER, gives new meaning to the phrase emotionally guarded, but she has her reasons.

When Kim and Jess meet, the attraction is immediate. Emotions Jess has tried to repress for years surface. But her interest in Kim also stirs dark memories. They settle for friendship, determined not to repeat past mistakes, but secretly they both wish things could be different.

Will the demons from the past destroy their future before it can even get started? Or will L.A. Metro be a place to not only heal the sick, but to mend wounded hearts?

BACKWARDS TO OREGON

Revised and Expanded Edition

Jae

ISBN 978-3-95533-026-2
521 pages

"Luke" Hamilton has always been sure that she'd never marry. She accepted that she would spend her life alone when she chose to live her life disguised as a man.

After working in a brothel for three years, Nora Macauley has lost all illusions about love. She no longer hopes for a man who will sweep her off her feet and take her away to begin a new, respectable life.

But now they find themselves married and on the way to Oregon in a covered wagon, with two thousand miles ahead of them.

HOT LINE

Alison Grey

ISBN 978-3-95533-048-4
114 pages

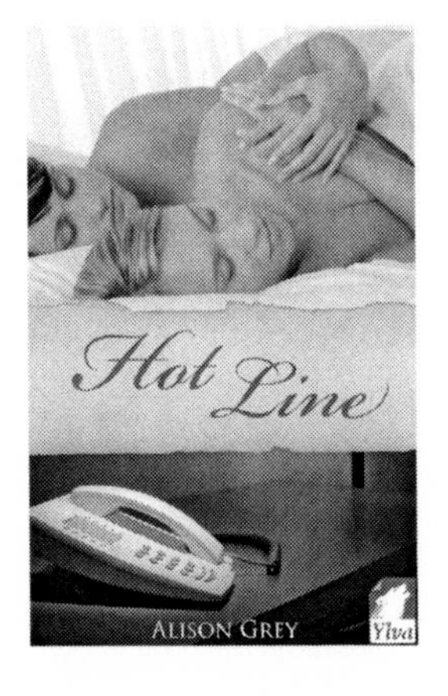

Two women from different worlds. Linda, a successful psychologist, uses her work to distance herself from her own loneliness.

Christina works for a sex hotline to make ends meet.

Their worlds collide when Linda calls Christina's sex line. Christina quickly realizes Linda is not her usual customer. Instead of wanting phone sex, Linda makes an unexpected proposition. Does Christina dare accept the offer that will change both their lives?

COMING FROM YLVA PUBLISHING IN SUMMER AND FALL 2013

SECOND NATURE

Revised Edition

Jae

ISBN 978-3-95533-030-9
Length: about 600 pages

Novelist Jorie Price doesn't believe in the existence of shape-shifting creatures or true love. She leads a solitary life, and the paranormal romances she writes are pure fiction for her.

Griffin Westmore knows better—at least about one of these two things. She doesn't believe in love either, but she's one of the not-so-fictional shape-shifters. She's also a Saru, an elite soldier with the mission to protect the shape-shifters' secret existence at any cost.

When Jorie gets too close to the truth in her latest shape-shifter romance, Griffin is sent to investigate—and if necessary to destroy the manuscript before it's published and to kill the writer.

CROSSING BRIDGES

Emma Weimann

ISBN: 978-3-95533-020-0

As a Guardian, Tallulah has devoted her life to protecting her hometown, Edinburgh, and its inhabitants, both living and dead, against ill-natured and dangerous supernatural beings.

When Erin, a human tourist, visits Edinburgh, she makes Tallulah more nervous than the poltergeist on Greyfriars Kirkyard—and not only because Erin seems to be the sidekick of a dark witch who has her own agenda.

While Tallulah works to thwart the dark witch's sinister plan for Edinburgh, she can't help wondering about the mysterious Erin. Is she friend or foe?

Lightning Source UK Ltd.
Milton Keynes UK
UKOW02f1032080615

253077UK00001B/67/P